T0278935

THIS is HOW you FALL in LOVE

ANIKA HUSSAIN

BLOOMSBURY

NEW YORK LONDON OXFORD NEW DELHI SYDNEY

BLOOMSBURY YA
Bloomsbury Publishing Inc., part of Bloomsbury Publishing Plc
1385 Broadway, New York, NY 10018

BLOOMSBURY and the Diana logo are trademarks of
Bloomsbury Publishing Plc

First published in Great Britain in 2023 by Hot Key Books
Published in the United States of America in February 2024
by Bloomsbury YA

Bloomsbury books may be purchased for business or promotional use.
For information on bulk purchases please contact Macmillan Corporate and
Premium Sales Department at specialmarkets@macmillan.com

Library of Congress Cataloging-in-Publication Data
Names: Hussain, Anika, author.
Title: This is how you fall in love / by Anika Hussain.
Description: New York : Bloomsbury, 2024.
Summary: Best friends Zara and Adnan navigate the twists and turns of fake
dating, family dynamics, and cultural stereotypes.
Identifiers: LCCN 2023030375 (print) | LCCN 2023030376 (e-book)
ISBN 978-1-5476-1450-9 (hardcover) • ISBN 978-1-5476-1451-6 (e-pub)
Subjects: CYAC: Dating—Fiction. | Interpersonal relations—Fiction. | Best
friends—Fiction. | Friendship—Fiction. | Family life—Fiction. | Bangladeshi
Americans—Fiction. | LCGFT: Romance fiction. | Novels.
Classification: LCC PZ7.1.H875 Th 2024 (hardcover) | LCC PZ7.1.H875
(e-book) | DDC [Fic]—dc23
LC record available at https://lccn.loc.gov/2023030375

Typeset by Westchester Publishing Services
Printed and bound in the U.S.A.
2 4 6 8 10 9 7 5 3 1

To find out more about our authors and books visit
www.bloomsbury.com and sign up for our newsletters.

*For Dadu, whose stories guided me through
the darkness of the night*

1

"Yo, does this pick-up line work, do you think?" Adnan asks, tossing his phone on my bed and interrupting my blissful reading of a juicy new romance in which the main character and the love interest arrive at a remote cabin only to discover that the last room available has one bed.

Knowing he won't give up, I put the book aside and look at the screen. I immediately shake my head at his message: *Have you been covered in bees lately? I just assumed, because you look sweeter than mishti.*

"You know, I can't stand you."

"And I you, Z," he responds with ease.

"She's not going to get it and you know that."

"Why do you say that?"

I tap onto her profile picture on Instagram, reminding myself of who the girl in question is. "Because she's as white as sugar?"

"Don't judge, Z. She might have some knowledge about Desi culture."

Somehow, I'm doubtful. But I'll let Adnan stay in dreamland for a little bit longer if it makes him happy. And nothing makes Adnan happier than flirting.

Being such a good friend, all I want is for him to find his happily ever after. Even if he is stupid and only meets girls by sliding into their DMs—I mean, *come on*, show a little imagination. Forbidden love or an enemies-to-lovers arc would be so much more fun. And don't even get me started on a second-chance romance!

"Anyway, I thought you were talking to that new girl, Camilla. What happened to her?" I swipe out of his DMs and look up Camilla's profile, lazily scrolling through her latest pictures, when I notice that Adnan hasn't liked a single post. "Playing hard to get, are we?"

"Don't like anything, Z," Adnan warns, his Adam's apple bobbing in fear as he prepares to lunge at me if I even consider hovering my thumb over the heart icon.

Seeing how desperate he is, I put him out of his misery and toss his phone back.

He grabs it midair, double-checking that I haven't accidentally liked any photos.

"So," I press, curious as to why he's so tight-lipped, "what happened with her?"

He shrugs. "Nothing happened. That's the problem."

"What do you mean, nothing happened?" I ask with a raised brow, because something *always* happens with Adnan and the girls he talks to. I don't know how he does it, but he's got some serious game, especially in comparison to me. I mean, you'd think that as someone who practically lives and breathes romance in any available format I'd stand a chance in the love department, but that would be a big fat nope.

"I'm telling you: nothing's happened," he says with a deep sigh. "Cami is a reserved person—I knew that from when we first started talking, but I thought . . . I don't know, maybe I could get her to lower her walls or something."

Even though I feel bad for him—I can see the disappointment clouding his eyes—I can't help but break out into a sly smile.

"What?" he asks, already rolling his eyes. "Scratch that. I don't even want to know—"

"You called her *Cami*," I say, ignoring him. "You never give girls nicknames."

"So?"

I poke him in the shoulder like an annoying child. "You *liiike* her."

"Shut up," he groans, but the grin on his face confirms my suspicions.

To be fair, I always knew he liked her; that Camilla—or, sorry, *Cami*—was going to be different from all the other girls he's dated since she joined our class. The first clue was the fact that Adnan *never* asks me to help him with girls. He really doesn't need it, despite his awful chat. Not with the cool-guy persona that he's perfected over the years, or his lean yet muscular build and his fashion sense—a mix between preppy and street. It also doesn't hurt that he's got eyelashes and hair that girls can't help but envy.

3

OK, *I* can't help but envy. It's seriously not fair. My lashes are never long enough to flutter wildly at people, and my hair, although straight and silky, has absolutely no life to it.

"You're thinking about my fabulous hair and eyelashes, aren't you?" Adnan asks. "You're doing that thing again with your face." He replicates my facial expression by furrowing his brows so hard he has to massage his temples—which is exactly what I did only ten seconds ago.

"Shut up," I say and throw a worn paperback off the stack on my bedside table at him. He expertly ducks and instead I nearly knock the framed photo of me, Baba, and Ma off my desk. "Oops."

"Zara!" Ma suddenly calls from downstairs.

"Ma!" I call back.

"Dinner's ready!"

"OK, coming!"

"You guys really need walkie-talkies or something," Adnan notes as I slide into my slippers.

When we get downstairs, the table is set for a feast rather than a quiet dinner for six. Somaiya Auntie, Adnan's mom, and Ma finish up with making the salad as Adnan and I take our seats, practically banging our cutlery on the table in anticipation of food. Sumon Uncle, Adnan's dad, pours himself a glass of ayran and winks at me as he does so, and I can't help but shake my head at him.

"What have you kids been up to, then?" Uncle asks as he takes his first sip of the yogurt drink, his expression gleeful.

"Adnan's been trying to come up with pick-up lines for

the past hour, but they've all been pathetic," I reply for us. "It's no wonder he's single."

"I thought the mishti one was pretty good, you know."

"It really wasn't."

Adnan flicks me in the temple, and I retaliate by twisting his nipple.

Uncle looks at us with a glint in his eye—one I know far too well after having Sunday dinner with him for as long as I can remember. "I don't think my son's relationship status is the way it is because of his pick-up lines, Zara. You know, it would be so much easier if you two would just get together already. Everyone can see you're meant to be."

"I agree!" both our moms shout as they bring out two different types of salad to the table: one with Naga Morich and one without for Adnan, who can barely even inhale the scent of chilli without having a coughing fit. Even now, as Ma places the bowl meant for everyone but Adnan at the other end of the table, I can see Adnan eyeing it up like it's his mortal enemy.

"Would it really be so difficult for you two to at least *try* to date?" Ma asks as she takes her seat next to me.

Adnan and I share a glance, already thinking the exact same thing: *Why can't our parents be like other Desi parents?* Because our parents are absolutely *not* like your typical Desi parents. They're never über-strict and never forbid me from dating before marriage like you hear some South Asian parents doing. But perhaps that's because of the distance from their own parents and how hard they

5

fought against the stereotypes society placed on them as soon as they set foot on this country's soil.

Which, I can admit, is incredibly admirable, but also incredibly frustrating considering it means they are sometimes *overly* involved in my love life. In particular, the one that doesn't exist—nor will *ever* exist—between me and Adnan.

"Sumon!" Like a blessing in disguise, Somaiya Auntie disrupts my train of thought and steers the conversation elsewhere. She has the palm of her hand to her forehead and is trying to grab the glass of ayran from Uncle. "You can't drink that!"

Uncle only recently found out he's lactose intolerant and you'd think, from the way he's been crying about it for the past two weeks, that he was grieving a person instead of a type of sugar.

"I need it!" He dodges her attempts at grabbing the glass by chugging it all down in one go, much to Auntie's dismay.

"Don't you come crying to me when your stomach hurts, you hear me?" Auntie is wagging her finger in the air like a typical Desi mother and, in solidarity, so do Adnan and I.

"Farah?" Baba shouts Ma's name as he comes through the front door.

"Arman?" she shouts back, her voice echoing off the walls and practically shaking the wooden ornaments hanging off them.

"Walkie-talkies," Adnan whispers in my ear. "Seriously. I fear for your family's vocal health."

"Sorry I'm late." Baba kisses my head and Ma's cheek

before sitting down next to her. For a second, Baba frowns as he takes in the abundance of food in front of us, but then he dives into a story about a young woman who was picking up her prescription at the pharmacy where he works.

". . . And then I noticed this thing on her wrist. It was a birth control ring," he says, shaking his head. "She thought that was how it was meant to be worn! But you know the best part?"

"What?" we ask in unison, wondering how the heck it can get better than this.

"She came back a few minutes later with a pregnancy test and said, 'I think I might be needing this.'"

A deep, rumbling laughter fills the room. By the time my stomach stops hurting, Baba repeats, "Pregnancy test!" and gets me going all over again.

"We shouldn't laugh," Ma says, trying to be serious but unable to stop another giggle escaping. "Poor girl, her parents mustn't have been very open with her if she doesn't know how to use contraceptives."

She clears her throat in an attempt to change the subject before we all start laughing again. "Does anybody want cha and mishti?"

We all nod our heads except for Baba, who looks like he's got a stick up his bum.

"Arman?" Ma prods as she fills up the pot and places it on the stove.

"No mishti, but cha, please." He smiles but it's stiff and unlike him. It's only a few seconds later that we understand why. "But not doodh cha. And without sugar, please.

7

Turns out I'm diabetic," he says, his voice even, like he's not dropping a bomb on us.

"Ki?" Ma shrieks at the same time as I say, "You're kidding?"

"I'm not kidding."

"What do you mean, you're diabetic?" Ma abandons the pot, spurring Auntie to take the lead on our beverages instead.

"I'm absolutely fine, I promise."

"What did the doctor say?"

"Farah?" Somaiya Auntie interrupts. "I think there's something wrong with your stovetop. The gas isn't lighting."

But Ma doesn't respond to Somaiya Auntie's concern. She's glaring at Baba. "I didn't know you'd been to the doctor."

"I didn't want to worry you."

"You didn't want to *worry* me?" Ma asks the question like she can't believe the words that have left her husband's mouth. Adnan, Uncle, and I watch the back and forth between my parents like it's a tennis match while Auntie keeps fiddling with the stove.

"It's making a hissing sound, Farah, and it's not even on yet." The pitch of Auntie's voice increases and when I turn to look at her, I see that there are beads of sweat on her forehead.

"Let me help, Auntie," I say, getting up from the table. As I'm about to turn the knob, Ma's and Baba's yelling becomes louder.

"How could you keep this from me?"

"I wanted to protect you!"

"Protect me? How was lying to me protecting me?"

"I wasn't lying!"

"But you were withholding!"

I look over my shoulder at my parents. I've never seen them behave this way before. Adnan catches my eye, a tight-lipped look on his face.

"Farah, please, you need to—"

"I need to what? Keep listening to your lies?" Ma shakes her head. "No, I've heard enou—"

"Farah, I think the sto—" Auntie interjects at the same time as Uncle says, "I need to go to the bathroom. I think the ayran is ready to make its appearance."

But their voices are drowned out by my parents' yelling, nothing able to get through to them.

And then the stove explodes.

2

The fire in our kitchen wasn't too bad, mostly because I might have exaggerated the severity of it. The stove didn't blow up or anything, but a flame shot up and almost set our curtains on fire, which was enough for everyone to completely freak out.

While Baba called the fire department, Somaiya Auntie ran to check on Sumon Uncle in the bathroom and Adnan put out the fire and turned off the gas valve. As all this was happening, Ma simply sat at the abandoned table, a blank look in her eyes as she stared into the distance. I couldn't get her out of her catatonic state before the fire department arrived, so Baba and I had to take over Ma's usual hosting duties and explain to them what happened. The firefighters said there was a small gas leak that probably would have killed us in our sleep one day and we were lucky that nobody was hurt by the combustion.

At least, not physically.

Emotionally? It seems to have left scar tissue yet to be seen.

After the firefighters leave, along with Adnan's family, I perch at the top of the staircase and eavesdrop as Baba tells Ma that he'd suspected something wasn't right with his health for months.

"Months?!" she shrieks, leaving a ringing sound in my ears. "You're terrible at keeping secrets. How could you keep this one?"

"It was for your own good, Farah. I know what you're like," Baba responds.

"This is serious. This isn't like when you scraped the car and we had to pay more than what the car was even worth to fix it." Ma's pitch rises even higher. "This doesn't just affect you; it affects me, too. It affects Zara."

Hearing my name takes me by surprise. With all the yelling and the stove exploding, I haven't had the chance to think too much about how Baba's diabetes will affect me, but now that the seed has been planted, it's all I can think about. What *does* it mean that Baba has diabetes?

"All you would have done is worry."

"Then let me worry! Don't take the choice away from me."

As Baba weighs out his response, I lean my head against the banister and try to slow down the distress in my chest.

In the end, Baba doesn't reply. From here, I can't see how Ma responds to this, but her huffing makes me think she isn't taking his silence too well.

"I have no doubt you'll be *fine*," Ma continues, her voice breaking on the final word, "and your condition is beside the point—"

"Then why are you so mad?"

"I'm not mad! I'm . . . disappointed. I'm hurt that you kept this from me. That you took away my choice, that you . . ." Ma doesn't finish her sentence, she just sighs. "I'm going to bed."

"Farah—" Baba calls out, but Ma stomps away from him and heads in my direction. When she sees me sitting on the stairs her mouth wilts like a flower, but she doesn't say anything. She swallows and trudges past me, slamming the door to their bedroom shut behind her.

I've never seen my parents fight like this. Sure, they bicker—all parents do—and I know my parents aren't perfect, but I've never felt this tension between them before. In my mind, my parents' relationship has always been rock solid. Something nothing or nobody can come between. Over the years, even with all the romances I've read and rom-coms I've seen, it's always the small ways Ma and Baba communicate their love to each other that have filled my heart most: Baba rubbing Ma's feet after a long shift at the facility, even if her feet stink like tilapia fish, or Ma plugging Baba's phone into the charger before they go to bed because she knows he's useless at remembering to do it himself.

Some people have faith in a higher power; I have faith in my parents and their relationship.

I abandon my post on the staircase and take a seat at

the kitchen table where Baba is dipping a tea bag in and out of his mug, the liquid going from a bright red color to a dark leather I know he won't drink because of its bitter taste. Wordlessly, he pushes the mug toward me, and I place both my palms around it, the heat of the ceramic oblivious to its glacial environment.

"Why didn't you tell her?" I ask.

"I didn't want to upset her for no reason."

On the one hand, I understand. It would have stressed Ma out if he'd said anything because Ma stresses about *everything*. But on the other hand, I completely get where she's coming from. It's her husband; of course she wants to know if something is wrong with him.

"Baba?"

"Yes, beta?"

"Will you and Ma be OK?"

Baba's eyes soften. "We'll be OK. She just needs some time to digest the news. By tomorrow morning, we'll be back to normal."

I nod, but I note the bags under his eyes and the gray of his mustache.

"Will *you* be OK?"

Baba rubs his head and smiles thinly. "Of course I will be, beta. Many people live with diabetes without any problem. OK? Now go on. It's getting late and you've got school in the morning." Baba kisses me goodnight and heads upstairs, his steps soft and weak in comparison to Ma's angry stomps.

I stay seated at the table a little bit longer, not yet ready to head to bed. I pick up the mug, but upon the first taste I find myself recoiling and nearly spitting it out. It's bitter. Too bitter. Usually I wouldn't mind, but tonight I can't stomach it.

I pour the dark liquid into the sink.

3

When I came down for breakfast the next morning, my parents pretended like nothing was wrong, while at the same time refusing to speak to one another.

And it was the same the next day. And the day following that. And the one following that; their stony silence unwavering despite how much time had passed. I would have thought it would have blown over by now.

On Friday morning, I take a seat in front of Baba, who's got his glasses perched at the end of his nose, doing that thing where he holds his phone at arm's length as he reads the tiny text on the screen. Ma, still nervous about using the stove, opens and closes the fridge multiple times like she's typing a message on Snapchat only to delete it all a second later and then restart the process all over again in the hopes that it will send Baba an IRL notification and make him begin a conversation with her.

I butter my toast and take a bite, but with the tension around us it tastes like cardboard.

"Anything exciting today?" Baba asks, taking off his glasses.

I close one eye in thought as I rattle off my timetable for the day. "Study period, Media Studies, tutoring, and then English Lit."

"Any after-school plans?"

"I think I'm seeing a movie with Adnan, but other than that, not really," I say with a shrug.

"You *think*?" Ma drops a plastic bowl into the sink with more force than is necessary and then wipes her hands on a tea towel that reads BABY, I WAS BORN TO DRY. "You either are or you aren't—which is it?"

"We haven't decided yet. We're going to look up what's showing at the Odeon during lunch."

"Why didn't you decide sooner? Or at least tell me sooner that you were thinking of going to the movies today? So typical of you and your dad to keep things from me. Hmph."

It's not often that Ma acts like this, like a proper Desi parent who polices her kid. Especially when it's anything to do with Adnan. But this week, she's been more on edge than usual. She's been snapping at me for things she normally wouldn't, like not doing my dishes straight away or not picking my clothes up from the floor.

I want to turn to Baba for backup, but I don't think anything he has to say would comfort her right now. Inwardly, I seethe. Their fight should be over by now. It's been, like, what, almost five days? Why are they dragging it out for so long? But also, why are they dragging *me* into it?

"I'll text you as soon as I know, I promise." I try to be reassuring by shooting her a small smile, but it does nothing except infuriate her further.

"We have the family calendar for a reason, you know." She points at said calendar on the fridge. "We need to know about any commitments you're making beforehand. What if we had scheduled something for tonight, Zara? What then?"

I open my mouth to say that we hadn't scheduled anything and, even if we had, I doubt it'd be happening given her horrendous mood, but I stop when I see how Baba rubs the indents on the bridge of his nose, his eyes begging me not to aggravate her any further.

"Sorry, Ma. I'll do better."

She lets out a breath of impatience. "We just don't need any more surprises, beta, is all."

I swallow, ignoring her dig at Baba. "I'm going to miss the bus if I don't get dressed. I'll text you at lunch."

I quickly get dressed into my uniform—a gray pleated skirt with a navy-blue V-necked sweater thrown over a white blouse—and dash out the door twenty minutes earlier than usual, eager to escape the bad juju this house has been infected with ever since that damn stove exploded.

"You were right," Adnan says, taking a seat next to me on the common room sofa.

"I'm always right but do remind me what it is this time," I answer without looking at him, too focused on

17

finishing the last few chapters of the book I started last night about a girl who, after years of pining for her best friend's sister in secret, finally gets the courage to make a move on them.

"About the girl not getting it. You know, 'Have you been covered in—'"

"Hearing it once was enough," I interrupt. I put the paperback away in my backpack and face him, leaning my arm on the sofa cushion. "You need better pick-up lines."

"I thought that was a great one. Oh, I've got an even better one!" Adnan repositions himself on the sofa, his movements as quick as an excited puppy. "I need to break my fast, can I have a date?"

A few seconds pass before I ask, "Do you think it's possible to unhear something?"

"If it is, let me know how so I can unhear everything you say."

I pounce on Adnan in an attempt to twist his nipple, but he manages to grab my wrists before I can do any harm.

"Whoa, get a room already!" a familiar voice yells across the room. I turn to see my best friend, Sadie, entering with our other friends Ceri and Liam, and their friend and long-time crush of Sadie's, Joe.

I roll my eyes at the same time Adnan does. Just like our parents hounding us about dating one another, people at school are no different. Everyone assumes we're together—because obviously Desis *must* date Desis—and even though we deny it, and the revolving doors of Adnan's girlfriends keep spinning like there's no tomorrow, they don't believe us.

"I take it you guys are official now?" Sadie plops down beside us, while Ceri, Liam, and Joe go investigate the vending machine. "What couple name are we using? Zadnan or Adra? Alphabet? Ooh, maybe we should mash your last na—"

"Sadie," I groan.

"What?"

"For the millionth time, nothing is happening between me and Adnan. And nothing ever will."

We're endgame, sure. But we're endgame in a completely platonic way, and even though Netflix always shows you otherwise, that the girl and guy best friend ultimately get together, that is not what's going to happen here. I refuse to fall victim to the script people have written for us.

"Incest is not wincest," Adnan adds with an arched brow.

"You're not even related."

"You don't know that. You never know with Desis. We're probably related through some distant uncle."

Sadie's lips are pressed in a firm line, her eyes on the verge of rolling into the back of her head. "I know you're messing with me, but whatever."

I don't hold back the laugh that escapes me. Adnan and I are 1,000 percent not related—we checked using one of those DNA kits you can order online—but it's too good not to use as an argument whenever Sadie brings up our nonexistent relationship. Mostly because messing with Sadie truly is one of my favorite hobbies and one of the main pillars of our friendship. Especially because she dishes it out just as much back.

The bell rings promptly at ten to nine, signaling for us to get off our butts and head to class. As we walk down the corridor, Sadie jogs ahead to engage in whatever heated debate Joe, Liam, and Ceri seem to be having while Adnan and I trail behind.

"Hey," Adnan says, "are we still on for the movies tonight?"

I bite my lip, hesitating. "I don't know if I should. Ma's still on edge after Baba's diabetes bomb."

"She's not on edge after your stove exploding?" Adnan notes with a raised brow.

"Well, she is, but that's beside the point . . ."

"Wait, what's going on? Bombs? Exploding ovens?" Sadie asks, rejoining us. "Anything I can relay to ThermaeSecrets? I've been waiting for my moment to shine, you know."

Ugh, that *stupid* Insta account. You'd think we were in *Gossip Girl* with the way the wannabe Insta ThermaeSecrets—named after the famous posh spa in town because the people who run the account thought it would be *classy*—actively seeks out scandal where there is none, baiting students with the promise of short-lived fame by chronicling everything that goes on at our school. Adnan and I have been posted on that page so many times for things that just weren't true, but which were twisted to look like it. Once, all he did was hug me as we separated for the bus and they made a whole post about our "undeclared love."

Also, it's creepy as hell that people I spend eight hours a day with are patiently waiting to snap a picture of me without my knowledge.

Allah, I can't stand that page.

"I don't think ThermaeSecrets would be interested in hearing about my dad's diabetes."

"Baba Farooq has diabetes?!" Concern flashes in Sadie's eyes. "Somebody fill me in ASAP!"

I was hoping I wouldn't have to tell Sadie the story, thinking it all would have blown over by now and been just a blip in the cosmos, but from my parents' behavior this morning it doesn't seem like that's happening anytime soon.

"Parents freak out about the most ridiculous things," Sadie says once I've explained about the eventful dinner and how Baba keeping his health concerns from Ma caused a fuse to blow both literally and figuratively. We pause at our lockers so we can leave our bags and not have to lug them around for the rest of the day. "You'd think your mom would be more concerned about your dad having diabetes than him not telling her."

"I know! It makes no sense, honestly." I shake my head as I cram my bag inside my locker, still struggling to understand just *why* Ma is so mad at Baba. "I mean, there are worse things he could have been hiding. Like—"

"He could have a whole other family like on *Ackley Bridge*," Adnan interrupts.

I shoot him a pointed look. "I was going to say 'like a secret stash of money.'"

"Oh, that would be more plausible, wouldn't it?" he says.

"Only a little," Sadie interjects. Turning to me, with a grave expression, she asks, "But Baba Farooq is going to be OK, right?"

"For sure. Diabetes is *totally* manageable"—I know because I googled it, extensively—"and nothing to worry about if you look after yourself, which Ma should be *helping* Baba with rather than telling him off for."

Sadie places a hand on my shoulder, her lips firmly pressed together in thought. After half a minute she says, "I was trying to come up with some comforting advice, but I have absolutely nothing and it's making me feel awkward, so I'm just going to leave you now that I've got the intel I came for and let you take out your frustrations on your handsome lover instead. Ciao!"

Before I even have the chance to tell her off about referring to Adnan as my lover, Sadie is already halfway down the corridor in her quest to catch up with the others.

"So, movies. Yes?"

I slam my locker shut and start down the corridor again. "Did you not hear anything I just said? I need to be in Ma's good books until this all blows over." Under my breath, I mutter, "Whenever that is . . ."

Adnan begins to guilt-trip me but suddenly stops midsentence, his eye caught by something behind me.

I follow his line of sight and see what, or rather who, has literally taken his breath away. Cami is effortlessly beautiful as she walks past us, even in our plain-as-all-hell uniforms, tucking a lock of her dark blond hair behind her ear, drawing attention to a pair of dainty crescent-moon earrings. A flicker of a smile appears on her face as she locks eyes with Adnan before quickly looking down at her feet, her arms squeezing more tightly across the book she's holding to her chest.

I nudge his shoulder.

"What?" he asks, his voice low and far away, like he's on a different planet.

"I take it you guys talked?"

He tries to suppress the grin spreading across his lips, his irises practically melting into the shape of hearts as if he's a cartoon character. "We were up until four in the morning talking about the universe, about the beauty in the burning balls of fire in the night sky, about the phases of the moon and how, even though it's a different version of itself every night, it's always there watching over us."

Ah, hence the earrings. And the stupid look on his face. "Have you asked her out yet?"

"Not yet."

"Why not?"

Adnan shifts his jaw a little. "I just don't want to mess anything up. She's . . . different."

"Yeah?"

"Yeah. I don't even want to use my stupid lines on her. I want her to know the real me, you know? I don't just want to be 'Adnan, the funny guy' to her, I want to be . . ." Adnan holds his hands out in front of him, making a frame by connecting his thumbs and pointer fingers. ". . . 'Adnan, the boyfriend' who can be funny *and* something more."

"Then ask her out. Nothing's ever going to happen if you don't *make* it happen."

"Cami's just . . . complicated."

23

"Complicated how?"

"She's just got some things going on with her family." Adnan rubs the back of his neck, his furrowed brows indicating that he's not willing to tell me the whole story just yet.

"Well, unless her family is as complicated as mine, I still think you should ask her out." I pause, a brilliant idea coming to me. "In fact, why don't you take her to the movies tonight?"

"Maybe," he says, but I know that he's already asking her by the way his fingers are flying across his screen.

As we shuffle into homeroom, I'm a little jealous of Adnan and the smile on his face. I have yet to find my person. It's not that I haven't dated or am overly picky about who I date; it just hasn't happened for me yet. I guess it doesn't help that when you grow up with parents like mine, where even just looking at them feels like being tucked under the coziest blanket in front of a roaring fire while heavy snow falls outside your window, it's hard to feel that spark with just anyone.

And it doesn't help that all my fictional boyfriends have raised my expectations even further.

"You gonna be OK at home?" Adnan asks once we've taken our seats in the back.

"Yeah, I'll just stay out of the way. My parents need to make up and fast, but there's not really anything *I* can do."

"You could give them some good news?" Adnan suggests.

"Like what? It's not like I do anything newsworthy."

"True. You are unremarkable in every way. Do you

even *do* anything but sit on the sofa and daydream about your knight in shining armor?" Adnan teases with a self-satisfied smirk.

I respond by raising my hand as if I'm going to scratch my face but instead I flip him off. Adnan simply shakes his head.

As Mr. Wright takes attendance, I feel my phone vibrate. I sneakily glance at the message on the screen.

I know you're worrying but we'll figure something out.

We'll find a way to help them.

Your parents will be OK. I promise.

I shoot Adnan a strained smile, comforted by his reassurance even though I don't believe him.

I mean, how do you help fix your parents' relationship when you've never been in one yourself?

THE COOLEST PERSON YOU WILL EVER MEET (S♥)

Today 20:04

Sadie

right

review time of that new rom-com on Netflix

you know the one about the couple at the chalet?

Zara

Oh yeah

How was it?

Sadie

gross

the love interest was NOT likeable

he was misogynistic af

if i wanted to spend two hours watching a man who refuses to evolve and STILL gets the girl, I would have called my deadbeat uncle

and it would have been for free

and also they tried to do the whole secret billionaire trope and it just wasn't working

26

Zara

How many stars?

Sadie

2

1 for being entertaining

the other 1 for making me want to turn my brain off

could have been a 3 if you were to hate watch with me

Zara

Ugh, wish I could

But Ma is still on a rampage

Not sure she'd let me come over

Sadie

even if you tell her it's for educational purposes?*

*not that we'd study, obvs

Zara

Obvs

But no

Don't think so

Sadie

is she working this weekend?

'cause Baba Farooq is fine with you going out, right????

Zara

Yeah, Baba doesn't seem to mind

And the usual Sunday dinner has been canceled since Ma has a late shift tomorrow she couldn't get out of, so, maybe I could sneak out

Sadie

turn that maybe into a yes, missy

because tbh, in the nicest—and most selfish—way possible, I think you need some time away from the fam

also, I need help brainstorming for a film comp coming up and you can't leave me hanging when I'm in dire need of your assistance

and you KNOW I've been dying to make a film ever since we saw that new JLo movie

Zara

That was a horrendous movie

Sadie

EXACTLY

so I need to make something better
than that so people don't think
all rom-coms are like that, and to do
that I NEED your help!!!

Zara

You do make a convincing argument

Sadie

would you be even more convinced
if I said we just did a grocery run
and the pantry is filled to the brim with
chips and that the latest Rowan
Blanchard film has just been released
on Disney+?

Zara

One sec

OK

I just checked Ma's schedule

She's working until 9 on Sunday
so I'll need to leave by 8:30

29

Sadie

YAS GURL

this feels very forbidden love-esque

Zara

You know I can't resist a good
ol' trope xxx

4

"Come on!" Sadie yells, jumping to her feet in frustration and gesturing wildly at the television like it truly is the bane of her existence. "It's not *her* you like, it's her sister! Just admit it already!"

I let out a belly laugh at how into this movie Sadie is, reminding me of the very first time we met and discovered how we were equally obsessed with rom-coms, to a degree others would find ridiculous.

We were at a big box store and I must have been twelve, only just allowed to watch movies where the main characters kissed (even though I read plenty of books under the covers where they kissed way before that). I remember wandering around the store while Ma and Baba were chatting with a salesperson about the latest vacuum cleaner model. I hid away at the back where all the TVs were, sucked into the vortex of screens showing a fit blond guy sitting under the stars with his brunette co-star. Even without any audio, I couldn't help but be mesmerized by them, anticipating the big kiss.

I was in the middle of trying to see if I could figure out what the characters were saying, mimicking their lip movements, when a girl blocked my view by standing right in front of me.

"Excuse me," I said, irritated that somebody would have the audacity to interrupt my viewing. Could they not see that the kiss could happen any second now? "You're in the way."

She flashed me a sheepish, apologetic grin and moved to the side without a word. I went back to focusing on the screen, again trying to discern what they were saying by gauging the context of the scene, when the girl sat down next to me.

"What's this about?" she asked.

I let out a frustrated breath. "I don't know but I'm guessing they're declaring their love for one another and are going to kiss soon. At least I think so from how long they've been sitting on that beach."

"Hmm. I don't think so, actually," she said, and then, cozying up next to me, she started pointing at the characters. "This looks like classic enemies-to-lovers. See the way her face is all hard and moody? Or how stiff her posture is? I think this is just the point where he lets his walls down and she realizes that *this* is the mome— Why are you looking at me like that?"

My eyebrows froze in a sky-high position on my face as I tried to understand what this random girl had just said. Rom-coms aren't difficult to figure out, the plot line is always stupidly simple, but I'd never met anybody who actually *analyzed* them. Her attention to detail had beaten my own and *I* should have been able to spot that this wasn't the first-kiss moment but rather the part where their chemistry develops.

"I didn't spoil the movie for you, did I?" she asked after I failed to respond, her fingers drumming against her thighs with impatience.

"No, I'm just impressed you figured it out."

She blushed, her cheeks flaring up as if she was a tomato. "I watch a lot of romantic comedies with my mom. It's stupid, I know."

"No, not at all! I love rom-coms, too!" I nearly stood up with excitement.

"No way!" she squealed, as excited as me. "Have you seen the one with . . ."

She started reading off a list on her phone where she'd scored all the rom-coms she'd ever seen, and I knew from that moment that I had to befriend her.

Which I did, obviously.

And now, just like in the store, Sadie stands with her arms across her chest, a perplexed look on her face, but this time not because she's trying to figure out where we are in the movie but because she's frustrated by the characters' hesitance to show their true feelings.

Sadie dramatically slumps into the sofa, the back of her hand pressed against her forehead like a damsel in distress. "I know it's all going to work out in the end, but this is capital S stressful!"

"That's why we love rom-coms, though, Sades. You always know that the characters will find their way back to each other in the end."

"Well, can you give Joe the memo? Because he's taking far too long making his way back to me."

Sadie's had a crush on Joe ever since their meet-cute at Sainsbury's two summers ago when they both reached for the last pint of Ben & Jerry's Vanilla Pecan Blondie, and, because of their mutual politeness, they each insisted the other take the pint. In the end, Joe paid for it and insisted they share it in the parking lot. They ended up chatting for so long that by the time they remembered the pint of ice cream it had already melted in the afternoon sun. In accordance with the typical romance storyline, it would have been the perfect moment for a first kiss, but before that could happen, Joe was quickly pulled away by an emergency at home and, unfortunately for Sadie, she didn't manage to get his number or ever see him again.

Until this year, that is. She was hoping they could pick up where they'd left off, but Sadie, ever the traditionalist, insists that Joe should be the one to initiate things.

"Sadie, you can't just expect him to make a move on you. You could make a move on *him*, you know." I nudge her with my shoulder, but the wistful expression on her face remains. "What?"

"I don't want to look like a dork."

I don't agree with Sadie. She's missing out on something great with Joe on the basis of a "what if?" when she could be spending time with the person she likes more than anything. I get it—looking like a dork sucks—but that shouldn't hold you back. At the same time, it's not just Sadie who's not doing anything. Joe's not been making any moves either. Maybe he's just as afraid as she is.

"That's what you're doing with Adnan, isn't it?" Sadie asks.

I shake my head. "Definitely not. Adnan and I are just best friends. We always have been and always will be."

Sadie sits up straight and turns to me, her legs crisscrossed like a child listening to a story. "Why though? You always say you'll never get together, but *why*? You guys are best friends, everybody already ships you, and you've got so much chemistry that it gives me radiation burns just from being in your vicinity. It would be perfect."

"On paper, sure. But in reality, no." I let out a deep breath, a little exasperated to have to explain this to Sadie for what is probably the twentieth time. With Sadie so desperate for a love story with Joe but too scared to do anything about it, she's clinging onto my supposed story with Adnan as if it's her lifeline. "He's just not what I'm looking for."

"Then what *are* you looking for?"

I don't even hesitate as the answer slips off my tongue. "I want someone who takes me by surprise. I want somebody who makes me feel comfortable and not on edge. I want somebody who can bring out the silly side of me without me feeling stupid about it. I want somebody who wants to be with me for *me*." I take a breath. "That's all I want. I want something reminiscent of my parents."

"Same, girlfriend." Sadie chews on her lip as she mulls over her next thought. "How do you know when you love someone? And once you love someone, do you think you'll always love them? Or do you think it fades over time?"

"Those are some deep questions, Sades," I joke.

"It's just . . ."

"What?"

"It's just made me think that maybe for the Cinemagic competition, rather than making a short film, I could make a documentary about love."

"A documentary? About *love*?" I ask the question like I physically cannot grasp the concept.

"Yeah. Never did I think I would make a documentary, but as we've been chatting I think it could be interesting, and it's not really something people make documentaries about. It'll probably help me stand out!"

It's actually not a bad idea. Sadie's always wanted to work in film, and I just know that she'd absolutely smash it. The short films she's made for various classes and the awards that came with them are proof of that.

Sadie sits taller, her eyes shining with her vision. "It'll be an observational documentary and I'll film it on my phone. So many documentaries are expository and shot on these high-end cameras, but there's something so raw about observing somebody firsthand, almost like you're close to your subjects, you know?" Sadie puts her hands on my shoulders like she wants to shake some sense into me. "I'll interview couples at our school, ask them to tell us about how they got together, how they knew they were in love, and all that. I could even capture couples in the making like the ones Thermae-Secrets posts about."

There's a weekly post on ThermaeSecrets about couples who've been, as they describe it, "bringing the heat." Essentially, it's about people who are in the talking stage and could very quickly move on to the relationship phase.

"So, what's the first step?"

"Well, the first is to nap," she says with a serious tone that makes me burst into laughter. "What? I'm shattered from all that planning!"

I return home a couple of hours later, racing to get back before Ma does, and snuggle underneath my blanket so that when Ma does come in, she will see me in the exact same position as when she left, and she'll be too annoyed at how lazy I am to even consider the idea that I might have snuck out to see Sadie.

But the joy of crafting the perfect cover-up doesn't last long. Even with Sadie's enthusiasm about the documentary, and our discussion of the prospect of one day finding my own great love, I feel drained. Especially with the frosty atmosphere at home, the absence of my parents' voices putting me on edge. I heard Ma come in about fifteen minutes ago and in that time she's not said a single word to Baba, despite his questions about her day at work.

I find myself scrolling through my camera roll until I find a picture from years ago when we were back in

Bangladesh, only a few months before Baba's sister got married. It's of my parents and me, along with Adnan and his parents, and we're outside the venue, with nothing but joy on our faces. We stand under a deep-azure sky, rain-washed green leaves hanging off a century-old tree in front of a grand house with lights strung up all around it. We're wearing our finest outfits: Ma and Auntie in silk saris with embellishments that sparkle in the sunlight, and Baba and Uncle in cotton sherwanis with delicate floral embroidery. Adnan stuns in a simple burgundy sherwani, while I rock a teal lehenga that makes me look like I've stepped straight off the set of a Bollywood movie. There is a night-flowering jasmine tucked behind my ear, the white petals contrasting with my raven-black hair and heavy eyeliner. The photo makes me feel warm and cold at the same time; the juxtaposition of the memory of what was, fighting against what currently is.

I decide to upload the photo onto my Instagram, having not posted anything in a few months but also because I don't want to be the only one to hold onto this memory. Ma and Baba don't have Instagram, but even so I feel the need to post it. Like if I post it, then it's out there in the universe, a memory never to be forgotten even if the feeling has long since passed. I caption the photo with a red heart, at a loss for the right words to adequately express how the image makes me feel.

But I shouldn't have. Only five minutes later, the picture is flooded with comments that make my eyes burn.

Omg you two are so cute together!!!

U can fo sure see the luv in their eyes
Look at that caramel love
You should deffo have this as your wedding photo one day
A + Z 4EVA
Cutie faces xxxx
Have u ever seen a fitter couple?

I lock my phone and toss it on the floor with a thud; it lands next to my desk chair across the room. Then I put a pillow over my face and scream into it. Why can't people just understand that Adnan and I are not, and never will be, a thing? I honestly hate the narrative that just because we're South Asian, we must date each other. White people never have to go through this crap. They can date whoever they want!

I remove the pillow from my face and breathe out heavily, staring at the glow-in-the-dark stars tacked to my ceiling. It sometimes feels like the stereotype of who South Asians are meant to be overshadows the reality of who we are. It'd be easier to date outside our culture if there wasn't such bad representation of us. There've been a few shows with South Asian girls dating people of other ethnicities, but even so there doesn't appear to be a widespread change in attitude. Because of those shows, it's almost like the industry has closed the door even more tightly for future representation because they think that's enough, when in reality one or two stories about South Asian people is not nearly enough. There are so many stories out there to tell, but the chances to do so are few and far between.

I try to think of something else, anything else, but the irritation of the comments gets to me. You'd think people would get over it by now, that they'd see that after all these years of pestering, and the fact that Adnan and I (OK, mainly Adnan) have been very open about dating other people, there is simply nothing romantic between us.

Maybe I need to do what celebrities do when they break up and write a lengthy statement on my story. I should research how other people have addressed romances that are pure friendships and see if I can use that as a template. I throw the blanket off me and head over to my desk, cracking my fingers like I'm gearing up for a fight. But as I make myself comfortable in my chair, I accidentally roll over my phone, which I've forgotten I chucked across the room only a few minutes ago.

"Shit!" I jump up to investigate the damage.

Fortunately, it still works.

Unfortunately, the screen is shattered. So shattered that I'm unable to read any incoming notifications.

Crap! Ma is going to be furious if she notices that I've cracked my phone screen *again* after we got it repaired only a few months ago.

OK, this is the plan: I'll just hide it in my bag and take it to the repair shop after school tomorrow. Maybe I could even do it during lunch. We'll have to see. Either way, Ma *cannot* find out.

To calm myself down, and to stop from crying about how stupid I am, I go back to bed and pick up the book on my nightstand. It's about a couple who try to have a relationship while always maintaining a six-foot distance because of their respective illnesses. The characters are just deciding to take a break because they can't bear to endanger the other when Ma calls for me from the hallway.

"In here!" I shout back and sit up in bed. I dog-ear my place in the book and put it back on the nightstand.

Ma drifts into my room, an oorna wrapped loosely around her head as she walks around with her tasbih. She must have just finished praying. As Ma slides the beads from one side to the other, I note how she gives the hairbrush on my desk a death stare. Even with her silence, I know exactly what she's thinking: the hairbrush is grim, and I should clean it without her reminding me to do it for the umpteenth time. To be fair, she's not wrong. It *is* grim—there's probably an inch of loose hair strands stuck in between the bristles, and who knows how much hairspray/dry shampoo/volume mousse is stuck in there as well? Even so, I can't be bothered. Mostly because it's a lost cause at this point and it truly would be easier just to buy a new brush.

Ma kisses the tasbih and gently places it on the desk, making sure it's nowhere near the brush, before joining me on the bed.

"What are you doing, beta?"

"Just reading," I say with a shrug that I hope conceals the fact that I'm totally freaking out inside about the fact that when I got back from Sadie's I forgot to put away my jacket that's currently resting at the foot of the bed.

41

"Anything good?"

I nod. I want to tell her about the book, like I usually do, but refrain when I think about the content. I'm not so sure Ma would like to hear about sick people in love.

"What have you been up to all afternoon, beta?" Ma asks, changing the subject.

"I've just been doing some homework. And reading. And scrolling on my phone." I shrug again. "The usual."

Ma slowly nods, waiting for me to continue. When I don't, she asks, "That's all?"

"That's all," I respond, crossing my fingers behind my back.

It's quiet for a moment, my heart racing in my chest as I wait for the moment when Ma will kiss me goodnight and I can be assured that my little venture out was successful.

"It's warm in here, don't you think?" Ma asks while fanning herself with her hand.

"Uhm, no. I don't think so."

"Really?" The corners of Ma's mouth drop, her eyes clocking the jacket for a brief moment. "I'd think you'd be burning from the lie you just told me."

Crap. She knows.

"Ma, I—"

"Zara, how could you lie to me?" Ma's voice rises several octaves. "Who were you out with?"

I find myself raising my voice right back at her. "Sadie. All we did wa—"

"I don't want to know what you did!"

"But, Ma!"

"But what, beta?"

I struggle to find the words, but when I finally do they come rushing out. "I just wanted to get away from this house and forget about you and Baba either yelling your heads off or not saying anything at all!" I exhale like I've just run a marathon, but I keep going anyway. "I knew you wouldn't let me go to Sadie's if I asked, because you're being ridiculously unreasonable at the moment with everything going on with Baba, so I just thought it would be better not to ask and not get on your nerves any more than I've already been doing, but I guess that didn't work because somehow you figured it out!"

Ma's face temporarily blanches before tears begin snaking their way down her cheeks. I've never yelled at her like that. Whenever we yell, it's with affection, like a call to prayer.

As soon as Ma begins sobbing, I let my guard down and throw my arms around her. "I'm so sorry, Ma, I didn't mean it."

"But you did," she says through the tears.

"No, I didn't. It was stupid." I squeeze her even more tightly. "I'm so sorry."

"But, beta," she says through her sniffles, "there is nothing to forgive. You are completely right."

Her words make me draw back slightly. "What do you mean?"

She uses the end of her oorna to wipe away the tears and takes a second to collect herself. "I have been unreasonable, I know that. I know I've been hard on you and it's not fair.

43

You should be able to go out with your friends at the last minute and not worry about what mood I'm in when you ask me for things."

"Then *why* are you being like this?"

Ma lets out a deep breath. "Because of your father's health."

"Baba is fine, Ma."

"I know, beta, I know," she says simply, but I can tell that there's more behind her words than she is ready to reveal.

I don't keep on with my line of questioning, able to see that I won't get any answers tonight. "I wish there was something I could do."

"There's not much you can do." Ma gently rocks me, soothing my guilt from yelling at her.

"Would good news help?" I ask.

"Do you have any?" she asks with a meek laugh.

If I were a mother what would I want to hear from my daughter? Well, I know what *I* would want to hear—that my kid has won the lottery and I no longer have to work a day in my life—but I feel like Ma would want something else . . .

"Would it help if your one and only daughter finally came to her senses and stopped denying her feelings for your best friend's son?"

Ma immediately looks at me like she can't believe what I've just said. I quickly add, "I'm just kidding. I have no feelings for Adnan whatsoever."

"What a shame," Ma whispers. She goes back to gently

brushing my hair with her fingers as my eyelids grow heavier, all the energy suddenly sucked out of me after what feels like a battle. "Maybe one day."

I don't respond. The gravity of what the world wants for me versus what I want for myself is weighing me down so deeply there is nothing left to say.

THE COOLEST PERSON YOU WILL EVER MEET (S♥)

Today 07:04

Sadie

MATE

DEBRIEF AT LUNCH

THE BEST NEWS

!!!!!!!

5

"Zara! Breakfast!" Ma yells from downstairs the next morning. "There's croissants!"

I shuffle into my fluffy pink slippers, and as my eyes adjust to the brightness of my room, I wonder why Ma is the one waking me up. Did I not set my alarm? As I scan the room for my phone, my stupid mistake from yesterday comes rushing back.

I go through my bag to confirm the memory and, yup, still cracked and unusable. I've got a couple notifications, judging from the WhatsApp and Instagram icons, but nothing I can open until I get the screen repaired.

"Zara!" Ma yells again. "You're going to be late!"

"Coming!" I shout back and descend the stairs. But as I near the bottom, I hear laughter that stops me in my tracks, the sound so unfamiliar to my eardrums after a week of stony silence and heated arguments.

When I step into the kitchen, I'm even more confused. The laughter is coming from *Ma*, who is on the phone.

"Of course, Somaiya. See you later, yes? Khuda hafiz! There you are, sleepyhead!" Ma says with a wide smile as she locks her phone, Baba sitting closely next to her at the dining table with a big smile.

My eyes dart from one parent to the other, my brain unable to comprehend what's going on. They look . . . happy, which is what I wanted, but how did this happen? They must have talked, but when? I start to think back to last night, trying to remember if I heard anything through our walls, when I realize that I don't really care. All that matters is that they made up and they're now back to normal. There's a little bounce to my step as I take a croissant.

"The water has already boiled," Baba tells me, pointing to the kettle.

I shoot him a thumbs-up and a smile, too stunned to formulate my confusion into words, and I pour the water into my "YOU'RE A HOT-TEA" mug. I dunk the black tea bag into the mug before leaning against the kitchen counter, blowing on the warm liquid. I expect my parents to make conversation, but instead they're grinning at me like two creepy Cheshire cats.

I raise a questioning brow.

"So?" Ma says, looking at me expectantly. "Anything you want to tell us?"

"Er, like what?"

"Come on. You must have something to say, Zara."

I put down my mug. "I'm glad you're speaking to each other again?"

"Anything else?" Ma prods, her eyes wide with anticipation.

Honestly, *what* is going on? Am I missing something?

"Cat got your tongue?" Baba teases, causing Ma to playfully swat him on the shoulder.

I tilt my head to the side like that might help me understand what's going on, but it does nothing except make my brain hurt even more.

"Well, when you're ready to talk, we'll be here," Ma says.

"Ready to talk about what?" I ask.

Ma and Baba look at me for a moment, and I think they must finally be catching on that I have no clue what they're talking about, but then they burst into laughter.

"No, no, we shouldn't laugh," Ma tells Baba. "She must still be in shock."

"Perhaps she just needs some time. It hasn't been that long. Maybe after . . ."

Ma and Baba keep talking like I'm not there as I try to get to the bottom of their cryptic behavior. What are they expecting me to tell them? Why would I be in shock? I chug the bitter tea and head upstairs, wondering what the hell happened with my parents while I was asleep.

If things were weird at home, they're even weirder at school. People keep looking at me like I have a giant zit on my nose as I walk past. Scared I might *actually* have a zit on my nose, I check my reflection in the compact mirror I carry around in my bag for situations just like this but there's nothing there.

"I got you a chai latte with extra cinnamon," Adnan says as I approach my locker, a Starbucks paper cup in his hand.

"Thanks, I guess?" Adnan doesn't normally bring me a hot drink, but I'll take what I can. Nobody can resist a steaming chai latte.

"You didn't answer my texts this morning," he says as I take my first sip.

Allah, that is godly.

"I broke the screen by accident yesterday so it's out of use until I can get it fixed." I take another sip, nearly rolling my eyes into the back of my skull with enjoyment. "Why? What'd you send? Please tell me it's not another pick-up line."

Adnan scratches the back of his neck, looking a little uncomfortable. Finally, he throws his arm around me. "Look, there might be something I have to tell you. I migh—"

But he doesn't get to finish his sentence because Sadie chooses that exact moment to engulf us in a hug, jumping and screaming, "FINALLY! I KNEW IT ALL ALONG!"

What is going on today? Why is Sadie this freaking happy? Why were my parents acting all weird at breakfast? And why are people still staring at me like they know something about me that I don't?

"Why didn't you tell me as soon as it happened? We were together literally yesterday! Wait! Is that why you were rushing to leave my house?" Sadie claps her hands in excitement. "I knew it! That must be why! I knew you having to get home before Mama Farooq was just an excuse! OMG, I am *definitely* making the doc now!"

"Sades, wh—"

"Hey, Sades," Adnan interrupts, "do you mind giving me and Z a minute? We haven't really had a chance to talk and . . ."

Sadie holds up her hands, already backing away. "Say no more. I'll catch you later for the deets!" As Sadie shuffles into our homeroom, I whip my head toward Adnan, who's wiping away the beads of sweat on his forehead.

"Before you freak out, let me explain."

"I'm already freaking out."

Adnan chews on his upper lip. "Let's sign in and then find a quiet spot to talk in the library."

We quickly sign in for study period and then, as soon as we can, sneak away. I'm seriously on edge as Adnan heads toward the back of the library, past the wooden tables and the decade-old computers. I follow but stop to pick up a book along the way. Whatever he has to tell me, I'm not sure it'll be good—at least judging from the way he collapses into the green beanbag and immediately begins bouncing his leg up and down—in which case, being able to trace the embossed title will help to center and soothe me. With the book clutched to my chest, I take a seat on the yellow beanbag next to him and stare expectantly at Adnan.

"So," Adnan says, his voice suddenly scratchy, "you really don't know anything?"

"Know anything about what?" I ask with irritation, watching his face for an indication of what the hell is going on. His skin still has its summer glow even though summer vacation ended four weeks ago. Praise Allah, Somaiya Auntie, and Sumon Uncle for his blessed melanin, I guess. "Does this have anything to do with my parents? Because they were super weird this morning."

"OK, there's no easy way to say this," Adnan starts, but then quickly stops, his foot tapping rapidly on the dingy carpet beneath our feet. "I thought it was going to go one way and then it went another . . ."

I raise an eyebrow.

"I don't know how to say it." He taps the side of his head with his palms, delaying the words that I'm pretty sure are about to turn my world upside down. Immediately, I feel tears sting behind my eyes, my legs turning into jelly, as realization dawns on me.

He wouldn't drag something out like this if it wasn't bad. If it wasn't something that would hurt me. Suddenly, I wonder if this is how Ma felt when Baba told her about his diabetes. I brace myself for life-changing news as I ask, "Are you sick?"

His brows furrow in confusion.

"No! I'm totally fine. It's just . . ." He stops, then starts again. "It's . . . It sounds so dorky out loud." Adnan inhales deeply and then, in one breath, says, "Imayhave-accidentallyannouncedtotheworldthatyouandIareinarelation-shiponInstagram."

I pause for a second, tipping my head to the side in

thought. "I may be bilingual but even I didn't understand that."

He drops his face in his hands and shakes it before straightening his back to look me in the eyes, his own black and wide in a way I've never seen before. "I may have accidentally announced to the world that you and I are in a relationship on Instagram."

6

I drop the book onto the ground with a muffled thud, the words refusing to click into place in my mind no matter how much they play on repeat.

I may have accidentally announced to the world that you and I are in a relationship on Instagram.

"Z?" Adnan says tentatively. "Did you hear what I said?"

I nod slowly, my eyes focused on a point in the distance.

"OK, good, good . . . any thoughts?"

I refocus on Adnan—on his dark eyelashes, on the little scar above his eyebrow from when he ran into a glass mirror, on his naturally plump lips.

And I feel repulsed. So repulsed that I pick the book back up, jump on top of him, and whack him over the head with it.

"OW, OW, WHY YOU GOTTA BE SO VIOLENT?" he cries out, earning a disapproving look from a student in the opposite corner from us.

"Why do you have to be so *stupid*?" I hiss.

"I . . . panicked?" he says.

I hit him with the book again, this time targeting his biceps.

"Z, please, hear me out!" He tries to wrestle my weapon away, but his resistance is futile. Nothing he says can explain why he would do something as ridiculous as this. I mean, how the hell does him having a moment of panic lead to posting about a nonexistent relationship?

"Excuse me," a female voice interrupts from behind me. With Adnan's grip still on my wrist, I swivel my head to find the librarian staring at us with a cocked brow and crossed arms. "Should you two be here?"

"We're just here for study period before English Lit to pick out a book." Adnan looks at the book in my hand. "That one, actually."

"I see," she answers, not deceived by the blatant lie. "Would you like to check it out and take it with you to class in that case?"

"Uh, we still have to find another book," he says with the dazzling smile he only uses when he gets in trouble. "We're doing a unit on classics, and we have to write a paper on the different writing styles of the authors of the time."

The librarian looks at us with skepticism but turns a corner once Adnan adds the magic words, "We'll be quiet. We promise."

I nod furiously to second the notion and it seems to placate the librarian enough for her to tell us that she will only allow us to stay if we remain deadly silent and take a seat at the tables near the front desk.

Once we've disentangled ourselves and grabbed our backpacks, we follow her to the table like obedient children. When we sit down, I grab a notepad and a pen out of my bag and lay them on the table, afraid that a) the librarian might haunt us if we so much as utter a word and b) I might scream unless I communicate with him via the written word.

EXPLAIN, I write, underlining the word three times.

You take the left side, I take the right side.

"So, like iMessage, but without Wi-Fi and on paper? Old school," he jokes, but I'm too angry with him to find it funny. Sensing my irritation, and the glare the librarian is shooting, he places the pad and pen between us and whispers, "Here goes . . ."

As he writes, I interrupt his messages by writing my own like we're having a conversation in real life.

So. When you skipped out on the movies, I invited Cami, as suggested.
The movie was great, btw.
You woulda liked it, totally up your alley, what with all the pining and

Get to the point, Naan

That nickname is old

And you won't get the chance to be if you don't
explain why you told the world I'm your stupid gf

OK, OK, no need to threaten!
After the movie we kept talking over FaceTime
and then last night we decided we were going
to be a thing

What happened to taking it slow?

Well, it went a little fast

You don't say

I shoot him an icy stare, which makes him quickly scrawl
out the rest of his explanation.

ANYWAY
So we decided we were a thing and I just wanted
to tell someone, so I posted a pic of us from after
the movies to my story on IG.
Just like a soft launch.
You couldn't even tell who was in the photo and
I didn't tag her either.

But then I started getting loads of DMs asking who it was and I was going to say it was Cami but she called me in a frenzy telling me to take it down

Why?

Cami's got some stuff with her family and her dad's super protective of her seeing people so dating is pretty much out of the question. At least publicly

It's not like her dad's hanging on Insta stalking her

You say that but Cami's afraid that it'd get to her parents the same way it got to ours

I want to ask Adnan just how our parents found out because as far as I know, Ma and Baba don't even know how to use Insta. I mean, they can hardly handle Google! But before I'm able to ask the question, Adnan furiously scribbles something else down.

For real, Z, she won't even tell her friends from her old school because she's been burned before by them talking to her parents

And here I thought the Auntie Grapevine and ThermaeSecrets were bad

Exactly
So she's a little paranoid and seeing the picture majorly freaked her out

Why didn't you just take it down?

I was going to but you don't get it, Z, my DMs were FLOODED . . .
Like people were invested!

What people?
I thought we made a deal to keep our accounts private after Somaiya Auntie kept trying to shade us and use our "close friendship" as clout at dawats????

Well, yes, but . . .
I forgot to put it on close friends and put it on my main story . . .

I snap my head up in understanding, my chest constricting with terror. If he put it on his main, that means . . . No. It couldn't have. But as I register the wide look in his eyes, my worst fears are confirmed.

It didn't reach BD, did it?

Oh you know it did
Goddamn time difference meant they were all
waking up in Bangladesh, eating breakfast
and scrolling on their phones and you know how
aunties and uncles are . . .
They TALK

Someone told your parents

Their phones were lighting up like a disco ball!
And you know Desis, they have no regard for time.
Everyone was congratulating them on my
relationship, which they assumed was about YOU
since Amma and Abbu won't shut up about us to
all their siblings.
So they started interrogating me about our
supposed relationship
Meanwhile Cami was breathing down my neck in
tears about the whole thing.
So in a fit of panic . . .

You tell them it's me in the photo

Yup.
I tell them it's you and, honestly, Z, it was like
I told them I had just won the Nobel Prize or
something.
They couldn't believe it . . .
So freaking overjoyed about it they would
have run out into the streets and woken up the
neighbors if I hadn't stopped them

And then they called my parents

Exactly

I swallow as I read over his words, the letters spinning out
of control to concoct a story so mad and yet believable at
the same time. But there's one thing that doesn't make
sense to me.

Then why did you post it?
If you knew Cami was going to freak out,
why did you do it?
Because you must have talked about it, right?
About why Cami wants to be so low-key?

I knew she was private

61

She's hardly on anything social
But I didn't realize she'd freak like that.
I thought it'd be a subtle way to show the world I
wasn't single anymore without making a big deal
out of it—you know, just giving people a small
snapshot

My heart softens. I know that if it were me, I'd be bursting to tell the world all about my person, too.

But then I remember why we're here in the first place and I have to physically shake myself out of the sympathy I feel for him.

Why didn't you just remove the picture from your
story like any other normal person?

Dude
I can't just remove a soft launch after it's been
up—that'd look shady or like I'm desperate af

Ugh. He's right. If people had seen it or screenshotted it and then he'd removed it, he'd be in for a lot of questions today.

So if you just told the people who DM'd you that it
was me, how the hell does everyone at school know?

I had to get the heat off Cami
And she knows that people think you and I are
together
So we kinda agreed that I'd just reupload the
story with a Z and a heart to make people believe
you and I are actually a thing and it was kinda
perfect since you posted that pic of us with our
parents in BD

Allah, of all the days for my phone to break, it just had to be yesterday. If it hadn't broken, maybe I'd have seen the post and we could have taken it down immediately or at least come up with a different strategy.

"Give me your phone," I whisper to Adnan. "I need to see the damage."

He pulls it out of his pocket, handing it to me with a shamefaced glance.

I click onto Adnan's profile and tap on his story; the incriminating evidence is like a blow to the gut. As an outsider, I can see exactly why people would think it's me. In the photo, which is just a silhouette, Adnan's got his hand extended in front of him, Cami holding onto it as she looks away at the neon movie theater sign in the distance. Cami and I look alike, at least in silhouette form, there's no denying that. I look at the time stamp of the post: ten hours ago.

I groan. Allah knows how many people his post has reached. I check to see how many people have viewed it and nearly drop the phone altogether: 350! I shake my head and hand the phone back, feeling disoriented by the sheer number of people who think I'm his *girlfriend*.

And Cami's OK with people thinking you and I are together?

Yeah. She's obviously not ecstatic about it but she understands that it's the only way she and I can be together until she's on better terms with her dad again

Even so, there's still something gnawing away at me . . .

Please don't tell me this is some elaborate ploy so that I'll fall in love with you?
Or that you've secretly been in love with me this entire time and this is your way of making us a thing?

Gross, Z.
What would make you think that?

Because that's literally how every YA rom-com starts. Boy and girl are besties, they get involved in a fake dating plan, and then BAM they get together for real.

Definitely no chance of that happening.

So you have no romantic feelings for me?

10000000% no. You?

1000000000% no.

That's settled then?

But it's not. As selfish as it sounds, I don't see why I should go along with this plan. It's not like I'm gaining much, or rather *anything*, from it. Sure, it'll mean that Ma and Baba will stop pestering me about *trying* with Adnan, but it also means they'll want to get involved in our fake relationship.

Which is a huge *pain*.

But my parents *were* talking this morning. Which is a lot more than they have done the past few days. They were laughing and happy and back to how they used to be. All because they thought Adnan and I are together.

And besides, everyone else already thinks we're together. Even if Adnan hadn't posted the story, we'd still be hassled about our relationship. Prime example being the fact that I can't even post a nice picture of us with our parents without people commenting on how cute we are together. If I go along with Adnan's plan, could this get them off our back once and for all? Does it take us faking a relationship for people to realize that maybe some people just aren't meant to be together?

Maybe it'd be a win-win situation for everyone: my parents are happy that their only daughter is dating their best friends' son, Adnan gets to be with the girl he likes without fearing that her dad will interfere, Sadie and everyone else around us will stop nagging us about getting together, and, when we finally break up, people will see that we're not meant to be and stop shipping us once and for all.

As much as I hate the idea of pretending to be Adnan's girlfriend, since it plays into the narrative everyone's concocted for us, I can't help weighing up the positives of the ruse. Especially bringing my parents back together.

Z, what are you thinking?

I dig my nails into the palm of my hand, creating little crescent moons to ground myself in the tornado of questions flying around in my head. What am I thinking? I think it's a bad idea, that's what I think.

You really like her, don't you?

Adnan lets out a slow breath and looks up, staring hard at me with his coffee-colored eyes as he says, "I do. I really, really like Cami. And more importantly, trust me when I say I wouldn't ask just anybody what I'm asking of you, Zara."

I whimper in exasperation as I shut my eyes, bewilderment clawing at my insides. If I do this, everything will change. People will expect us to be all lovey-dovey and I'm not sure how I feel about pretending to be in love when I'm not. Especially with my *best friend*.

But I also know I don't really have a choice because it's what I need to do to keep my parents talking to each other.

And I'll do anything to keep them happy.

Shit. This is *not* how I imagined my love story would go. Usually fake dating is for enemies, not best friends! Although maybe because we're subverting the trope—and the end result, because no way will I fall in love with Adnan!—it means my chances of a great love story won't be completely squandered. Sure, I might be in a "relationship" for a bit, but it probably won't even be long enough that I'm missing out on anybody else.

"Promise me one thing," I whisper.

"Anything."

"Mates before dates. Our friendship always has to come first."

"Wait," Adnan interrupts, "does that mean . . . ?"

I let out a sigh and, with a heavy eye-roll, ask, "What's our ship name?"

Like a tween girl, he squeals and throws his arms around me. "Thank you, thank you, Z. I owe you big time, I swear . . ."

Adnan starts talking at a million miles per hour and I flash him a smile.

What could possibly go wrong?

67

7

Despite six excruciating hours of class spent trying to ignore all the people whispering about my new relationship status and dodging Sadie, who won't stop texting me for details, I agree to meet with Adnan and Cami at the local Costa to go over the game plan. Fortunately, next door there is a phone repair shop and I manage to hand mine in and order myself a drink before Adnan and Cami even arrive. I order a soy chai latte—honestly, they're superior—and take a seat toward the back, out of view of any curious eyes. A few minutes later, Adnan and Cami walk into the café, beelining for me once they've ordered and received their drinks.

"Z, this is Cami," Adnan says as he perches on the edge of the sofa opposite me. "Cami, this is Zara."

You'd think I would have met my bestie's love interest before this, but Adnan's always been good at keeping the girls he's interested in at arm's length.

"Hey, nice to finally meet you." I reach my hand out to her, almost like I'm greeting her for an interview. Well, in this case, I'd be the interviewee, considering I'm applying for the position of Adnan's fake girlfriend.

"Likewise," she says with a smile. Her grip on my hand is firm, her eye contact consistent, as she shakes it twice. As she sits down, she flicks her ash-blond hair over her shoulder, a healthy distance even Allah would approve of between herself and Adnan. Well, I guess, as his *girlfriend* I shouldn't exactly be expecting that they'd be all over each other. At least, not in public.

There is a moment of silence between the three of us when all you can hear is the bustling of the café and our breathing.

"This is weird, isn't it?" I say.

"So weird," Cami responds with a relieved laugh, which immediately puts me at ease. "Let me be the first to apologize that it had to be this way."

"*You're* apologizing? I think the person who should be apologizing is that one over there." I point at Adnan and squint at him like I'm one of our old aunties scrutinizing his whole being.

"I already said I was sorry . . . ," Adnan mumbles.

"I think Zara's going to need a whole lot more than 'sorry' for having to pretend to be your girlfriend." Cami nudges Adnan's shoulder, her face cracking into a much bigger smile now that the tension seems to have dissipated. "You better find her the love of her life after all this."

"I'd like to second that."

"Lord, help me put up with these women," Adnan says, his gaze directed at the ceiling.

"You're the one with two girlfriends, why are you asking for help? We're the ones who have to put up with you." Cami winks at me. "And just so you know, Zara, this isn't forever. I don't know how much Naan has to—"

"Oh my God, you call him that, too!" I am unable to contain my glee.

"Of course. It's right there! How could you not?"

I like this girl already.

"Like I was saying, I don't know how much he's told you, but you honestly have no idea how grateful I am to you for doing it for us, which is why I want to reassure you that this will only be for a little while. My circumstances will change soon, promise." Cami takes a long sip of her drink, shielding her face with the enormous white mug. I want to ask her why she needs to conceal her relationship in the first place, curious about the little dusting of information Adnan told me earlier about her dad being super protective, but I keep my interest to myself. "I just need some time to figure out how to do that."

I shoot Cami a small smile. "It's fine. If I have to make this one sacrifice and earn all the good karma, I'm up for it."

"Thank you. I know you probably think I'm ridiculous, but it wouldn't surprise me if my dad had a lurker account and was following that profile on Insta. What's it called again? ThermalGossip?"

"ThermaeSecrets," I correct with a sigh. That stupid Instagram account tries so hard to be DeuxMoi on a

70

budget and without any actual celebrities. Especially considering it's just a school account. "I honestly hate it. The number of times they've made a huge deal out of nothing is amazing."

"Remember that time they snapped a picture of you crying and me just standing there with my arms crossed?" Adnan groans. "They made it seem like we were breaking up when, you know, we weren't even together."

"I wasn't even crying. It was my stupid hay fever!"

"I don't know how you've put up with it for so long," Cami comments with a sympathetic expression.

"Yeah, me neither." I let out a deep breath. I haven't checked the page today but I'm betting good money we're on it. "The devil lives on social media," Cami and I say simultaneously, mimicking a viral YouTube video of a parent on a rampage about their kid's terrible attention span now that TikTok has made us all unable to focus on anything longer than thirty seconds. We both laugh.

"Girlfriends in sync," Cami says, raising her mug.

"Girlfriends in sync," I repeat, and raise my own mug to cheers hers. "So, uh, how should we do this?" I ask, wanting to get this over and done with as soon as possible, even though we're all having a laugh and not silently fuming about how this has turned our lives upside down. "Is there like a story we should be telling or . . . ?"

"I guess we could just pull bits from how Cami and I actually got together," Adnan suggests. "We'd need to tweak it, but it could work."

Cami bites her lower lip and looks down at her feet.

"What's wrong?" Adnan says, his hand reaching for hers before he realizes he can't do that in public anymore unless he wants cheating rumors circulating. I look around quickly to see if there's anybody from school in the shop, but fortunately we're the only ones in uniform.

"I just . . ." She tucks a strand of hair behind her ear. "I'm not so sure we should do that."

I suddenly understand: she's already sharing her boyfriend with me; she shouldn't have to share something as significant as their origin story, too. In books and movies, even when the way the characters meet isn't like a stereotypical fairy tale, it will still matter to them; they will still look at it fondly, and in the way they retell it, you can see the affection tucked beneath their words or how they longingly look at each other as they recount their memories. Origin stories infuse significance into a moment that would have otherwise passed by, giving a relationship both a beginning and a history. Stealing someone's origin story is like taking a part of their soul.

"We can just make something up," I say, to reassure her. "We'll rip off a storyline from a show or something."

"Thank you," Cami says with a soft smile.

Following a brief silence, she and Adnan gaze at each other, unspoken words flying between them, and soon enough, Cami leans in with a mischievous grin, her bangs concealing her eyes as she does. Adnan restrains himself from kissing her on the forehead as she rests her head on his shoulder for a second, but I see the circumspect squeeze he gives her leg before they separate. The sight makes me want to barf in my mouth, because this is Adnan we're talking about, practically my brother, but it also makes my heart falter.

I wish I had that. I wish I had someone who I could just speak to via eye contact, someone who made me feel sick but in a good way.

I want someone to look at me the way Adnan looks at Cami.

But mostly, I want to look at someone the way Adnan looks at Cami.

"We'll have to change our lock screens as well, Z," Adnan says, drawing me back into whatever conversation they had while I spaced out. "So, say goodbye to Machine Gun Kelly."

"But he's my bae!"

"As far as our parents know, I'm your bae now. And if we're going to sell this, we need to do it the right way. We can't half-ass it. And I'm looking hella fine right now."

I roll my eyes. "My phone is at the shop. We'll have to do it some other time."

Adnan nods in agreement. "Sure. Look, I've got to run. I want to get in a quick gym sesh before we meet at yours, Z. Cami, I'll call you later?"

"Wait." I wave my hands out in front of me, grabbing Adnan's attention. "We're having dinner together?"

"Of course we're having dinner. Don't you think your parents want to meet your new boyfriend?" He wiggles his eyebrows jokingly. "Also, we missed Sunday dinner yesterday so it's only right we make up for it by having dinner today. When I left this morning, Ma was even telling me that Auntie was making biryani."

Wow. Biryani. She's really bringing out the big guns. I mean, I knew Ma would be over the moon if Adnan and I ever got together, but I didn't think it would be biryani-level happy.

Oh Allah, this is not going to be easy. But knowing that it's worth it just to see my parents in a good place, and to quash the idea of Zara and Adnan forever when the time comes, is enough to remind me why I'm going through with this in the first place.

"Hey." I gently grab Cami by the arm as we exit the café, allowing Adnan to walk ahead for a second. "Are you sure you're OK with this? I know we agreed it was a weird situation to be in but . . ."

"I know this isn't going to be easy," Cami says with a shrug. "But it's what I signed up for, and I trust you."

Her words surprise me. She doesn't even know me, yet she trusts me. "Are you on something? Because if you are, that's OK, but I'd like to know what life-altering drugs you're taking because no girl would be as chill as you are right now."

Cami lets out a laugh. "Adnan thinks the world of you and I'm not going to distrust him just because his best friend is a girl. He's assured me that there's nothing between you two, and seeing you together confirms it. You act more like brother and sister than boyfriend and girlfriend." She pauses before adding, "You're also doing me a huge favor, so I can't hate you, can I?"

I snort. "Probably not."

"It'd be nice to be friends with you. I don't really know anybody here since we moved, and I'd much rather not be the girl who only hangs out with her boyfriend. Which will be hard considering I can't really hang with him in public by myself anyway."

My heart suddenly feels like mashed potatoes. I don't know much about Cami except for the fact that her family moved here at the end of the summer. And now the added information about her dad being super protective. It must be hard to be new *and* in a secret relationship.

"I think we'll get on just fine," I tell her.

8

"I'm home!" I say as I kick my shoes off and throw my backpack onto the floor before quickly picking it back up and digging into it to make sure the brand-new screen on my phone hasn't cracked again from the impact. The guys at the repair shop charged a fortune to fix it in record time so no way am I breaking it again. After carefully investigating it for any cracks and finding none, I slide into my slippers, the soft padding a comfort to the soles of my feet after such a draining day.

But obviously, that doesn't last very long.

"Zara!" Ma exclaims in surprise when I enter the kitchen, her right hand on her chest. "You nearly scared me to death. Why didn't you say you were home?"

"I did!"

"In any case, come, have some cha." She fills up the kettle before I even have a chance to tell her that I've had enough hot drinks today. I know liquid intake is very important, but I genuinely fear for the state of my bladder.

"Thanks, Ma." I take the mug by its handle and am just about to head upstairs when Ma loudly clears her throat. I turn around to see her leaning against the counter. "What?"

"Well, aren't you going to talk to me?" she says, a mischievous grin on her face as she bobbles her head in the knowing Asian-mother way.

"About what?"

Ma rolls her eyes in exasperation as she takes a seat at the table. "About you and Adnan."

"Oh." Right. It would be naive of me to think that getting together would be enough. Of course Ma would want to know every little detail. I take a seat across from her and decide to stall until I can think of a viable story. I take a sip of my drink, the warm liquid reminding me of the times we visited Bangladesh during monsoon season, sitting on the balcony to watch the rain sizzle on rooftops made of aluminum while we huddled together under thin blankets, our hands warming around our cups of sweet cha with honey. A simpler time.

"Beta, come on, tell me."

I sigh, sensing the impatience growing in her voice. "There's not really much to tell, Ma. It kind of just . . . happened."

"But *how*, baba?" She practically pounces on me, her eyes alight with a glow I see in her whenever she looks at wedding videos on YouTube. "Did he ask you? Did you ask him? What was it that made you finally realize he was the one for you?"

The way Ma talks about it you'd think I was getting married. I guess in Ma's mind there is nobody more perfect for me than Adnan. And even though Ma pretends to be the hip, cool Asian parent who doesn't want to dictate who her daughter dates, I could always tell from the way she sized up the few guys I brought home before that she not-so-secretly wished I would end up with Adnan.

"Can we talk about it later? When Auntie and Uncle come? I just want to see all your reactions to the story at once," I deflect.

"Of course. But I want *all* the details at dinner, OK? Your baba and I have been itching to hear about you and Adnan since we found out."

Ma mentioning Baba makes me perk up. It's exciting to think that me and Adnan "getting together" is what's gotten them over their spat, at least temporarily, and talking again. But just as quickly as that joy appears, it disappears, replaced with a spine-chilling alarm that vibrates throughout my body. And when I look at Ma, a wide smile pressed into her cheeks, I know *exactly* why.

"What?" I ask, already shutting my eyes with fear.

"Oh, I'm just thinking about all the pictures I am going to take of you and Adnan tonight!"

"Ma, please, no."

"Zara." She says my name with an edge that tells me there is no disputing this. "I have been waiting *years* for this. Let me have my moment."

9

An hour and a half later, the doorbell rings. I unplug my curling iron and rest it on its little stand before running my fingers through my hair. As I pinch my cheeks to give them some color, I suddenly feel an uncomfortable flutter in my stomach.

It's just Auntie and Uncle. I see them every week. They're practically my second set of parents. So why the hell am I so nervous to have dinner with them tonight?

"There she is!" Somaiya Auntie exclaims as I descend the stairs. "Assalamu alaikum."

"Walaikum assalam, Auntie." I go in for a hug, breathing in Auntie's signature scent, the subtle notes of black currant filling the air just enough so as not to bring on a migraine.

"Ki obostha?" Uncle asks.

"I'm good, thank you," I answer politely. Behind Uncle stands Adnan, who is looking surprisingly dapper. His hair is poofy, probably from showering at the gym, and he's wearing the designer shirt Ma gifted him at Eid last year. What a suck-up.

"Hey," I croak as I twist the ring on my middle finger.

"Hey," he responds, rubbing the back of his neck.

Adnan and I stand by our parents, who exchange pleasantries, just like they usually would, but they keep glancing at us as if waiting for one of us to make the first move. For us to do something out of the ordinary. For us to behave like the couple we're supposedly meant to be.

"Uhm, we'll just go upstairs then until dinner is ready?" I tentatively ask. Usually, this is what we would do anyway—head to my bedroom and wait until we're called down for food—but I'm not sure how we do things now. Will Ma stop us from hanging out on our own and make us sit in the living room while the parents are in the kitchen?

"Of course. You may as well go do something else, while we wait for your father," Ma says, ushering Adnan toward me.

"No need to be too encouraging," Uncle comments conspiratorially. "We've all been teenagers before."

Adnan groans and shakes his head. "Let's go before Abbu starts reminiscing about his player days."

"Keep the door open!" Ma shouts as we ascend the staircase. "No hanky-panks!"

Who needs to buy blush when you could just have your mother's embarrassing words release hormones in your body free of charge?

"That wasn't too bad," Adnan notes as he lies down on my bed, hands behind his head. I kick some clothes from the floor into my wardrobe and shut my half-opened drawer of panties, suddenly feeling like he shouldn't be seeing them even if nothing has actually changed between us.

"I don't know what world you were in but that was awful. Also, why are you so dressed up?" I roll my chair out from underneath my desk and take a seat, resting my feet at the end of the bed.

"I'm meeting the parents; I've got to look good."

"You've met my parents before. I don't see why you had to get all dressed up."

"Yeah, but never as your boyfriend."

Boyfriend. What have I done?

"Besides, it's not like you didn't make an effort either." He gestures at the off-white floral dress with a sweetheart neckline I'm wearing. "I mean, I don't think I've seen you in a dress since we were kids."

Maybe I did put in a bit more effort than normal. But Ma did say she was staging a photoshoot, and no way in hell am I going to look basic in pictures that I am sure will end up plastered all over Desi social media.

"You look nice, actually. Less like my sister-slash-best-friend and more like my girlfriend." His cheeks flare up and, Allah, is he lucky he got the good melanin genes because otherwise he'd look like a ripe tomato. "You know what I mean?"

As much as I love watching Adnan dig himself into a hole, I decide to let him off on this occasion and open up Spotify on my phone. Blackbear blares through the

Bluetooth speaker on my desk. I bob along to the beat, properly feeling myself for at least a solid half-hour before Uncle ruins the mood.

"Don't think we can't hear the kiss-shaped silence through the music!" he calls from downstairs, fueling raucous laughter from our moms.

"That better be the bass and not the bed thumping!" Ma yells, a giggle in her words. A second later, she adds, more soberly, "I'm serious! I don't want any grandchildren yet!"

I let out a guttural groan. "Kill me now, please."

"It's just banter, Z. They'll settle down eventually," Adnan says without looking up from his phone. Judging from the enormous grin on his face and the way he's been tapping away at his screen the entire time, I assume he's deep in Cami-land and away from reality.

"Hey!" I shout, getting his attention.

"What?"

I hold up a fist and pretend to crank it until my middle finger is fully lifted.

Adnan rests a hand above his heart. "Thanks, I really feel the love."

"Speaking of love, I almost got us busted earlier when Ma asked how we came to our senses and decided to date."

"Really?"

"Obviously she's going to want to know every single detail. Didn't Auntie ask you anything?"

"Not really." He shrugs. "But I guess that's more of a girl thing than a guy thing."

"Way to stereotype."

He holds his hands up by way of apology. "The patriarchy still rules over South Asian women, so sue me."

I glare at him, my eyeballs itching to roll into the back of my head. "We need to nail down a story. Because I bet you a tenner they're going to interrogate us at dinner. And as much as I would like to scam you of your money, I'd much rather not scramble for a lie on the spot."

"Let's brainstorm then." Adnan scoots forward, perching on the edge of the bed with his elbow on his knee, his biceps bulging more than usual because of the position. I roll my chair nearer to him, my legs resting on the end of the bed, his thighs merely inches away from my feet. As we delve deep into what would constitute a plausible explanation for our "getting together," I can't help myself from getting distracted. The veins on Adnan's forearms are so prominent despite the deep coffee color of his skin. And the way his index finger is rhythmically tapping the center of his bottom lip where the skin is slightly cracked is almost hypnotic. A feeling I can't put my finger on runs through me as I note the details of his body and I have to scoot away just to shake it off me. Adnan doesn't seem to notice, though. "What about . . . ?" he starts to say.

"Adnan! Zara! Dinner!" Ma yells, interrupting our planning.

"I'll think of something," Adnan says. "Now let's go down before another stove explodes."

10

The heavy fragrance of saffron-infused beef biryani hits me as soon as I go down the last step, nearly missing it altogether because of the enchanting smell.

Our table is big enough for six, with Ma and Baba at opposite ends of it and Auntie and Uncle sitting together on the same side. Adnan pulls out a chair for me and it's only then that I take note of how formal tonight's dinner looks. There is a stack of plates and a bowl of hot water in the center of the table for us to wash our hands in between courses. Napkins, folded in triangles, are placed in front of us and Ma's pulled out the fancy glasses we pretty much only use on special occasions.

It almost feels like we're at a wedding.

Before we dig in, Baba leads us in prayer, like he does whenever we are celebrating a special occasion, and even though I wouldn't call myself religious, I can't help but mouth along to the words he recites, grateful to have my family on speaking terms again.

"Bismillah ir rahman ir rahim," we all say as he finishes.

"Farah, this looks absolutely delicious," Somaiya Auntie says, her eyes admiring the steaming rice in front of her.

"No borhani?" Sumon Uncle teases, only to hold his hands up in concession a second later when Somaiya Auntie gives him the glare of death.

Ma pointedly clears her throat and looks at Baba out of the corner of her eye. "We're trying to keep the surprises to a minimum, this time."

"No surprises here," Baba responds with a smile. "Except maybe the one of our children getting together so suddenly."

Everyone looks between Adnan and me expectantly.

"Well—you see—we kind of—" I stammer, annoyed at myself for not rehearsing our origin story, but it doesn't matter because Adnan jumps in.

"It was at the movies a few days ago," Adnan says, his lie silky soft. "We'd just seen this rom-com, upon Zara's request, *obviously*. I didn't really want to watch a rom-com—you know how much I hate them—but she said she needed to get out of the house." I sheepishly look at my parents, who clear their throats and do their best not to let their guilt show. "And afterwards we were talking about the movie, and Zara was just going *on and on* about how meant-to-be the main characters were and droning on about love like her whole life depended on it. At first, I thought she was just being typical Zara with her rose-colored glasses, but then I actually started to see her point. And it didn't seem so silly anymore." He turns his head toward me and the look in his eyes makes my knees quiver. "Obviously, I wasn't going to tell her that, so to shut her up I kissed her."

I bark out a laugh at the same time that everyone else does. I don't know how Adnan came up with that on the spot but it's so realistic that even I almost believe it. I hope that my actual origin story, whenever that comes, is something similar. Effortless. Real.

But most of all? Easy. Like there's no hesitation.

I look to my parents to see if they've bought the tale Adnan has spun and, judging by the stars in their eyes and how Ma briefly squeezes Baba's bicep with affection, I think it's safe to say they have.

"We were both shocked that it happened. I mean, Zara nearly fell over and got hit by a bicycle after the kiss, but a second later, she bounced right back and we both just knew it was right."

"Is that how you remember it, Zara?" Somaiya Auntie asks. "Because you've got to get these details right early or it'll cause problems along the way. Adnan's father and I *still* cannot decide on how we got together."

"It was the first email. You always remember it wrong," Sumon Uncle declares with a grin so wide I bet it could be seen from space.

"Of course, jaan," Auntie responds with an exaggerated wink. When Uncle shakes his head in defeat, she brings her attention back to me. My skin grows warm under her scrutiny, and I force myself to answer her original question.

"Yeah, definitely."

"I thought you didn't go to the movies in the end," Ma

observes, ever the detective. Her forehead creases, deep ridges above her brows. I suck in a sharp breath, ready to spin another lie just to keep up appearances. However, before I can, she backtracks. "But I suppose I may have been a bit preoccupied." She clears her throat, the apples of her cheeks brightening in embarrassment.

I swallow hard and move some rice around on my plate, the yellow coloring of the biryani staining my nails. With our story told, and our parents reminiscing about their own, I tip my head in Adnan's direction with a questioning brow.

"What?" he whispers.

"What was *that*?" I have to restrain myself from allowing my jaw to drop. "I thought I was the one who religiously watched rom-coms here, not you."

"What can I say? Seems I'm just a natural romantic."

"As if."

Adnan beams with a self-satisfied smirk. "You liked that, didn't you?"

"Shut up."

"Guess after all these years I just know what it takes to tug at your heartstrings. Now, come on. Let's take selfies for our lock screens," he says. Grabbing my phone off the table, he holds down the camera icon on the lock screen and immediately starts tapping away, taking pictures of himself from different angles, before handing it back to me. "Pick your favorite. But honestly, if I were you, I'd just make a collage out of them since I look *fire* today."

I choose a picture at random and make it my lock screen before picking up Adnan's phone. "Let's do yours now."

I try to replicate Adnan and take selfies from different angles, but I look so stiff in each and every one of them and just end up deleting them in the end. Eventually, Adnan pushes his chair closer to mine and gets in the frame with me.

"You're obviously in need of dire assistance," he says simply before making silly faces at me until I laugh so hard I feel like my stomach is cramping. He finally captures a photo of me where I'm in the middle of an open-mouthed smile and he's looking fondly at me.

"That's the one," Adnan announces. He makes the photo his lock screen, before tuning in to a heated conversation between Baba and Uncle about the Premier League.

As Adnan talks to Baba like the perfect son-in-law, Ma and Auntie toy with the idea of hosting a dawat in the near future to celebrate our union.

"Ma, please, no," I whine. "We don't need a party."

But Ma doesn't listen to me. Instead, she simply waves me away and continues to chat Auntie's ear off about various decorations she could get shipped from Bangladesh.

Even though I tune out of the conversation, I can't help but feel my heart growing exponentially. All the arguing has been forgotten. It really does seem like, with the help of Allah, our little announcement has reignited something in Ma and Baba again. Something's changed. This joy . . . it's like they've won the lottery or been invited to Buckingham Palace.

Except it's all built on a lie.

No, I can't think about that. I'm doing this for a good

reason. The good will outweigh the bad. I shake my head in the hopes that it will kill the brain cells that conjured that ugly thought. I refuse to let anything ruin this evening.

"Beta, what's going on in that beautiful head of yours?" Somaiya Auntie asks from across the table, shifting everybody's attention. "It looks like you're trying to solve a complex math problem."

"I was just thinking . . . that this is nice. Seeing you all so happy about Adnan and me." I shrug, trying to shake off the strange butterflies flitting about in my stomach. Underneath the table, I incessantly spin the ring on my finger. "It just makes me happy that you're happy."

"We're happy because *you're* happy, baba," Ma says with a jovial smile. "All we've ever wanted is to see our children happy. So how can we not be when they are?"

I respond with a small smile, unable to verbalize my emotions, or rather lack of emotions, and shovel some beef into my mouth, hoping they'll take that as a signal to carry on with whatever conversations they were previously having.

"Look at you being all soppy." Adnan nudges my shoulder with his and I promptly tell him to shut up and never speak of it again. "I knew everything would be right with them after our news."

But that persistent ache in my chest is still there as I think about the duplicity of all that we are doing.

89

FAKE DATING PLAN

Today 07:24

ADNAN created group

ADNAN added you

ADNAN added Cami

Zara

Gee what a great name

Tell me how often does Auntie find your phone face up?

And how often does she take a peek at your phone when it lights up?

Also remind me, did you ever do that thing to your phone where you remove the preview of the messages?

Adnan

can't be bothered

Cami

TBF Naan, Zara has a point

That is probably the most obvious name you could give a group chat

ADNAN renamed group "BESTEST FRIENDS EVER"

Zara

You know Sadie is going to murder you if she sees you named the chat this

She's going to get jealous

And she will see it, I can tell you that now

That girl is pro at reading texts over your shoulder

ADNAN renamed group "GROUP"

Adnan

that good?

Cami

Not the most inventive group chat I've been in

But I haven't been in any for a while so this will have to do!

Zara

Once we've introduced you to the gang, we'll get you in on our main chat

Not that you'll see much other than pics of Liam and Ceri making out

91

Adnan

anyhoo, Z

Cami and I want to meet this Saturday

Zara

OK?

Adnan

which means we'll need you there

Zara

Why?

Cami

We can't be seen together without you

You are his "girlfriend" after all

Zara

Oh yeah, sorry, duh

Still getting used to living a double life

What are you guys even going to do?

Cami

Well, my parents aren't home

And they're always home

So, this is the perfect opportunity to spend time together

We were thinking about staying in and watching a movie

Zara

So what am I meant to do while you two are sucking each other's faces?

Cami

I've got a home theater

We can all watch the film together?

Zara

I do love to spend my weekends third-wheeling!

SHAH RUKH KHAN 2.0

Today 07:59

Adnan

Z

Zara

A

Adnan

please

Zara

I DON'T WANT TO SIT IN THE DARK
AND WATCH YOU TWO MAKE OUT

Adnan

we'll watch the movie with u!!!

Zara

That's what you say but I KNOW
that you'll end up making out

Adnan

dude

Zara

Dude

Adnan

come on

i'm begging you

Zara

I can't stand you

GROUP

Today 08:04

Zara

Fine. I'll be there.

Cami

YAY!!

Thank you thank you!

Btw, you'll have to take two buses

I'll send Adnan the information

And oh, wear boots

You'll have to walk through some fields to get to my house from the bus station

SHAH RUKH KHAN 2.0

Today 08:13

Adnan

thank you

Zara

Two buses???

You owe me

Big time

95

Adnan

i know i know

Zara

I just don't get why I have to be there

It's not like you're going somewhere public

I doubt someone from school
would catch us by her house

Adnan

she gets paranoid about these things

it's just in case her parents come
home early

or her cousin comes over

he lives nearby and pops in sometimes

Zara

Dude

What did this girl do that her parents
have her on lockdown 24/7?

I am wholly intrigued

Adnan

a story for another day

oh, I should also mention that we're going there early

Zara

How early we talking?

1pm? 2pm?

Adnan

more like before noon

Zara

If it's before 11:59, I am going to be pissed

Adnan

we're leaving at 10

Zara

Why would we get up that early?

What is there even to do that early?

Adnan

her parents get back at 6

i want to spend as much time as possible with her

Zara

Ffs

And what do we tell our parents we're doing at 10am?

Their bullshit radar is going to go berserk

I don't think Ma's ever seen me get up before 3 in the afternoon on a Saturday

Adnan

we'll make something up

Zara

That's how we got into this mess in the first place

11

"Where's your boy toy?" Sadie asks, stuffing her face full of fries before we've even had a chance to sit down for lunch.

"He's only four months younger than me, Sades. I don't think you can call him a boy toy if the gap is that small."

"Oh, mate, you're so wrong." Sadie goes off on a tangent, something about a dating formula she saw online to back up the facts she'll include in her documentary, which calculates the acceptable minimum age for dating someone, and usually I'd shut down her rambling within seconds, but I make an exception this time because at least then she's not focusing on Adnan's absence.

It's only been a few days since I became Adnan's fake girlfriend, but it feels like a lifetime and it's honestly already starting to feel like a chore. There's the stupid date tomorrow and then there's now, where, when Sadie is done with her rambling, I'll have to pretend I don't know where Adnan is, and act all bothered about it like a girlfriend would.

". . . so, technically," Sadie says, squinting with one eye as she holds up a finger, "he's your boy toy."

"If that's what gets you to sleep at night." I steal one of her fries.

"There's Mr. Romance." She points her chin in the direction of the door through which Adnan is walking. "Dude, where've you been? I've had to keep an eye on this one for far too long."

"Sorry." Adnan pants as he comes to a halt, his hair all ruffled and less than perfect. In fact, he looks very unlike himself. His cheeks are rosier than normal and his lips almost look swo—Oh my Allah, he's just come back from a make-out sesh with Cami! "Been busy, y'know."

"So busy you don't even want to say hi to your girl-friend?" She affectionately punches him in the shoulder. "She's been waiting forever."

Adnan's cheeks redden with heat as he takes a seat next to me, leaving Sadie by herself across the table. "Sorry, I keep forgetting that we're a couple."

My eyes widen. How can he say that? And in public? I mean, I get what he means but people are going to figure out that this is all fake if he comes out with stuff like that.

And we *cannot* have people figuring it out. Not yet at least. Ma and Baba may be on speaking terms, but I wouldn't say they're totally back to the way they were before.

"It's just . . . for so long, my feelings for Zara have been repressed and now that they're all out in the open, it just feels a bit weird," he says quickly, saving himself. "I never could have imagined a day when I'd get to sit next to you like this. As your boyfriend and not just your childhood best friend."

To stop myself from rolling my eyes at how sappy he's sounding, I focus on a leaf in his hair, so small and dark you wouldn't be able to see it unless you were really looking. I carefully pluck it out, noting just how soft his hair is. I've never had any reason to run my hands through his hair before. Reminding myself that Sadie is watching, I hide the leaf in my palm as I remove my hand from his silky strands. I smile for the imaginary cameras, even though I know we are currently acting for an audience of one. To further sell the picture, I lean in to whisper something in his ear. "Here." I locate his hand underneath the table, pressing the leaf into his palm. "Save it as a memento of your time with Cami." I mean for my words to be playful, but they come out with a twinge of annoyance.

Adnan's eyes flash. He puts an arm around me, his lips against my hair as he quietly mumbles, "We'll be more careful next time."

"Awww, you guys!" Sadie coos, and it's only then I notice she's got her phone out.

"Are you . . . filming us?" I ask, feeling on edge.

"Obviously." Sadie literally zooms in on us. "Now that you're a couple, I thought I'd make you guys the focus of the doc!"

"What are you talking about?" Adnan asks before I can freak out about what Sadie's just said.

"Sadie's entering Cinemagic, this film competition, and she's filming a documentary on love," I explain quickly, feeling like I'm about to be sick.

"And I was originally going to ask couples around school for their stories and try to figure out a focal point from there, but now that you've got together it's only fitting that I make you guys the focus!"

"But . . ." Adnan glances at me before asking the same question on my mind. "Why us?"

"Because you're just at the beginning stages of your great love story and I can actually follow you as you fall in love." Sadie pauses her recording. "Also, it'd be a bit weird to follow around people who aren't my besties and ask them to divulge every single detail about how they fell in love."

Now we have to act for the *camera* as well? I'd better earn an Oscar for this.

"OMG, I just had another brain wave!" Sadie extends her hand across the table and stares deep into my eyes. "I could call it *This Is How You Fall in Love*." She lets go of my hand and pretends to drop the mic while my stomach also drops. "How brilliant is that?!"

"Incredible," I manage to say, once the lump in my throat passes. At the same time, Adnan lets out a simple "Wow."

"I just can't believe the timing—it's so great. Can you believe, Z, that it was only a few days ago we talked about love and the doc and now you have a whole *boyfriend*? How wild is that?"

"Wild," I repeat. "So wild."

"Now you two just have to stay together, since your story will make up the bulk of my documentary and it would be a pain to edit you guys out," she says with a laugh. "Also, it's out of selfish reasons. I like you both too much to have to choose sides if you break up."

I stiffen. I'd forgotten that breakups, even fake ones, require people to take sides. And I don't want people to take sides. I don't want Sadie to have to choose between me and Adnan. I know I'm the one who's closer to her and, because of how fiercely loyal Sadie is, that she'd take my side—especially if, after our breakup, whenever that is, Adnan "moves on" with Cami—but I don't want that. I want us all to be friends after this is over. I want everything to go back to normal. And it's not like we'll ever be able to tell Sadie the truth without her a) being devastated that it was all a ploy, b) being pissed that she wasn't included in the plan, and c) holding it against us for all eternity as leverage for doing whatever the hell she wants us to do on her behalf because of our betrayal. And, oh, d) it's not like we'd ever be able to tell Sadie the truth without revealing that her documentary is based on a complete lie.

Damn, fake relationships are so much harder than they show on TV.

"By the way, you two are yet to give me the official deets on how you got together. Don't think just because I'm knee-deep in researching interviewing techniques that I've forgotten about your story. And, oh!" Sadie kicks my foot, activating my knee-jerk reaction so that my leg bangs into the table. "Did you hear that blackbear is doing a last-minute gig in London this weekend?"

I stop rubbing my kneecap long enough to squeal, "You're joking!"

"I wouldn't dare joke about blackbear," Sadie says, dead serious.

"He's not even that good," Adnan comments.

Sadie and I stare at him through the slits of our eyes. I'm about to rip into Adnan about his substandard taste in music when Sadie says, "While I would like to debate the merit of blackbear versus the so-called musicians you listen to, I'm more interested in why that girl over there is staring at you."

I follow Sadie's gaze across the cafeteria. Cami is watching us from a table in the corner. I sigh internally. If we want this to work, we're going to need to introduce her to the group sooner or later, but the question is, how will we explain her newfound presence in our friendship group? And beyond that, can she and Adnan be trusted to keep their hands off each other in public spaces? I mean, they were making out on school grounds! Even if Sadie and I didn't catch them, somebody else could have.

And I can't have that. Not if I want to keep the ruse up.

"Do you guys know her or something?" Sadie asks.

Adnan's eyes widen as I spit out the first lie that comes to me. "We're in book club together."

"Book club?"

"Yeah, uhm, Ma's friend's daughter hosts it."

"Really?" Adnan asks me, and it takes everything I have not to smack the back of his neck.

"Yes," I say through gritted teeth. "And I met her there. Cami. At the club."

Sadie contemplates my lie, her head tilted to the side as she looks between me and Adnan to Cami. Sweat pools in my lower back as the gears in Sadie's brain turn. Can she see through the blatant lie?

Finally, Sadie says, "Is she into rom-coms?"

"Uhm, I think so."

"In that case, you should ask her to sit with us. We could always use more people on our side."

I exhale with relief. Spared for another day. "Yeah, I'll talk to her."

"Anyway . . ." Sadie redirects the conversation and pulls out her phone to retrieve her emails. "Here . . . The gig is tomorrow."

"Did you say tomorrow?" Adnan asks at the same time a weight forms in my gut.

"Yeah. Why?" Sadie lifts a brow. "You're not away at one of your parents' thingies, are you?"

"Dawat," I correct. "And no. We're not, but—"

"We have plans this weekend," Adnan jumps in.

"Can't you reschedule? It's not every day blackbear pops to the UK."

"You're right, Sadie. It *isn't* every day that blackbear is in the UK." I turn to face Adnan, hoping he can read the pleading in my eyes. "Can't we reschedule? I'm sure we can hang out next weekend."

Adnan looks at me with desperate eyes. "I don't know, Z. It took a lot of planning to make this Saturday happen in the first place."

Is this how it's going to be from now on? What I want doesn't matter as long as Adnan gets what *he* wants with Cami?

I know I shouldn't be annoyed with Adnan, I do, but I feel salty that I am missing out on a great concert just so he can hang out with his girlfriend. Like, what happened to our number one rule? Mates before dates.

At the same time, I can't help but think about why going along with the date, and the whole charade in general, is the right thing: my parents. How happy they were at dinner the other day. How they're finally on speaking terms again after what felt like an eternity.

"Look, if it's that big of a deal, we can skip it," Sadie says softly, reading the tension between us. "It's not a massive thing, just an intimate concert. I won't go either, Z. So it's not like you're missing out."

I appreciate the solidarity, but it still doesn't make me feel any better.

"Thanks, Sades." Adnan fist-bumps Sadie across the table before she heads off to the library to read up on filming techniques.

"I'd better have the time of my life tomorrow," I tell Adnan as we walk to class five minutes later.

"You will, I promise. It'll be a day you never forget."

12

"When's the next bus? I'm freezing."

"The app says it's coming." Adnan blows into his hands in between words. It's only the middle of October but it feels like it might as well be December. "Give it another minute or so. You know what buses are like in the middle of nowhere."

Other than an old man, we're the only ones at this random bus stop in Thickwood. It honestly wouldn't surprise me if we saw farm animals roaming the streets at this point.

"Why does she go to school in Bath if she lives all the way out here? She must get up at five a.m. to get there in time."

"Long story," Adnan says simply.

I gesture at the empty road and then the app, which has been telling us that the bus has been due for the past fifteen minutes. "We've got nothing but time."

Adnan grimaces. "The gist is that her dad works in the city so he drives her to and from school. So, it only takes her about twenty minutes or so since the route is a lot less convoluted by car than it is by bus."

Well, if it's so darn convoluted, I still don't understand why *I* have to be here.

"Her cousin—Z, you already know this," Adnan responds, somehow reading my mind. Finally, the bus chugs into view and he holds his arm out to signal it to stop.

There's hardly anybody on the bus or anyone waiting at the stops along the way, but even so we practically crawl forward. I open up the Pokémon GO app on my phone and start spinning PokéStops.

"Dude, that is so 2016. Are people still even playing that anymore?"

"Obviously," I say, though it's been at least a year since I've spotted someone other than me playing it. Not that I play it often, but it's a good way to kill time every now and then.

"But why?"

"You know why. You were as obsessed as me, if not more, when it came out."

"Yeah, because I was *ten* and didn't know how to talk to girls."

True. But I don't admit that. Nor do I tell him that it's the only thing that can calm me down when a book ends on a cliff-hanger and the next installment isn't due for another year. Instead, I deflect by asking, "How else am I meant to get my exercise in?"

"Going to the gym?" Adnan presses the "Stop" button

as we pass by the Lucknam Park Hotel & Spa, which is apparently only a five-minute walk across the fields from where Cami lives. "And just because the app thinks you're walking doesn't mean you're actually walking. You can't take that distance tracker seriously."

"I'm buff enough as it is. I don't need to go to the gym." I kiss my nonexistent biceps through my jacket as we get off the bus. "Also, Ash Ketchum told me to—and I quote—'catch 'em all.' So that's what I'm doing."

"You're such a nerd."

"Says the guy who knows the names of all the first-generation Pokémon." I walk ahead of him, only turning around to shout, "In order of *Pokédex number!*"

Adnan drags his hand across his face as he catches up to me. "Why you gotta do me dirty like that?"

"Growlithe, Arcanine, Poliwag, Poliwhirl . . ." Adnan names Pokémon the entire way to Cami's, barely stopping for breath. "Poliwrath, Abra, Kadabra, Ala— Whoa. This must be it."

Tucked away at the end of a quiet cul-de-sac, the three-story building looks out of place amid its green, rustic surroundings. While the neighbors have all opted for a brown color for their exterior, Cami's parents have chosen a shade of pure white. On either side of the house there are built-in garages, and a concrete walkway with a marble finish leads to the front door.

"I now see why you date her," I whisper to Adnan as he messages Cami to get the all-clear to enter the house.

"She says to go around the back," he says, ignoring me.

"Up here!" Cami yells from a second-story balcony when we circle the house. We come to a standstill when we see the connecting staircase with glass panels. We cautiously make our way up, vertigo kicking in at the grandiosity of it all.

"Hey." Cami gives me a quick hug before flinging her arms around Adnan's neck, practically hanging off him as she tips her head back to kiss him. "Sorry I can't let you in through the front. Dad installed a doorbell cam after—" She cuts herself off, her eyes wide with something I can't quite read. But just as quickly as it appeared, it disappears. "He's just big on safety."

Ignoring the awkward vibes, and because we're good Desi kids, Adnan and I slip off our shoes before following Cami into the house. Cami slides the glass door open and I immediately feel like I need to sit down. She leads us downstairs to the kitchen, which reminds me of those Scandinavian ones you see on home decor shows, complete with an island, hanging copper pots and pans, a built-in oven and microwave, and a stainless-steel fridge with an ice dispenser.

"Help yourselves," Cami says, pointing to a platter of cheese and crackers. "And, oh, Zara, I got you some chai latte pods you can use in our coffee machine since I know you like them so much. At least, Adnan said you liked them. But I wasn't too sure of the brand, and I know they all taste different, so I got you a couple of options." Cami speaks a mile a minute, only stopping when my

110

mouth falls open at the sight of the mountain of chai latte pods on the counter. "What? Did I get the wrong brands? I knew it—"

"No, this is . . . wonderful." I pick up the pods, my mouth watering at the sight. "Thank you, this is so kind of you."

"Well, Adnan told me you were missing a concert today, so I felt bad." Cami bites her lip and it makes it all the harder to be upset with her. "Here, I already made you a cup. It's still hot."

I take a sip of the chai and almost forget how annoyed I am at missing the concert today. With the mug in my hand, we follow her on a tour of the rest of the house, including through an immaculate living room with a chandelier Ma would 100 percent kill for and a master bathroom with his-and-hers sinks.

But even though the house is grand and everything I wish my house looked like, it feels sad. There are no tacky pictures lining the walls as you go up and down the staircase. The furniture in the living room looks unused; the books on the shelves are gathering dust. And I don't know why this is what saddens me the most, but the house doesn't smell like anything.

People always say that when they step into my house, they're immediately hit by a blend of spices. I can't smell it myself because I'm so used to it, but I understand what they mean—the sentiment behind it. After so many years in the same home, even after airing it every day, the smell of Ma's cooking has managed to seep into the walls, lingering for decades. It's weird to be somewhere with no smell at all.

"Nice house," I say once she's concluded the tour and brought us back to the kitchen.

Cami shoots me a tight-lipped smile.

For a beat, nobody says anything. The three of us simply stand around the island, looking anywhere but at each other. Or, at least, that's what I'm doing. God, is this how parents feel when they supervise their kids on dates?

"Er, so, what should we do?" Adnan laughs nervously, trying to remove the veil of tension surrounding us. "Should we watch a movie or something?"

Cami nods. "Sure. Naan, will you get a couple of glasses from the cupboard and the bottle of Pepsi from the fridge? I'll grab the snacks and set up for the movie."

"I'll help you." I drain my chai and pick up a few bags of chips while Cami retrieves a huge bag of chocolate, and then I follow her down into the basement. Now, when Cami said she had a home theater, I assumed she meant a little room with a few old chairs and an overhead projector.

Obviously that's not what she meant. Cami's family theater room consists of six actual theater seats, a projector screen, a little cart with freshly popped popcorn, and a massive L-shaped lounge sofa. And, oh, there are, like, a bazillion speakers in every corner.

"Dude. This is *sick*," I say, unable to contain my shock. If Sadie were with us, she'd be running wild at the prospect of having our movie nights here. Imagine being able to gawk at Jordan Fisher in 4K. Or even a shirtless Adam Demos!

Cami lets out a strained laugh. "Glad I've got your seal of approval."

"Why wouldn't you have had it before?"

Cami shrugs. "You must think I'm some sort of irrational person considering I'm making both of you pretend to date just so I can be in a relationship with him."

"I mean, maybe a little?"

"Knew it. Adnan owes me five quid."

"But," I add, not wanting to make Cami feel bad, "I get *why* you're doing it. Not, like, specifics or anything, but it sounds like you're in a tricky situation with your dad."

"Yeah, you could say that."

Cami looks like she's about to cry so I put the bags of chips on the table, freeing up my arms in case she needs a hug. I expect her to elaborate and tell me all about what's going on with her dad—I mean, we're friends, right? But she doesn't. Instead, she changes the subject entirely by asking me to pick out a movie.

"Netflix or Prime?"

"I have both."

I decide on Netflix because Prime feels too much like that random bin full of discounted crappy DVDs you find in supermarkets. "You happy to watch a rom-com?"

"Sure," Cami responds just as Adnan expertly navigates his way to the sofa, his arms full of glasses and a big bottle of soda.

"Seriously, Z? A rom-com?" Adnan groans as he sets down the glasses and starts pouring soda into them.

I shoot him a look that says you-made-me-come-here-when-I-could-have-been-at-a-concert-so-now-you-must-suffer-the-consequences and hope he gets the message that this is one part of our so-called relationship that I am not backing down from.

After a twenty-second staring match, he concedes. "Fine, we'll watch a rom-com."

I raise my fist in the air as a sign of victory.

"Are we watching something we've seen before or something new at least?"

"New," Cami says just as I say, "Old."

"Flip a coin?" he suggests.

"Here." Cami hands him a coin.

Adnan flips the coin into the air, and I hold my breath like they do in the movies right before their fate is decided. I don't necessarily mind the newer rom-coms, especially with them being more diverse than the older ones, but there's just something about movies from the late 90s and early 2000s that I love. They're so fun, while also telling a story that hits you right in the heart. For an hour and a half, you can just let go.

And if I'm going to spend time with Adnan and Cami while they gaze longingly at each other, I *need* to let go.

"Heads," Cami calls right before Adnan clamps one hand over the other. When he uncovers the back of his hand, the coin glistens with tails.

"Sorry, babe." He kisses her on the temple.

I pick *10 Things I Hate About You*, my absolute favorite enemies-to-lovers movie that never fails to make me smile. I guess it's kind of appropriate as well with its fake-dating plot. Cami and Adnan lie on the sofa while I take one of the theater seats, plopping down my glass in the cup holder. I curl my feet up under me as the movie starts up, happily filling my stomach with the warmth of the buttery popcorn and feeling like I've hit the jackpot. It feels just like being in the movie theater—except better, because it's free.

But then I remember why I actually don't like going to the movie theater very much: people making rude commentary throughout sex scenes, the unpleasant sound of loud chewing, and, most of all, the obnoxious couples making out in front of me.

And Adnan and Cami? They. Won't. Stop. Sucking. Face.

And we're only ten minutes into the film!

I clear my throat, loudly, but either they don't hear me or they're choosing to ignore me.

I try to focus on the movie, forcing myself to concentrate on the chemistry between Kat and Patrick rather than the heat radiating from Adnan and Cami, but it's impossible. Especially when I notice how high up Cami's leg Adnan's hand is traveling.

I spring up, flinging kernels of corn over the carpet. "I'm just gonna . . ." I trail off, not even bothering to finish my sentence. I slip out of the room and am immediately surprised by how bright it is. I check my watch: only twelve thirty. Five whole hours left.

"*It won't be like that,*" I mimic in a stupid high-pitched voice that's meant to sound like Adnan's.

I head to the kitchen and munch on a sad-looking cracker. I scroll on my phone for a bit but that quickly gets boring. Usually when I've got nothing else to do I read, but for some reason I didn't think to bring a book this time or download an audiobook in advance.

Oh, wait, I know exactly why: because Adnan said I was going to have fun and that he and Cami weren't going to be making out the whole time!

What a lie, what a lie, what a lie!

I sigh and place my phone face down on the table while I wistfully look out at the fields. The tall grass waves at me. Birds fly over the house, chirping away to a melody only familiar to them. And . . . there's a group of random people just hanging out.

Wait. It's not just one group of people. It's *multiple groups* of people. And they're all looking down at their feet. I used to see this all the time when Adnan and I played Pokémon GO back in the day. It can only mean one thing: there's a five-star Poké Raid either in progress or about to happen.

I quickly pick my phone back up and go onto the app. Before it's even finished loading, I slip into my boots and head in the direction of the strangers in the field, praying that I'm right and get there in time.

If nothing else, it's an excuse to avoid the kissfest going on downstairs.

13

I'm practically out of breath as I near the giant tree where people are milling about, and I'm cursing my phone for not loading the app quickly enough. I stomp through the field, the wet ground clinging to the heels of my boots.

"Come on," I mutter under my breath. I keep shifting my gaze from my phone to the cluster of humans, watching them for signs that they've joined the raid already. From the way I'm stressing, you'd think legendary raids were uncommon or something, which they aren't, but where I live, nobody really does them and you've got to have at least a group of four or more people to win a raid, since the boss is ten times more powerful than regular Pokémon. And considering none of my friends play, and I don't have enough devices or hands to play with multiple accounts, I'm not exactly equipped to do them on a daily basis.

I stand a couple of feet away from the group, not brave enough to actually socialize with them, before clicking on the gym with the legendary raid. But I can't see any other players in the lobby. When I look up, the reality only settles in further as I see thumbs tap away, the sound of nails against glass deafening in a way I never thought it could be.

I'm too late. I can't believe I missed it.

"Good game, guys!" A boy with a burgundy beanie and Skullcandy headphones says, fist-bumping the girl next to him. "Anyone get triple fifteen?"

"Nah, mate—fourteen, fifteen, twelve," one girl says.

"Eleven, eleven, fifteen," someone else says.

"I'll probably do another one. Need a better one," the guy with the headphones says.

"Fair," this other guy, with thick glasses and a scruffy beard, says. "See you at the next one?"

My head snaps up. Of course. The pro-gamers, the ones who practically breathe the game, don't just do one legendary raid and then call it a day. They do several, building their teams with maxed-out Pokémon. And from the sounds of it they're heading to another one.

I check the app and see that there's one egg hatching in about five minutes not too far from here, probably less than a quarter of a mile away from the looks of it on the map.

I walk toward the gym, keeping an eye on the timer for the raid. When I get there, there are a few people hanging about but not as many as at the previous raid. I sit underneath a giant oak tree despite the wetness of the mud seeping into my jeans. I watch my phone the same way I watch a pot of boiling water, my feet nervously tapping.

I wait two minutes.

Then five.

Then ten.

At fifteen, my butt is numb from the cold and my fingers feel like they're about to fall off.

I don't get it. Why are people still hanging around here if they're not going to battle? They're all looking at their phones in anticipation, their fingers hovering over their screens.

And then it hits me: they're not joining because they're waiting for someone else to take the plunge. It's like a party: nobody ever wants to be the first one, but if there are already one or two people there, others are more likely to come.

Following that logic, I enter the lobby, watching as the timer counts down from 120, the maximum amount of time anybody has to join before it's just me.

120, 119, 118 . . .

I place my phone on my thighs as I blow air into my hands, the heat softening my palms. Surely, now that I've joined it, somebody else will, too? But when I check my phone, nobody else has. There's only my character on screen.

76, 75, 74 . . .

It's fine. Loads of time left.

69, 68, 67 . . .

Oh! Someone's joined! I knew it. Being the first one is always scary but soon enough people come to play and—

They left.

53, 52, 51 . . .

Nobody's going to join, are they?

46, 45, 44 . . .

I should have just stayed at Cami's.

37, 36, 35 . . .

"SolusZ26?"

I tear my gaze away from my phone upon hearing the username I use on about every platform ever. I try to locate the voice but there's nobody in front of me or even behind me.

"Up here!"

My neck aches as I bend it backward to see where the voice is coming from. Right above me sits a boy probably not much older than me, his legs dangling from the branch.

"Jump out of the lobby. Nobody's going to join you," he shouts down.

I furrow my brows as I read how many seconds are left: twenty-nine. When it hits twenty, nobody else will be allowed to join. I have nine seconds to make a decision. On the one hand, I don't want to give up my free raid pass of the day for nothing. On the other hand, I'm going to lose the battle. There is no way I can take down the legendary on my own; it's just not possible.

"If you jump out now, you won't lose your pass!" the boy shouts down.

My thumb hovers above the exit button in the upper-left corner of the screen. Can I take the word of a stranger?

"I'll log a message on Discord and put out a call for help, promise."

I do that stupid thing they do in movies and bite my lip in contemplation. Four seconds—it's pretty much now or never.

I tap the screen, holding down the circle with the running man until I arrive back at the main menu. I let out a breath of relief, seeing that my pass hasn't expired.

The boy jumps down from the tree and takes a seat next to me on the ground. He turns his phone in my direction and with an easy smile says, "We've got three other people who are willing to do the raid in about fifteen minutes. You going to stick around?"

I nod my head, not sure if I'm doing so because he's helping me or because of the way his smile lights up his face. He's got that scruffy look that instantly makes me melt: dark, tousled hair with sweet eyes and a sharp jaw. He looks like the kind of guy who could wave 'bye at me and I would still think about that one interaction with him seven weeks later.

He's impossible to look away from.

"Do you want to dance?" the boy asks out of nowhere.

I meet his eyes, which are glinting with mischief. "Sorry, did you just say *dance*?"

"Yeah, I did." He shoots up and it's only then I realize just how tall he is. As he towers above me, I note that he must be at least a foot taller than me. He's slender with a perfectly straight posture, not bent awkwardly like so many of the guys at my school. "It's just, you look a bit stressed and my gran always told me that when you're stressed you should get up and dance. So . . ."

But he doesn't dance. Instead, he starts jumping. On the spot. But rather than jumping as if he's on a trampoline and waving his arms around to gain some height like most people do, he stands with his arms close to his sides as if he's a pogo stick.

"That's not dancing," I respond, in shock at what I'm witnessing. Who *is* this person? Is this why parents are always advising you not to talk to strangers?

"This is just the warm-up. Didn't you ever learn to always prepare your body before a workout?"

"I wouldn't exactly call dancing a workout," I retort, restraining myself from smirking. "It's more like an excuse to look like a dork with music on in the background."

"Well, in that case, we're about to look like dorks. Now, come on," he says, his words strained from the effort. "Don't leave me hanging!"

I shake my head. No way am I jumping around in a field in the middle of nowhere. And I'm not dancing either. Dancing is not a thing I do. It wasn't a thing when Ma made me take Bollywood classes when I was younger and it will never be a thing in the future.

If I do ever dance, Sadie and Adnan know to call someone and tell them that aliens have taken over my body.

"Fine," the boy says when it becomes clear that I am not moving. "You can just watch me then. I don't mind an audience."

I can't help the smile that snakes its way across my face at how ridiculous he looks.

But also, you know, ridiculously hot. I've never met

somebody who could make *jumping* look sexy. Especially as his hoodie rises up slightly to reveal the olive skin of his stomach. But beyond that, it's his eyes. As he moves, his eyes never break away from mine, the eye contact confident without being cocky. Even when I look away briefly, wondering if I'm imagining it altogether, only to return a second later, he hasn't broken eye contact.

On top of it, he pairs the eye contact with a smirk that makes my cheeks blush.

"Just know," he says, "that actually jumping is *way* more fun than watching somebody else jump. I'm telling you, my endorphins are skyrocketing right now."

"Unlike you," I quip.

He stops in place and grins at me, before resuming his jumps. "Well, between the two of us, at least I'm closer to skyrocketing, Mrs. I'll-Just-Sit-on-the-Ground-While-My-Ass-Goes-Numb."

He's got me there. Also, did he just inadvertently say he's noticed my ass? I don't have time to mull that over in more depth because when he beams at me, it's like all my brain cells go out the window. Case in point: I find myself pushing up from the ground, shoving my phone in my back pocket, and jumping, just like him. Because, why the hell not?

At first, my jumps are pathetic, but then I fully get into it, swinging my arms to build some energy. But even then, I hardly make it past his shoulders.

"No fair, you're taller!" I shout at him, which elicits another grin that makes my insides tickle. "I wasn't prepared! Also, we look stupid as all hell!"

"Doesn't matter. Hello, endorphins, goodbye, cortisol and that frown on your forehead!" he responds.

I can't stop myself from laughing as I jump. But I do when he seamlessly transitions from jumping into a dance routine that looks like something straight out of a viral TikTok. This guy is *good*. Like, he's got actual moves. Even without any music, his body is fluid, hitting all the beats. I can't take my eyes off him to the point where, when his phone buzzes and he stops to check it, I find I've almost forgotten why we were dancing in the first place.

"Saved by the literal bell. You have been spared from dancing today thanks to the raid."

We sit back down and as I catch my breath I watch him use the sleeve of his black, oversize hoodie to swipe away a few beads of sweat that have formed on his forehead. A second later, he takes the hoodie off entirely, revealing a slim but toned figure, covered only by a thin T-shirt picturing some anime, and the briefest glimpse of a trail of hair on his lower stomach. I have to look away to hide the heat creeping up my cheeks.

"Let's go in," he says, and we enter the raid lobby.

A smile tugs at the corner of my lips as three more people join us within fifty seconds.

I'm actually doing this. I'm participating in my first ever five-star raid. I'm going to catch a legendary! And, just like this guy said, I'm actually not feeling that stressed about catching the legendary anymore. In fact, all that's left in me is sheer excitement.

We get three hundred seconds to take down the

legendary, but we only need about seventy-three, no thanks to me. When I finally come face to face—virtually, that is—with the legendary, my hands are shaking. I have thirteen attempts to catch it, but legendaries are renowned for being hard to catch. Out of the thirteen, two miss the Pokémon entirely, three are headbutted away, and five are broken out of. I've only got three left and I'm starting to feel like even with another jumping/dancing session, I'm never going to catch it.

"Do you need any help?" the boy, whose name or username I still don't know, since there were so many of us in the raid lobby, asks me.

I shrug in response.

"Maybe I can try?" he says, part question, part directive, effortlessly charming. I nod and he hooks two fingers around my PopSocket, the tips of his fingers touching mine, sending sparks up my arm.

He scoots closer to me as we huddle over my phone. "You've got to wait until the circle is really small and then throw it. And don't forget to use the Golden Razz Berry. And you should . . ."

He keeps talking, giving me pointers, but it's hard to focus on his words when his scent makes my hormones go out of this world. He smells like lemons and chai with a hint of olive blossom but also tobacco and coffee; it's the most unique smell ever and I think it ingrains itself into my brain cells.

"There you go," he says, handing me the phone back. "All caught. And it's a perfect one as well."

125

"Wow, thank you," I say, my voice thick with gratitude. But also something else. Something I can't identify just yet.

"No problem," he replies with a broad, easy smile. "I'm Yahya, by the way, otherwise known as VelasY74." He holds his hand out for me to take.

I shake his hand, his palm rough against mine. "Zara, otherwise known as SolusZ26. But you already knew that."

"Well, you *were* the only one in the lobby."

My cheeks flush. "Thanks again for helping me out. I really do appreciate it."

"No worries," he says. "I'm just impressed by the fact that you joined the raid all on your own. I wouldn't have the ovaries to do it."

For some reason, the fact that he said "ovaries" and not "balls" makes my insides flutter. "Impressed or flabbergasted?"

"Impressed, definitely."

"Why?"

He shrugs. "There's something admirable about a person who takes on a battle they're not sure they can win. It means they're willing to take a chance. It means they've got hope."

"That's pretty deep, like something straight out of a John Green novel."

"Is that the dude who wrote that book about towns being made of paper?"

"Yeah, but it's not literally made of paper."

A little dimple appears in his cheek. "I only remember because in the movie, they sing the theme tune for *Pokémon* when they're in that weird storage space and one of the guys says, 'You don't get scared if you sing' or something."

And then he sings the *Pokémon* theme song. And, because it's impossible not to, I sing along with him. His dimples flash again and his eyes light up as we belt out the final notes at the top of our lungs, our voices carrying across the stillness of the field, the other players having left long ago. When we've finished, we're fighting for breath, our chests heaving.

"Well, that's something I've never done before." He laughs and it feels like Ma's kichuri on a rainy day.

"Me neither."

"So, wha—" he starts, but is interrupted by the ringing of my phone.

Adnan calling

"Sorry, I've got to take this," I tell him before walking a bit away from where we were sitting. "What?" I answer with irritation.

"Where are you?" He sounds out of breath, like he's run a marathon.

"Out."

"Where?"

"Just in the fields behind Cami's house."

"Doing what? Why?"

"Playing Pokémon. What else am I meant to do? I wasn't going to sit around and watch you two get all cozy."

"Well, you can come back now. Cami's parents are coming home early."

Yes! I can finally go home and get on with my day. I'm

about to leap for joy when I look back toward Yahya, who smiles at me with a slight tilt of his chin. My hands suddenly go clammy and my stomach feels like it's full of fizzy pop.

"When will they be there?" I check my watch for the time: 1:19. Have I seriously been out here for almost an hour?

"Soon. So we've got to go. Like ten minutes ago."

I sigh. "Be there in five."

I end the call and clutch the phone to my chest.

"Everything OK?" Yahya asks as I return.

"Yeah, I'm fine." I take a small step toward him. "But I've got to go now, actually."

"Oh, OK." He glances at the ground. "Well, maybe I'll see you around? We're always on the lookout for more people to join our raids."

"Yeah, maybe."

"And I won't even make you jump next time. Promise."

I smile. *Next time.* "Yeah, but only because you'd just make me dance instead."

"I *will* get you to dance," he says.

"Will you now?"

"For sure."

I suppress the smile that threatens to overtake my face. "We'll see."

He holds my gaze and I find myself not wanting to break it. I swallow, feeling parched all of a sudden. I don't want whatever's happening between us right now to end, but when my phone violently vibrates in my pocket, I know it's time to go.

And it seems Yahya does, too. "It was nice meeting you, SolusZ26."

"You too, VelasY74."

I turn away, afraid that if I stay any longer I'll say something stupid, and decline Adnan's call. The wind carries me back to Cami's despite my heavy heart. Even though Yahya said the words "next time" like he truly meant them, chances are I'll never see him again. Like Adnan said: Cami's parents are rarely out of the house, so who knows when I'll be back here? And if I am, who's to say that he'll be here?

I shake my head. Whatever. It's not like it matters anyway. He just wanted somebody to do raids with. He didn't show any indication that he was interested.

Not that *I'm* interested in *him*.

Not at all.

14

After the early rise, Adnan's make-out fest, and my adventure in the fields, the exhaustion is real, leaving us without any energy to speak as we jump from one bus to the other.

When we get back to town, Adnan stops off at the corner store for a snack. I wait outside and finally take my phone out of my pocket, where it's been incessantly vibrating for the past five minutes.

When I pull up the screen, I have four missed calls from Ma and one from Baba. Obviously, they've followed up with messages.

Ma

At what time are you planning to come home?

You've been out for quite some time

Baba

I think it is enough now

Ma might be ecstatic that I'm with Adnan, but she's still a control freak who wants me in her vicinity at all times. And Baba just goes along for the ride, to be honest. It's not like they're demanding that I come home, which is how you'd read it if you didn't understand the intricacies of Desi parents, but more like they're manifesting it out into the universe that their offspring return home or they'll shrivel into raisins, their life having no meaning if their only child is not with them.

Yes, it's dramatic. That's Desi life for you.

When Adnan returns, we slog our way through the final leg of our journey to my house. As we approach my front door, I can practically feel the softness of my bed deep in my bones.

"How was your first date, baba?" Ma says, opening the door before I've even had a chance to put the key in the lock.

"Fine," I say at the same time that Adnan says, "Great."

I slide off my boots and socks in the hallway, my toes grateful for the ability to fan out, and Adnan scrunches up his nose. Good. It's the least he deserves after cutting my time with Yahya short.

Not that I'm salty about that. At all.

"That's all I get? *Fine*? *Great*?" Ma harrumphs. "Details, beta!"

"Ma," I groan. "Can we talk about this later?"

Ma scrutinizes me for a second but gives in to my request, bobbing her head in approval. "Of course, baba. You must be tired from your day out. Cha?"

I swear, Desis think tea fixes everything.

Stuffy nose? Cha.

Tired? Cha.

Death in the family? Cha.

Lose out on getting a hot guy's number? Cha.

Even though I doubt the healing abilities of cha, I say, "Yes, please."

Once Ma has brewed us a cup each, we plonk ourselves down on the sofas in the living room. I prop my legs up on the stool, remote in one hand and tea in the other, channeling my inner Homer Simpson as I flick through the various shows until I land on *Ackley Bridge*.

"Z, is everything OK?" Adnan asks when there's an ad break.

I take a sip and nearly burn my tongue. "Yes."

"You sure? Because you seem . . . off."

Even though Yahya didn't explicitly show an interest in me, it's hard not to be off with Adnan when I feel like I missed out on a potentially epic make-out session—but I'm not so sure I want to tell Adnan about it.

"I'm fine," I tell him. And then, because I don't want to deal with any follow-up questions, I quickly add, "Do you know what Discord is?"

"Yeah. It's like Messenger but for gamers." He raises a brow. "Why?"

I shrug as nonchalantly as I can and make something

up. "When I was playing Pokémon around Cami's, I heard some people talk about it. Thought it might be handy for me to have. Since, as you so kindly pointed out earlier, I'm such a big nerd and all."

Adnan fake gasps. "I'm going to lose you, aren't I?"

More like you tossed me aside . . .

I fight the lump in my throat, ignoring what I wish I could say, and shift my focus back to *Ackley Bridge*. "A girl's gotta do what a girl's gotta do. And this girl needs her Pokémon fix."

After dinner with my parents and after Adnan has left, I retreat to my bedroom. In my pajamas and snuggled under my weighted blanket, I read a book about a boy who keeps getting sent back in time to save his girlfriend only to learn that he risks the lives of others. After a while, I'm startled by Ma knocking on my door.

"What are you reading?" Ma asks, standing in my doorway having just done her twelve-step nighttime skin care routine.

"Just something I picked up from the library."

Ma smiles thinly as her eyes flicker across my bedroom before landing on the hairbrush on my side table. She lets out a loud groan.

"Zara, how many times have I told you? You need to clean your brush more often." Ma picks up the brush to investigate it as if it were part of a lab sample. "When was the last time you cleaned this?"

I shrug sheepishly.

"You're inviting bacteria to breed!" Ma uses scissors to cut through the hair lodged in my brush and holds it out for me to see with an expression that says child-look-at-this.

She shakes her head as she mumbles something in Bangla. When she's done being disappointed in me, she takes a look at my hair and shakes her head all over again. "No wonder your hair is this way—you can hardly use this as a brush!"

Ma goes off with the brush, huffing and puffing like she's the Big Bad Wolf, and then returns a minute later. "I've washed this so I can sort out this mess on your head. Turn around."

I do as she says, too exhausted to disobey her.

"My amma used to tell me to brush my hair one hundred times a day, you know."

I roll my eyes. "Nanu also said if you don't wear a hat, your brain will freeze. And that cucumbers make you smart. And that—"

"Chup," Ma shushes. She hums a tune I'm sure I've heard before as she drags the brush through my hair, the bristles getting caught in the tangles as soon as it makes contact with my head, forcing her to unpick them. I shut my eyes, reminded of how Ma used to do this every morning before school when I was younger.

"Baba?" she asks softly.

"Hmm?"

"Is everything OK with you and Adnan?"

"Of course."

"Are you sure?"

"Yes, why do you ask?"

"Because I know when you're lying to me, baba."

My eyelids flutter open, my back stiffening. "I'm not lying to you, Ma."

Ma puts the brush aside, grabbing my shoulders to rotate me so that I'm facing her. "You can talk to me, you know. I used to be young once."

I roll my eyes.

"Just because I'm your mother doesn't mean I won't understand you or the things you do."

Would she, though? Would Ma really understand if I told her my relationship with Adnan was all a sham because it was the only thing that had any chance of putting her and Baba back on speaking terms?

"Come on, baba," Ma whines. "I thought we were friends."

I let out an involuntary laugh. "We're *best* friends, Ma."

"Then tell me, beta! You know I won't judge you."

Ma knows. She has to. She wouldn't be so insistent if she didn't. Even when Ma's curious, she's never this tenacious in her questioning.

But even if she didn't know . . . *could* I tell her? I fight down the giant lump building in my throat. If I tell her, then that's it. No more pretending.

On the other hand, if I did tell her, it would mean admitting to lying and keeping a secret from her in the first place—just like Baba did about his diabetes, which is what started this whole mess in the first place!

"Relationships are tough, beta," she continues, "and they're even harder when you're in one with your best friend." Ma tucks a lock of hair behind my ear. "Just know that I am here for you if you need me. We can talk about anything you want. About how—I don't know—Adnan kisses, if you want to buy some nice clothes for him, about taking the next st—"

"OK, Ma, stop." I wave my hands in front of me, begging her not to go any further, equal parts relieved and guilty that she's still buying the ruse, but mainly mortified that she's trying to give me an after-school special right now. "I appreciate it, I do. I guess I'm just not ready to talk about it yet. But when I am, I'll come to you."

"Promise?" she asks with a firm squeeze of my hand. She's being weirdly insistent, even for Ma.

"Ma, what's going on? Because I know this is about more than just me and Adnan."

Ma's grip tightens. "My mother—your nanu—and I didn't have the best relationship. And it was all down to secrets, down to not speaking to each other openly enough. If I could go back in time . . ." She inhales a ragged breath. Ma doesn't talk about Nanu often, but I do know, from what Baba has told me, that it's a sensitive subject. Even more so following her passing a couple of years back. "I don't want us to have a relationship like that. I want us to be better. I want you to come to me for everything, little or big." Ma cups my face in her hands, a fierce look in her eyes. "Promise me, baba, that you will talk to me always. That we will not keep secrets."

I swallow, my stomach twisting like there's no tomorrow as I utter the word "Promise."

"OK then. Get some sleep. We've got to go to the store and get some more rice in the morning." Ma kisses the top of my head before leaving my room, shutting the door behind her.

I push my face into a pillow a second later. Why did Ma have to bring up Nanu? I already felt bad knowing Ma and Baba's joy was nothing but a by-product of false advertising, but now Ma's had to bring in her relationship—or lack thereof—with Nanu, adding another wrench in the works. Ma can never know that what Adnan and I have is fake. That it is all just a ruse to help her and Baba while they find their way. Otherwise it might break our relationship just like it broke hers with Nanu.

No. That would never happen. This is just one tiny little secret I'm keeping to myself. Besides, it's healthy for moms not to know everything about their kid, right?

To distract myself, I open the Pokémon app, hoping I can catch something from my bed. But all it does is remind me of Yahya and how I'll probably never speak to or see him again. And even if I did see him, it's not like I can date him, because I'm meant to be in a couple with Adnan.

"You suck, universe," I say, looking up at my ceiling.

Even so, I try to stalk Yahya by looking him up on Instagram—I do have his Poké username after all, and it wouldn't surprise me if he used it on other platforms—but nothing turns up. The same with TikTok. And Snapchat.

He *did*, however, mention Discord, so maybe he's on there with his Pokémon handle?

But obviously I'm not *so* desperate that I'm going to create an account on a platform I don't really know anything about just so I can stalk him down.

That would just be silly.

DISCORD REGISTRATION

Hey SolusZ26

Thanks for registering an account on Discord!
Before we get started, we just need to confirm
that this is you. Click here to verify your email
address.

ADD FRIEND
You can add a friend with their Discord tag.
It's cAsE sEnSiTiVe!

Enter a Username#0000

ERROR
We need VelasY74's four-digit tag
so we know which one they are.

15

Why can't Discord be like Instagram or TikTok where all I need to stalk a person is a username? Why do they have to add a personal four-digit code to the end of the username?

I mean, I suppose from a safety perspective I get it. You wouldn't want just anyone to find you on a whim.

But from the perspective of a teenage girl who just wants to, maybe, talk to what seemed like a nice boy who made her insides go all mushy? I don't get it.

16

The weeks following the Pokémon fiasco are excruciating. Not only because Yahya's running around in my mind— man, he smelled *amazing* and something about him just instantly put me at ease—but also because Adnan and I are having to up our relationship game by actually, you know, pretending to be in one.

"I am not holding your hand," I tell him as we walk to class one morning.

"Zara, people aren't going to believe we're a couple unless we show some affection."

"How about I give you a compliment every once in a while? We could say *that's* our form of affection. You know, like our love language. It's all over TikTok at the moment."

Adnan screws up his face like he's in agony. "I guess. But I'm not sure that alone is going to sell it."

"Why not?"

"If this were one of your books, you'd expect the couple to show some affection through physical touch, right?"

OK, he has a very valid point there.

"Look, we don't have to hold hands *all* the time. Just every once in a while."

I groan. I don't want to, but at the same time I know I *need* to in order to sell the picture of the Alphabet Couple, not only at home but also at school. And he's right: if we were an *actual* couple, we'd be cuddling up to one another at every given moment or longingly gazing at each other when we thought nobody else was watching.

Still . . .

"Is there nothing else we can do? I thought sitting together at lunch in ridiculously close proximity was enough."

"Well," he starts, the word far more drawn out than it has to be, "we could kiss."

Our eyes lock for a brief second, then our gazes shoot away from each other like we've been caught doing something naughty.

"Forget I said that," he says quickly. "Let's just hold hands."

And that's how, twenty minutes later, we enter class holding hands. Unlike Yahya's, Adnan's palm is smooth, probably from years of Auntie telling him to moisturize, and, surprisingly, holding it is not actually that awful.

"Aww, my angels!" Sadie squeals as we approach her. She's got her notebook propped open—furious scribbles, timelines, and to-do lists filling up the page. As she closes it, I can see that she's customized the cover to say *This Is How You Fall in Love—Documentary BTS*. I didn't realize just how invested she was getting. "Honestly, I'm disappointed it took you so long to get together considering how perfect you look together."

"Well, disappointment we are no more." Adnan brushes the pad of his thumb over my knuckles, sending unexpected shivers running up my spine at the intimate gesture, as he beams at me with that golden-boy smile.

I mirror his expression, and something funny buzzes throughout my body as I do. Somehow, despite my reluctance, it doesn't feel as difficult as I would have thought to hold his hand and play the picture-perfect girlfriend.

It feels even easier at lunch when we take it up a notch by Adnan putting his arm around my waist, the warmth of his fingers radiating against my skirt.

Today, it's not just Sadie but also Joe who joins us.

"Think we need to get together next, Sades," Joe says before pointing at the corner of the cafeteria where Liam and Ceri are sucking each other's faces. "With everyone else all loved up, it's only us left."

Sadie rolls her eyes at him in dismissal, acting non-chalant, but I can see from the way they slide back to him only a millisecond later that she wishes he wasn't joking. Sometimes I want to shake Sadie by the shoulders and yell at her for not telling Joe how she feels, because he's *clearly* waiting for her to make the first move. He's just as afraid as she is of being rejected.

Fortunately for her, I'm interrupted from communicating this to her by a kick under the table.

"Can I sit here?"

I turn in the direction of the words to see Cami standing there with her tray of food. I swivel my head in Adnan's direction in confusion. I know we told Sadie we'd introduce her to Cami at some point, but I wasn't aware that it was going to be today!

"Sure," I say, gathering myself together and scooting a bit to my right so Cami can take a seat on Adnan's left. "Guys, this is Cami. She's in my . . ." I try to remember the line I fed Sadie when she asked how I knew Cami but come up with a total blank.

"Book club," Adnan finishes for me, quickly glancing in my direction with panic in his eyes. I really need to get my head screwed on, but seeing Cami has rattled me.

"Nice to meet you, Cami," Sadie says with a big grin. "This is Joe."

"Hey," he says, leaning back but also closer to Sadie, almost like he's staking his claim. Honestly, the "Will they? Won't they?" between them is killing me.

"Nice to meet you," Cami responds. "I've heard so much about you from Adnan and Zara."

You'd think the conversation would flow from there, but if anything, it's like there is no sound at all; my ears feel like they do as soon as you step off a plane—everything a little bit muted. I can feel how Adnan hasn't let out a breath since Cami sat down.

Maybe I'm not the only one who's rattled by her presence. We never did discuss how we would act with Cami around, only how we would act when she *wasn't*.

"Zara told me about your documentary, Sadie," Cami says to create conversation. "How's that going?"

"Oh my gosh, great!" Sadie practically claps her hands in excitement. "I've been really enjoying researching love and how it's been portrayed in different forms of media. Like how it's depicted in books versus films versus magazines and all that. And then there's this whole other angle about how love is just an illusion that the media has created and, honestly, it feels like I'm spiraling, but it's, like, good spiraling that I kind of don't want to stop!"

Cami lets out a little laugh. "That sounds really cool. Sounds like there's so much you can do with it."

"Yeah, almost a bit *too* much. I think I might need to whittle it down a bit. Especially now that the Alphabet Couple are going to be my focus."

"Alphabet Couple?" Cami asks, her brows furrowed, at the exact moment that Adnan and I say, "Please don't call us that."

"You know, these two." Sadie points at me and Adnan, her eyes turning to hearts as she speaks. "Because their names start with the letters A and Z, the beginning and the end of the alphabet. Withstanding whatever comes in between."

"Oh." Cami's smile drops, her expression crestfallen as Sadie keeps going on about how it was meant to be for me and Adnan from the moment we were given our names. My heart breaks for her, but at the same time I can't do much about it, considering we wouldn't be in this position if it weren't for her and Adnan not going public.

"They were basically a rom-com waiting to happen—everyone could see it but them," Joe finishes for Sadie. "Typical friends-to-lovers, no, Sades?"

Sadie can hardly contain the blush that creeps into her cheeks. "Exactly." Quickly shaking off the heat, she looks to Cami, who's poking at her wilted salad, and shoots me a subtle glance, the question clear in her eyes.

What's up with her?

I shrug in response. I get why Cami is upset—it must be horrible to hear all about your boyfriend and his supposedly perfect match who isn't you straight to your face—but she shouldn't have sat with us, or asked about the documentary, which is all about love and us as a couple, if she couldn't handle reining in her feelings. Besides, it's not like *she's* the one who has to do anything. She doesn't have to pretend to be in love with her best friend and hold his hand all the time or lie to pretty much everyone in her life.

Cami's reaction to the Alphabet story makes even Adnan change his manner; his arm has disappeared from my waist and he rubs the back of his neck nervously.

What have we been doing all this for if Cami is just going to go ahead and blow it by being as obvious as daylight?

I quickly scoot closer to Adnan, nudging him with my elbow to put his arm back where it was.

"What are you guys reading in book club, Cami?" Sadie asks, to end the awkwardness. "Zara hasn't really said much about it other than the fact that it exists." Sadie mockingly shoots daggers with her eyes in my direction.

"Oh, just this book about a couple who fake date and eventually fall in love."

My eyeballs nearly pop out of my head and Adnan bursts into a fit of coughs, feigning choking on a fry.

Quickly, I add, "That was last month's book, Cami. This month it's a retelling of *Jane Eyre*, remember?"

Cami turns in my direction, holding my gaze before responding. In her eyes, I see something territorial. For a moment, I think she's about to blow the ruse right here and now, fed up with being a secret, as I predicted she would be, and my heart feels like it's in my throat.

But as quickly as the fire lit up in her eyes, it fades away. Underneath the table, I can see that Adnan has touched her leg with his foot. "Of course. Silly me!" She lets out a giggle that reminds me of the Cami I first met.

"That's cool," Joe says, like he really is interested in the conversation. "Do you prefer the retelling or the original? I already know what this one would choose." He points at Sadie with his thumb. "She's a sucker for originals."

"I think retellings are fantastic, actually. Sometimes they're even better than the originals." Cami doesn't look at me when she speaks but something in the air shifts. "Retellings are brave, you know. I think it takes guts to take something original and change it, breathing new life into what once was or what people expected."

Honestly, it's like she's not even trying to be subtle about it at all.

"I think retellings allow characters to evolve. Kind of like sequels. Take *Legally Blonde 2*. The original was great but the sequel added some much-needed depth to the characters."

Sadie and I look at each other. She did *not* just delve into rom-com territory. *Especially Legally Blonde.* "Sometimes, a character is fully formed and doesn't need 'some much-needed depth,'" I say, hardly able to contain the irritation in my voice.

"I agree with my girl Z here," Sadie replies, extending her hand across the table to me, which I gratefully grab. "Originals are better than retellings or sequels. It's a fact of life. Just read the reviews on Rotten Tomatoes. Besides, you can never beat the feeling of returning to your favorite characters."

Cami opens her mouth but before she can say anything, Joe jumps in. "Don't even try. They're not going to budge on this one. You've just got to accept it as a fact of life from here on out."

Yes, Joe!

"Well, we can't all agree on everything." Cami looks back down at her tray like it has personally victimized her. God, why can't she just *pretend*? It's what we've been doing!

"What's everyone doing this weekend then?" Joe asks us all, picking up on the weird vibes. I can't help but notice how he glances at Sadie out of the corner of his eye.

"I haven't got any plans, and even if I did, I know there's no point in inviting Zara. She's too loved up to hang with me anymore," Sadie jokes. "She's bailed on our last few weekend hangouts!"

I inwardly sigh, wishing I could tell her the truth—

I'd much rather be spending time with her than sneaking around going on secret three-way dates with Adnan and Cami.

"We're going to that silent disco at the Tobacco Factory, right, Z?" Adnan asks.

We are? This is the first I've heard of it.

"Remember?" he prods further but I definitely don't remember this.

Cami looks up from her salad and immediately I realize that I'm not being forgetful; I've been forgotten.

I can't believe this keeps happening. Adnan and Cami just go ahead and make last-minute plans without checking with me first, expecting me to go along with them like I don't have a life. So much for our golden rule. But I can't call them out on it now, not in front of an audience.

"Of course. Sorry—brain fart." I laugh it off and flick my temple.

"Silent disco?" Sadie furrows her eyebrows. "Like, everyone wears a pair of headphones and listens to the same song? Why not just go to a house party and, you know, not look like a total weirdo?"

"Kind of, but not really. The Tobacco Factory does it their own way. Everyone gets a set of headphones, but you don't listen to the same song. Usually, you can change stations and vibe to whatever you want, but at this one there's a bit of a difference," Adnan explains, gesturing wildly with his hands as he gets more and more excited. "The goal of the disco is to find the person with the same song as you and have the ultimate dance party."

"How would you know if you had the same song?" Joe asks, leaning forward.

Adnan shrugs. "You wouldn't, but you could probably guess by the rhythm of how they dance."

"So, you dance with the same person the entire night?"

"There are different playlists and they're all shuffled so you might dance with the same person the entire night, or you might not. It's all up to fate."

Sadie pointedly looks to me, fully knowing that I'm not one to dance ever since Ma made me take Bollywood classes when I was younger. "And you agreed to this?"

I sigh. "Adnan really wanted to go."

And what Adnan wants, Adnan gets.

"We should all go!" Joe slaps his hands together. "If it's all right, I'll invite Ceri and Liam—I bet they'd be up for it."

Adnan's eyes light up with panic. He clearly didn't expect anybody else to want to go. I guess that's what he gets for telling me his plans only when prompted by others, rather than telling me in advance.

"The more the merrier," I say.

"Sadie, want me to pick you up? I can ask my mom to drop us off." Joe and Sadie live only a few streets apart.

Sadie smiles widely, like a five-year-old who's just been granted all the candy in the world. "Yeah. That'd be great."

With both Joe and Sadie agreeing to join the outing, Sadie looks to me before subtly pointing at Cami with her eyes, silently prodding me to do the decent thing. I mean, she's going to be there anyway; at least this way it won't be such a surprise to everyone when she does turn up.

Letting out a deep breath, I put on a smile I usually reserve for aunts and uncles in Bangladesh. "Cami?"

"Yeah?"

"Do you want to come, too?"

As if she doesn't know whether she wants to go, she takes a few seconds to ponder the question, tilting her head in thought. "Sure, why not? It could be fun!"

The table goes on to talk about what to wear on Saturday, Cami being invited to give her opinion like she's now part of the group.

And I guess, unbeknownst to everyone else, she one day will be.

SHAH RUKH KHAN 2.0

Today 13:32

Zara

Next time you want to make plans, involve me, please

I know I'm not your real girlfriend but I'd really appreciate being in the loop

Adnan

sorry, Cami sprang it on me this morning

Zara

It's fine, don't worry about it

But just keep me in mind, yeah?

I know you don't want to be a shitty friend

Adnan

:(

we OK otherwise?

you seem a bit off

Zara

~~Just tired of pretending to be somebody I'm not~~

~~Just tired of feeling like somebody is going to figure us out~~

~~Just tired of lying to Sadie~~

Yeah, I'm cool

I don't want to screw it up for you and Cami

I know how much you like her

Adnan

thank you, Z

you're honestly the best

i love you

Zara

Love you too, bro

17

The afternoon of the disco, I know something's wrong as soon as Ma knocks on my door. The second indication that things are out of the ordinary is when Ma asks, "Zara, are you decent?"

It might not seem strange to anybody else, but it is to me because Ma never enters my room by asking whether or not I'm decent. It's almost like she's incapable of doing so. And if she does bother to knock, it's a quick one with her other hand already pressing down on the handle. When I've called her out on it before, all she's said is, "I've seen your naked butt before, it won't be anything new now."

But this knock is soft, tentative, and she actually waits for me to reply. When she steps into my room, she's not empty-handed. My eyes follow her from the door to the end of my bed, where she perches with the bag in her hand.

"What's in the bag, Ma?" I ask, skipping any kind of formalities.

Wordlessly, she places the bag in front of me. There's pink tissue paper sticking out of the top. "Open it," she says.

I remove the tissue to uncover . . . underwear. But not just regular underwear. Thongs. Thongs in neon, in leopard print, in lace. And, oh, Allah, there are condoms!

"Ma, what is this?" I shove the bag away like it physically pains me to touch it.

"I'm not stupid, Zara. I know what it's like to be a young girl. I know you have needs—"

Oh, Allah. I thought the benefit of being a South Asian child was that your parents never give you "the talk." Then again, maybe I should have seen this coming after I shut her down when she tried to give me that after-school special about "next steps" with Adnan.

It was foolish of me to think I could evade Ma once she had her mind set on something. And, unfortunately for me, that something seems to be the sex talk.

"Please, no, Ma. I don't want to have the 'talk.' "

"Baba. We should discuss this."

"But why? I'm not even thinking about doing it," I lie, obviously. I am a teenage girl, after all. "You don't have to worry or buy me . . . underwear." My cheeks flush. I can't believe I'm having this conversation with Ma.

"Sex is not a bad thing, but you must know the consequences of it."

I sigh, having heard this exact thing in sex ed previously. "Unwanted pregnancy, I know."

Ma smiles wistfully, like she expected my reply. "Not that, baba. Your uterus is not the only thing you need to protect. You need to protect your heart as well. Your uterus and your heart are both powerful organs."

"Thank you, Ma. I'll be careful, promise," I grit out, cringing on the inside. "With my uterus and my heart."

"Thank you, beta." Ma caresses my cheek before kissing me on the forehead and leaving my room, shutting the door on her way out.

I peek at the bag as if I think there might be a frog or something in there just waiting to pounce on me, until finally I shove it in the back of my closet. As nice as the gesture is, it's very much not needed.

Since I've got a few hours before I have to start getting ready for the disco, I lie down in bed with my tablet and read. I'm so engrossed in the second-chance romance that when Ma and Baba raise their voices from their bedroom across the hall, I think I'm imagining it as part of the dialogue in the book. To check it's not a figment of my imagination, I put the tablet away and crack my door open, allowing the sound to travel more clearly from my parents' bedroom to mine.

"I couldn't get hold of you!" Ma shouts, her voice as loud and clear as if she is standing next to me.

Shit. They're arguing again.

"My phone was low on battery, so I put it on Airplane Mode," Baba responds, his voice more muted. Level-headed. Calm. "How was I supposed to know they were going to call you?"

"Because I am your *wife*, that's how!" Ma croaks out the words. "I am your wife, and I should know where you are because I should be there *with* you. Why didn't you tell me you had an appointment at the clinic?"

"Because I knew you were working. I didn't want you to waste your time while they told me what I already knew—that everything is OK. It's just routine tests."

"Do you know how stupid I looked when they asked me where you were and I didn't even know you had an appointment?" Even though I can't see them, I imagine Ma crossing her arms across her chest with a dismayed expression on her face. "Where did you even go?"

"I just went to the vending machine on the next floor. I checked in with the nurse when I got there but the doctor was running late so I picked up a snack for later. Is that a crime?"

Silence ensues. Both probably participating in a staring match.

I'm grateful not to see. I gently shut my door and take a seat at the end of my bed. I thought they were OK again. Maybe I've been slacking in my performance.

Come to think of it, I haven't mentioned Adnan as much as I could have. Even when Ma came in here earlier, I wasn't really acting like Zara the girlfriend who is pleased that her mother is preparing her daughter for future intimate moments. Instead, I was acting as Zara the friend who gets disgusted at the mere thought of her best friend seeing her in her underwear. No wonder Ma and Baba's relationship is refracturing.

As the alarm on my phone rings, reminding me that I have an hour to get ready before I need to leave and meet up with Adnan, there's only one thought running through my mind: now, more than ever, I need to keep up the act.

And I need to do it *better*.

18

"You ready for tonight?" Adnan takes the window seat, his legs propped up on my lap as we settle in for the thirty-minute bus ride to the Tobacco Factory. We're a bit behind schedule, thanks to His Royal Highness's inability to choose a shirt, so the group and Cami are meeting us there. "I've been practicing my dance moves, you know."

He starts to wiggle his shoulders while pulling funny faces and it makes me think of Yahya and the way he surprised me by going from a weirdo who jumps in fields to a person I'd actually like to get to know.

"Let's just get it over and done with," I reply.

"More enthusiasm, please," he says, pinching my arm.

But I can't. Not with Ma and Baba's fight still fresh in my mind. When I left the house, I poked my head into the kitchen to see Ma angrily chopping up vegetables. When I asked her where Baba was, all she did was grunt.

To be honest, I'm shocked she didn't tell me to stay home.

159

"Why did you and Cami have to pick a silent disco as one of your dates? You know I hate dancing," I say, to deflect from the weight in my chest.

"I forgot?" he offers with a preemptive wince like he already knows I'm going to punch him on the arm.

Which I do, obviously.

"There's no way to forget my intense hatred of dancing." Ever since Ma made me take Bollywood classes when I was nine and we were forced to do end-of-session recitals, I've hated the entire concept of dancing. Not because I didn't like the dancing itself—that was actually quite enjoyable—but because of what happened at the infamous Pohela Boishakh of 2015. Let me set the scene: the room is abuzz with energy, the tabla's beat blares through the speakers, and the dancers part like the Red Sea as I take my place on stage to perform my coveted solo.

Except, a STUPID fly is buzzing around my head. Assuming it's a wasp, I start panicking, yelping and running around the stage, until I'm so disoriented that I misremember the order of my steps and ultimately trip and fall over my own feet in front of two hundred people.

Since then, I've vowed never to dance again.

Half an hour later, we're standing in the heart of South Bristol, outside the Tobacco Factory. The redbrick building, with its giant mural of our Swedish eco-queen, Greta Thunberg, is nothing if not awe-inducing. Part café, part market, and part art exhibition, the Tobacco Factory is like a Kinder egg: you never know what you'll get.

"Alphabet! Finally!" Sadie squeals, hobbling over to us in her heels. When she finally arrives, she immediately frowns. "I thought we were wearing jeans and a nice top?"

"My good jeans were in the wash. So, I had to go with this."

I'm wearing an oversize black T-shirt dress with a safety belt to give my body some shape over sparkly black tights and my trusty Dr. Martens. I thought it was a good outfit considering we were going for a casual but nice vibe, but maybe Sadie doesn't agree. Probably because it's the complete opposite of her look, which is a cropped red cowl camisole with low-waist black jeans and a pair of strappy heels.

"I think she looks great," Adnan comments just as he slides his hand into mine, his fingers finding the empty spaces between mine. It catches me off guard, not in an entirely unpleasant way. I distract myself by focusing on the weight of his ring, the one I got him for his birthday last year.

"Zara always looks hot. I was just so surprised by how *smokin'* she looks today!" Sadie spins me by the hand like I'm a ballerina. "I take it this is why it took a thousand years to get here?"

I'm quick to point the finger at Adnan. "Not my fault."

"What can I say? It takes a lot of time to look this good," he says with a drawl, like he's a brooding bad boy from the early 2000s.

"You are so full of yourself," Sadie tells Adnan with a playful shove. "You being slow worked in my favor anyway.

I've managed to interview some random couples for the doc and Joe even got to play Director of Photography for a hot minute!"

"I did indeed." Joe beams. "You could say that Sadie and I are now *partners*."

Color rushes to Sadie's cheeks, and as Joe says something else about the documentary and how they should move forward with their partnership, I can tell that Sadie's ready to run away from her surprise at the turn this conversation has taken. Fortunately for her, Adnan redirects it entirely.

"Oh, there's Cami," he says.

Cami comes strutting up to us wearing a white high-neck cropped tank top, a lacy wireless bra underneath, with a light blue pair of jeans and some heeled booties. Her make-up is flawless, a winged eyeliner with blended eyeshadow that perfectly matches the color of the stones on her rings.

"Hey," she says, her voice breathy and sultry yet somehow warm and inviting. She pushes a lock of hair behind her ear in that way girls do when they're trying to be cute, her dangly moon earrings glinting in the glow of the fluorescent lights above us.

"Hey." Adnan practically melts at her feet but quickly picks himself up when I loudly clear my throat. "Where are Ceri and Liam?"

"Inside," Joe responds, standing close to Sadie but not close enough to encroach on her personal space.

"Let's go!" Sadie exclaims. Putting an arm around Cami, she adds, "We're single and ready to get our moves on!"

I raise a brow in Sadie's direction. What is she doing? Is she trying to get a reaction out of Joe? If she is, it's working. He longingly gazes at her, the want in his eyes as clear as day.

But he's not the only one reacting to her words. Cami's face has gone blank. I try to meet her eyes but all she does is look at Adnan. To remind them both that they need to stop being so obvious, I put the hand that was holding Adnan's around his waist and lean against him. The action seems to jolt Cami awake, reminding her that she, like us, is a thespian, with Sadie and Joe as our audience.

"Let's show these couples what they're missing!" she says with mock enthusiasm and struts off with Sadie.

At the entrance, we hand over our fivers and grab large over-ear headphones from a little rack. Inside it's like a fusion between a disco and a club. There are silver disco balls twirling from the ceiling catching the bouncing gleam of the strobe lights that flash around the room. The DJs have already set up and people are dancing, their limbs moving to beats we can't hear. The best thing of all is the fog machine, which makes it look like everyone is dancing on clouds.

"Dude, these are great!" Sadie says a little too loudly, her headphones on already. "I can't hear anything!"

I remove the headphones from her head. "Then you probably didn't hear how loud you were."

Sadie laughs before winking and sliding her headphones back on.

The notes of Ariana Grande are bursting through my headphones before I've even slipped them on. Next to me, Sadie is rocking out to a punk song, judging from the way she's strumming an imaginary guitar, along with Joe, who is pretending to play the drums; their songs must have synced up.

Honestly, they are living in a romantic comedy without even realizing it.

I move away from them, just in case *this* is the moment one of them finally makes a move and they need their space, and head across the dance floor, noting where everyone else is. In the corner closest to the exit, Ceri and Liam are off making out, their headphones not even on. Meanwhile, Adnan is already in the center of the room, shuffling his feet like he's Marshmello as Cami sways along to the beat in her headphones near him. It's hilarious, really, hearing what I'm hearing and seeing what I'm seeing. How people's arms and legs are so out of sync with the beat of my music.

Again, Yahya infiltrates my thoughts, reminding me of how well he danced that day in the fields. How, unlike me, he is someone who wouldn't come to a silent disco only to uncomfortably bop along, waiting for the music to end so he could go home.

I shake off my thoughts about Yahya and decide to find someone who looks like they might have a similar song to me. Maybe that will help me get more into it. As I scan the room, searching for movements that are slow and relaxed, I feel my chest constrict when my eyes land on someone who looks like they could be dancing to my song.

He's here. Yahya is *here*.

He's with a group of guys in the far corner of the dance floor, his face illuminated by the strobing lights as he grooves his body to the song—*our* song—playing through his headphones. For a moment, I think I'm just imagining it, that there is no way that he could be here of all places. I take my headphones off, thinking somehow that the lack of music will help me to see better, and I find it surprising when it actually works.

There is no denying it: Yahya is here.

And now he's looking right at me. He's stopped moving and taken his headphones off, just like me. And, as clichéd as it sounds, I can't help but feel like my stomach is bubbling up with butterflies. He tilts his head to the side with a half-smirking, half-open mouth, like he can't believe he's seeing me either. I offer a stiff wave, which he reciprocates with the most beautiful smile I have ever seen.

I put my headphones back on—an alternative track that is way more up my alley is playing—and am just about to shimmy my way across the dance floor to Yahya when a group of people suddenly block my view of him. I manage to squeeze through them, but on the other side Yahya is nowhere to be seen. The corner where he was standing is now occupied by other people. The butterflies in my stomach drop.

Where is he?

I turn around, scanning the entire room for him. Which is when my eyes land on Cami and Adnan's bodies getting dangerously close in the center of the floor, Sadie's eyes bugging out in confusion as she watches from the DJ booth at the front of the room. Their songs must have synced up because they're dancing in a similar style. It would have been helpful if it was a rock song, but it seems more like a slow song, judging from their soft movements.

From Sadie's stance, I can tell she's about five seconds away from getting all up in Cami's face and asking her what the hell she's doing. I've got to defuse this before they ruin our plan. Because while trying to explain to Sadie and everyone else why my boyfriend is flirting with another girl right in front of me sounds like an absolute blast, I'm more focused on our relationship not ending too soon and Ma not finding out that it was nothing but a ploy. Not after her and Baba's argument earlier. Not after what I've seen our relationship can do for them.

I elbow my way through the crowd, feeling like I'm racing against a timer. They're getting closer and closer, their faces only a few inches away from one another. Across the room, I clock Joe nudging Ceri and Liam, while Sadie is also squeezing through the crowd to tear them apart.

Fortunately, I get there first, literally coming in between Cami and Adnan. I immediately latch onto Adnan's side and rest my head on his shoulder, hoping they'll get the memo that there are prying eyes. Adnan doesn't do anything at first, his arms hanging limply at his sides as I loop mine around his waist, but after the initial shock, he

166

snaps out of whatever trance Cami has put him in, and cups my face with his hand, his fingers trailing my jawline, the touch sending a shiver up my spine.

But I know this isn't going to cut it. Not for Sadie, who is behind Adnan and still glaring daggers at Cami, and not for Ma and Baba if they get wind of this. Which is why I do the only logical thing I can think of—the *only* thing that might just save the day—and kiss him.

The crescendo of an R&B song surges in my headphones just as our lips meet, one thought drowning out all the others: I see why girls keep coming back for more. He's gentle, his tongue delicately exploring the inside of my mouth, and his hands sliding down to my waist with such ease you'd think we'd been doing this for years. And even though this is something I never thought I would do with Adnan, something about his lips on mine feels . . . natural. Almost like I can't remember why I ever wrote him off as anything more than a best friend.

I come up for air, my lungs begging for a recess, and we both quickly separate, like we're magnets repelling each other.

What the hell was *that?*

But there's no time to think about it. Adnan's eyes widen as if he has just remembered Cami. When I turn, I see she's making her way through the crowd and toward the exit. We both throw off our headphones and scramble to get to her, but when we get to the doors separating the dance floor from the hallway, Cami's nowhere to be seen.

She's gone.

19

"Shit," Adnan mutters. "I need to fix this. I'll be back in a sec."

Adnan speed-walks down the hall toward the lobby, leaving me alone by the exit, the taste of him stinging my lips.

"What was all that about? Where's he going?" Sadie asks, coming up to me, her headphones around her neck, strobe lights highlighting her concerned features.

I can't stop pressing my fingers to my lips, still in shock. Did I seriously just kiss my best friend? "Consoling Cami, I guess."

"And you're OK with that?" she asks with a disbelieving look.

"I'm not sure what I feel, OK?" I answer honestly, because I can't think straight right now.

Why did I do *that*? Why didn't I just tell Cami to back off? Why did I kiss Adnan?

"Your boyfriend chasing after another girl? Sounds like trouble to me."

"I'm not worried. I know where I stand with Adnan."

Well, I used to. Not so sure after that kiss.

"You sure? Because what I saw on the dance floor between them was not halal, Z, and you know it."

I love Sadie and how hard she's fighting for me to get mad in this situation. If Adnan was my actual boyfriend, I would be mad. But he's not, and so all I feel is sick. Sick at having lied to Sadie in the first place when I should have just told her the truth, and sick at having to keep lying to her for who knows how long. If it weren't for my head spinning from that kiss and from Ma and Baba's fight earlier tonight, the guilt would be clawing its way up my throat and I would have spilled my guts out to her already.

"Look, I know Cami likes Adnan. We've hung out together and I've seen how she looks at him. But I also know that Adnan doesn't reciprocate it."

"You sure about that? Because he just ran after her!" Sadie looks at me like she wants to shake me by the shoulders. "You don't do that unless you like someone!"

"He's just being a good friend."

"There's being a good friend and there's being a good boyfriend. One takes precedence over the other. Seriously, Z, why aren't you bothered by this?"

Because I'm freaking out over the fact that I just kissed my best friend!

And also, because a guy I met in a field this one time and haven't been able to stop thinking about ever since may have also been on the dance floor and I might have ruined everything if he saw what I just did.

"Z . . ." Sadie takes my hands, gently approaching me like I'm an easily rattled fawn. "He's being a bad boyfriend right now and you know that. I know your relationship has been a long time coming and you're probably scared of messing it up, but you're allowed to be mad at him when he does shitty things like run after another girl. You don't deserve to be treated like that. If you need me to, I'm more than happy to kick my karate skills back into gear."

"Please, don't. We don't need the police involved again."

"That was one time!" she whines, the echo of her voice drowned out by the cacophony of people's feet. "Seriously. Just give me the word and I'll do it."

I swallow the metallic taste in my mouth and keep back the tears threatening to escape. I don't deserve Sadie and her friendship.

"I need some air," I say.

Before she can stop me, I make my way down the hallway and into the lobby, but I can't see Adnan or Cami anywhere. Maybe they've gone to the makeshift refreshments station. I clomp my way upstairs, my shoes feeling heavy and uncomfortable, the weight of the night dragging me down.

I thought I'd ruled out any possibility of me and Adnan ever being a thing, of me ever having any feelings for him. But that kiss . . . it made my insides feel all funny. And not in the way I'd expected. I thought kissing him would be quick and simple, kind of gross because he feels like family, but it wasn't. It felt like the first ice-cream bite of the summer; at first, chilling, until all there is left is this light, airy sweetness that stays with you long after you've finished your ice cream.

But the taste of the kiss disappears as I think about how Adnan chased after Cami. I would have thought that after what happened he would have at least stayed and talked about it. Not that I know what there is to say . . . but still, *something* should have been said.

I'm not sure what the kiss means, for any of us. All I know is that I need to find them. And I need to do it sooner rather than later.

Upstairs, I scan the floor but still don't see Adnan or Cami anywhere. I check my phone but there are no messages. I tap it against my palm in thought, wondering whether I should go downstairs again. I can't imagine them going back to the others and pretending like everything is normal. That would be far too awkward. No, they must have just found a quiet corner somewhere in the building.

I order myself a Fanta at the counter, deciding that if they're going to hide, I should hide as well. I need to get my story straight before I face Sadie again anyway.

And I just need some time to *not* think about that kiss and *not* think about how annoyed I am at Adnan for running off. Actually, no, I'm annoyed at both of them. I wouldn't have had to kiss him if they hadn't been making out with their eyes. How could they do that? How could they be so reckless and selfish? They knew our friends would be watching! I've had to sacrifice so much—for *them*!—so why can't they suck it up for one night and act like they're just friends?

171

To calm myself down, I take down a nearby Pokémon gym on my phone. It helps, being able to take out my frustrations on random strangers, until I hear the notes of a familiar husky voice. "Ah, come on, I just put my Pokémon up there."

Looking up, I find myself unable to hold back a smile, the bubbling bitterness morphing into excitement. "VelasY74."

"We meet again, SolusZ26." He grins. "But seriously, don't kick me out just yet. I need the coins."

I tap my chin with my phone. "What's in it for me?"

"A drink?" he offers.

I grab the tall glass of Fanta. "Seems I've already got one."

"Ah, I've got nothing," he groans, and it makes my stomach flutter with giddiness.

I bite the bottom of my lip. "How about you offer me some good company instead?" I ask. "I can't in good conscience kick you out of the gym if you're in my direct line of vision."

Yahya orders himself a Sprite before joining me at a table in the corner of the bar that overlooks the street below. It's not that late, only 9 p.m., but from the stars that light up the raven-colored sky, you'd think it was almost midnight.

"You know, I'm glad to see you here," he says, taking a sip of his drink. "For a second, I thought I'd imagined seeing you at all."

"Oh yeah?" I look down at my drink, not sure whether I should feel flattered about him being glad to see me or nervous about *what* he might have seen. "How so?"

"Well, I caught your eye for like a second and then you were gone. I kept looking for you in the crowd, but it was like you just disappeared." Yahya pauses before letting out a small laugh that makes my heart melt. "Guess I know why, now. You just had to take the gym down, didn't you?"

"The grind never stops," I say, trying to keep my cool about him looking for me.

Yahya takes another sip of his drink while peering at me over his glass. I'm going to take it from how friendly he's being, and the fact that he hasn't said anything about it yet, that he didn't see what happened with Adnan downstairs.

"Who are you here with?" he asks.

"Just some friends. How about you?"

"Same. We got here a while ago, though, so we just went for some fresh air."

"Where are they now?"

"They've left," he says with a casual shrug.

"And you're still here because . . . ?"

"I guess I didn't feel ready to leave just yet."

Because I'm here?

I wish I could ask the question, be as direct as the voice inside my head, but the words dig their heels in.

"You know, part of the reason why I thought I might have imagined seeing you downstairs is because I'm actually quite surprised to see you here of all places."

"And why's that?"

"Well, you were pretty adamant about not dancing the last time I saw you. Yet here you are."

I nod. "Here I am."

"From what I saw, though, you had some good moves, so I—"

"You don't need to lie to me," I interrupt.

"I'm not!"

"Oh, you totally are!" I accuse. "I have no moves and that's exactly why I don't dance."

"You can't be that bad," he counters.

"Oh, but I am. Trust me."

He leans back in his chair, gesturing for me to prove it.

"No way."

"I'll only believe it when I see it."

When I don't move, Yahya sighs and I think for a moment that I have disappointed him; my brain yells at me for screwing things up with him before anything's even started, but then he follows up with "I'll let you off. *Again*. But next time, I'm getting that dance out of you."

Unable to verbalize my shock at his promise of another meet-up, I change the subject to something more neutral that *won't* raise my heartbeat exponentially. "So other than dancing, what do you do for fun?"

He laughs. "Why does this suddenly feel like a job interview?"

I cross my legs and pretend to check the time on my watch. "My next candidate is due in a few minutes, so you'd better get a move on if you want the job."

"Well, I think I need a reminder of the job description. Just so I can outline how I match the person specification."

"Let me just check the paperwork here . . ." I pretend

174

to shuffle some papers and imitate Baba when he reads the news on his phone by holding the imaginary paperwork in front of me at arm's length. "Ah, yes, you've come in for the position of . . ." I try to think of a job title but come up blank until I spot a poster across the room advertising for volunteers at the annual Skate at Somerset House in a few weeks. "Ice Rink Hand Holder."

"Ice Rink Hand Holder?" Yahya snorts.

It's difficult to fight the smile that creeps onto my face and rearrange it into the stern look of a CEO.

"Sorry, but that's the only position available at the company and if you'd rather walk, then please, go ahead."

"No, no!" Yahya sits up straighter and clears his throat as if he really were at a job interview and it makes me feel all warm inside that he's playing along. If I were him, I certainly wouldn't have. "I think I'm the right candidate because, well, I've got great hands, for one."

"Do you now?"

"Here, feel them." He reaches his hand out across the table. "Go on, inspect the goods."

My heart begins to race as soon as my finger trails the lines running along his palm. I pretend to scrutinize each and every crease, as if I know what the lines represent. "Not bad."

"They feel even better when you're fighting for your dear life on the ice."

"Shame there's no ice rink here."

"That's a real flaw of this interview. You should probably raise it with your superior, you know."

"Noted, with thanks." I pretend to scribble something down with an invisible fountain pen on the tabletop. "Now, if we can ju—"

"Actually," he interrupts, "I think it's best we run through a simulation. Just so you know how I'd be on the ice."

Before I can ask him what he means, he stands up, pulling me with him, his fingers tightly wrapped around mine, and starts swinging our arms wildly while at the same time moving about in a zigzag motion. "I know you're scared, but it's OK. I'm here to be your professional Ice Rink Hand Holder and I won't let anything bad happen to you."

"Except giving me vertigo."

"Yes, unfortunately that is part of the job," he responds gravely. "But I'll be here with you the entire time."

We look ridiculous and we're being far louder than the crowd in here, but I don't care. I smirk at him, surprised he's gone along with the fake interview for as long as he has, but I guess I shouldn't be surprised considering he was jumping in the middle of a field the first time we met.

After a lap of fake skating around the bar, we call it a day and sit back down.

"Did I get the job?" he asks, beaming like he's just retrieved his favorite candy from the bottom of the pick'n'mix bag.

"I'll have to think about it. I've still got a few candidates to see, you know."

"Ah, yes, of course." Yahya drains his drink and my body begins to refill with uneasiness. I'm going to have to go back downstairs at some point and face the music. I crane my neck and scan the premises for Adnan and Cami again but have no luck. "Sorry, am I boring you?"

"No, not at all." I shake my head, my annoyance bubbling to the surface again. "Two of my friends had a fight earlier, so I'm looking for them but haven't really gotten that far."

"Sorry about that." He smiles sheepishly. "I must have halted you on your hero's journey."

"You know about the hero's journey?" I say, surprise lacing my words.

"Just 'cause I've got a pretty face doesn't mean I don't read."

"Cocky, too, are we?" I tease.

"I just know what I bring to the table. In fact, I'd like to say that I *am* the table," he says, holding my gaze.

His confidence makes my stomach flutter.

"To go back to your question . . ." I tear my eyes away from Yahya's stare, in the hope of regulating my body temperature, and redirect the conversation. "I'm more like the sidekick—there to ensure everything goes the way it should."

"Want to talk about it?"

Absolutely not. Unless you somehow find girls who are in fake relationships to make their parents happy an attractive quality?

I'm saved from answering by my phone beginning to vibrate.

Adnan calling

"One sec," I tell Yahya, stepping away from our table.

177

"Where are you?" I ask, my heart racing as I accept the call.

Adnan lets out a slow, long, shuddering breath. "I'm with Cami across the street, at Aldi."

"What are you doing at Aldi?"

"Something about grocery stores soothes her, so we've just been walking around for the past twenty minutes browsing different aisles."

"Well, when are you coming back?"

Adnan doesn't say anything for so long I wonder if the signal's dropped.

"Hello?"

"I don't think we are. Honestly, Z, I think we're just going to get on the next bus home."

"What? Why?"

"Cami feels humiliated. She wasn't ready for . . . *that*."

The way he says "that" makes my skin crawl with fire ants. "I wouldn't have had to intercept if you two hadn't got all cozy and almost given us away."

"We were just dancing!"

"It sure looked like more than just dancing." I feel the volume of my voice increasing as my frustration reaches boiling point. "I could practically see the drool dropping from your mouth and if I could see it, what makes you think nobody else could? I had to kiss you or someone was going to figure out that you're actually dating Cami rather than me. I mean, what kind of girlfriend just lets her boyfriend dance like that with another girl?"

The line goes silent again.

"Adnan, you've got to realize, I did it for you. For us."

"Well, it's not just about us, Z. We didn't think about Cami," he finally says, his voice sad and low.

"And Cami didn't think about *me* when she almost kissed you in the middle of the dance floor," I hiss. "This isn't just about her, you know? There are other people involved now and if we don't sell them the lie of being an actual couple, then everything will implode and Cami won't be the one on the firing line: I will. Do you think Ma and Baba will take well to me lying to them? Will Sadie, who is basing a major part of her documentary around us?"

There's something conclusive in the stillness that follows. As I wait for his response, I feel tears pool in my eyes.

"She's my girlfriend and we need to be more considerate of her feelings," Adnan croaks out.

Whatever I want to say next dies on my tongue because what's the point? It's not like he'll listen to me. It's all about Cami now. Never mind the fact that we've been best friends for sixteen years. Cami wants to hang out, so I have to come, too. Cami is upset, so we have to leave. Cami doesn't want to tell her dad she's in a relationship with Adnan, so I have to pretend to be his girlfriend while they live happily ever after. Cami, Cami, Cami. I want to tell him off, tell him he's being an asshole, that girlfriends come and go, that he and I are forever.

But of course, I don't. Because Adnan's my best friend and I'll do whatever it takes to make him happy. Even if this is breaking my heart.

"I'll meet you at the bus station in ten," I say and hang up.

As I stomp my way back to the table, I can't stop myself from squeezing my fists in anger, fueled by the unfairness of it all. Again, they're cutting my date short. Again, I'm missing out on a chance to actually spend some time with a boy I might like.

"Everything OK?" Yahya asks when I get back to the table.

"Yeah, but I kinda have to go. I'm really sorry but it's those friends I was talking about. This girl, she's new to our school after some stuff went down at her old one or something—I don't actually know to be honest; she won't really talk about it unless it's with my best friend," I explain, my mind running at a million miles per hour as I try to extinguish the anger that is spreading through my body like a wildfire. "And right now they're not happy with me for something that happened downstairs, which wouldn't even have happened if it weren't for them in the first place and I ju—"

I stop talking when I notice the deer-in-the-headlights look on Yahya's face, which I'm presuming is his way of telling me without actually telling me that he's rethinking ever speaking to me again. No one wants to be with someone who's constantly surrounded by drama.

"That's . . . intense," he finally says.

"Yeah, it is." I deflate, the weight on my chest a little bit lighter for the briefest of moments. "But all that is to say: I need to go. Like, right now."

"Oh, OK. No worries," he says, but I can hear the disappointment in his voice. "Maybe I'll see you around? Or . . . maybe I can take your Discord? You know, maybe we could do a raid or something."

I offer him a small smile. "I'd like that."

"It's VelasY74#0189."

"I'm SolusZ26#2909," I say as I type the four digits of his username into my Notes app, a little rush running through my veins. "Well, I guess I'll catch you on the interwebs then, VelasY74." Sometimes I truly do wonder if there's an evil little person in my brain playfully pulling random strings that make me say the dorkiest stuff.

Thankfully, Yahya just laughs at my idiocy. And not in a mean way; almost like he finds it endearing. "Catch you on the interwebs, SolusZ26."

THE COOLEST PERSON YOU WILL EVER MEET (S♥)

Today 22:09

Sadie

mate, where are you?

Zara

Sorry, I'm leaving with Adnan

After the whole Cami debacle, not really in the mood for dancing

Sadie

everything ok with u 2?

can't have mom and dad break up

Zara

I thought Liam and Ceri were Mom and Dad

Sadie

more like grandma and grandpa

too boring for my doc

Zara

Don't be mean!

Sadie

it's good C-roll I suppose

might even upgrade to B-roll

CONSIDERING I GOT NOTHING OF YOU AND ADNAN TONIGHT

Zara

Sorry!!!!

Maybe your doc could focus on them instead of us????

Sadie

I know you don't like the spotlight but I am putting you in it

no offense to Ceri and Liam, but people have been waiting LITERALLY YEARS for you two

Zara

~~I wish they hadn't~~

At least you've got Joe there

Maybe you can finally tell him how you feel????

Sadie

fat chance

Zara

Sades

Come on

Sadie

not the right time

Zara

Is it ever?

Sadie

don't be pushy, Z

Zara

~~Unlike you?~~

Fine.

GROUP

Today 23:52

Cami

Can you ask Sadie to remove her Instagram story of you guys making out?

I don't exactly want to see that on my feed.

Zara

Since when were you following her?

Adnan

i'll talk to her

Cami

But don't make it obvious that I asked!

Just need it down fast before it's reposted on ThermaeSecrets

Adnan

i won't don't worry about it babe

Cami

Look, I'm sorry for freaking out.

I know we shouldn't have been so obvious, Zara.

But you guys can't do that to me.

I don't want to see my boyfriend hooking up with his best friend.

It's not cool.

Adnan

sorry babe

won't happen again

promise

Cami

There are other ways to keep up appearances.

If people are being suspicious, just upload pictures of you guys when you're at family dinner.

Or of you holding hands.

Something which doesn't involve you swapping saliva.

Zara

~~We're doing YOU a favor and you're making demands?~~

~~How about you grow some ovaries and tell your parents about your relationship?~~

Adnan

ofc babe

we'll think of something

Today at 01:32

**This is the beginning of your direct message history
with @VelasY74**

VelasY74
So I've been trying to figure something out
But I'm not getting anywhere

SolusZ26
I see we've skipped introductions

VelasY74
Well, I never know when you're going to have to head off
So I figured I better make the most of the time I have
when you're online

SolusZ26
Sorry about that

VelasY74
No!
That's not me being aggy
Just genuinely want to talk to you

SolusZ26
OK, I believe you
Now what were you trying to figure out?

VelasY74

Why SolusZ26?

SolusZ26

Oh haha

It's really stupid tbh

And not as deep as you'd think

VelasY74

Go on

SolusZ26

I got really into reading romance novels when I was like 11
and when I started signing up for things online, like fanfic
forums and whatnot, I bought into the whole
"readers are deep and mysterious and lonely" persona

VelasY74

You didn't

SolusZ26

Oh I did

So I googled what lonely is in Latin

Since obviously only serious people use Latin

VelasY74

Obviously

SolusZ26

And it was solus

And then since I was a word nerd and I had figured out
from my extensive reading that there are 26 letters in the
alphabet, mine being the last, I thought, "If this isn't super
deep and mysterious I don't know what is"

VelasY74

Wow

SolusZ26

Yeah

So I'm going to go hide under my duvet now,
thank you very much

VelasY74

No come back!

It's just quite funny

And cute, tbh

SolusZ26

You think?

VelasY74

For sure

I can just imagine an 11-year-old Zara thinking she's all
profound coming up with that username

SolusZ26

What about yours?

Why VelasY74?

VelasY74

It's nowhere near as entertaining as yours

Velas is my last name

Y for my first

And 74 because I had to pick a number hahah

SolusZ26

You're right

It wasn't

I was expecting something profound

VelasY74

I'm sorry to disappoint

☹

SolusZ26

Well, we can't all be perfect

VelasY74

Is that so?

SolusZ26

It's OK, I'll take one for the team

VelasY74

Anyone ever tell you you're pretty cocky?

SolusZ26

My mom

But she says a lot of things that aren't true

Things like cucumbers make you smart

SPOILER: they don't

VelasY74

You did not fall for that

SolusZ26

Look, my mom also used to say I'm perfect

So I believed everything she said at the time

Also I was five!!!!

VelasY74

I bet you were so cute back in the day

SolusZ26

You saying I'm not cute now?

Ouch

VelasY74

Opposite, actually

And in fact, I think your mom was definitely telling the truth about one thing back in the day

20

I wake up the following morning to the screeching sound of Ma vacuuming my bedroom.

"Do you really have to do that right now?" I grumble as I shove my head underneath my pillow.

"Time to get up now, beta. It's almost three in the afternoon!" she hollers over the vacuum cleaner. "You've slept so long your pasa has become massive!" Ma slaps my butt cheek, but it does nothing to prove her theory that your butt inflates in your sleep.

I check my phone to see that Ma's right. It's well past midday. I must have been exhausted from all the drama last night. Or it might be the fact that I was up until almost four in the morning messaging Yahya about I don't even know what, the fluttering butterflies in my stomach refusing to take a break and let me sleep.

"Come on, get up now." Ma throws my duvet off me, which is an effort considering it's weighted. "Adnan and his parents will be over for Sunday roast in a couple of hours, and I need your help preparing."

By "Sunday roast," she means a Desi Sunday roast, which consists of a roasted whole chicken marinated in a medley of all the spices you can find in our cupboard—garam masala, ginger, turmeric, cumin—with vegetable pulao and an assortment of chutneys.

But I can't even enjoy the idea of stuffing my face with Ma's wonderful food because sitting down at dinner means sitting down next to Adnan. Which is fine under normal circumstances but is absolutely terrifying the day after kissing one another, and we have yet to actually properly address it. On the bus ride back from the silent disco, we sat in a heavy silence that neither of us could break. Or rather, one that we *wouldn't* break. I, in particular, refused to speak to him after he put Cami first and our friendship second. We didn't even sit together; instead, we each took a two-seater and looked out of the windows, despite the darkness clouding our views.

"Come on, I need your help, baba," Ma whines, bringing me back to the present. She unplugs the vacuum cleaner and leaves it standing next to my wardrobe as she starts to fuss around in my bedroom. "And you need to wash your hair before they come over, you know. When was the last time you washed it? Have you been using coconut oil like I told you to? Your hair is so brittle already, you need to keep it moisturized. You're not taking the multivitamins I got you from the pharmacy, are you? You know you ne—"

"Ma!" I shout, unable to control the irritation that comes

with just waking up. "Can you stop micromanaging for just one second?"

"I'm not micromanaging. I'm taking care of you," she says, the hurt in her voice evident.

"Taking care of someone doesn't mean hovering over their shoulder like they're a child."

"But you are a child, still. My child."

"Baba isn't," I blurt out.

Ma sighs deeply, like she's run out of steam. "What are you talking about, Zara?"

I didn't want to bring it up, especially after the argument I heard them having yesterday, but the events of last night have left me with too many unreleased feelings and I'm afraid if I don't speak up now, I might explode later at dinner. "I heard you and Baba yesterday. Arguing about his appointment."

"Oh." Ma collapses onto the foot of my bed, like her knees can no longer support her. "How much did you hear?"

I swallow, the sharpness in my chest growing at the memory of their loud voices. "Enough. You shouldn't worry about Baba as much as you do. He's an adult. He knows how to take care of himself, and he doesn't need you managing his diary. You're a caretaker at work but you shouldn't have to be one at home." I move from my position at the head of the bed to where Ma is, my feet landing on the carpet with a low thud. "And besides, it's not like Baba is dying. Diabetes is a very manageable condition, you know."

Ma goes silent for a second.

"You remember your nanabhai?" she finally asks.

195

I shake my head. "Only that he died when you were nineteen, right?"

"I was away at university in Chittagong and your nanabhai and nanu were back in Mymensingh when it happened." Ma smiles softly, careful not to let the pain show. "Your nanabhai suffered a pretty big heart attack on what was the most beautiful day of the year. In fact, your nanu told me later that only thirty minutes before he was in their backyard, admiring the strawberries. He asked her, 'Aren't they just beautiful? Who could believe something so beautiful could bloom from only one seed?'" Ma stares past me, a tear threatening to slide down her cheek. "Ma found him on the sofa not long after that, his hand clutching his heart as he called her name in agony. Fortunately, the ambulance didn't take too long, and they managed to get him to the hospital, where they were able to treat part of the blockage in his heart. But they couldn't do it all without taking him into surgery." Ma inhales sharply. "They booked him a date a month from then and gave him medicine that he could take when he got home. To manage it."

I wait with bated breath as Ma takes a moment to collect herself. She's never spoken to me about nanabhai before.

"But he never got home," she croaks out, the words lodging themselves somewhere deep in her throat. I quickly scoot closer to Ma and put my arms around her. "They thought he was getting better but he had another heart attack despite all the work the doctors had done. And just like that, my father was gone."

196

I listen to the beat of my mother's heart as I feel the wetness of her tears on my scalp.

"As horrible as losing my father was, the worst part was that I wasn't there in his final moments. That nobody told me this was happening in the first place. Not my mother nor my aunties. They kept it to themselves." She smooths down my hair as she speaks. "They didn't want to worry me for nothing, especially when I was so far away from home. They thought it would be too difficult for me to leave my studies, even for a little bit, and didn't want to cause me any stress." Ma breathes out heavily through her nostrils. "How could they be so selfish not to tell me what was happening? How could they keep something as momentous as a heart attack a secret from me?"

I stay silent, understanding finally clicking into place about why Ma reacted with anger—or rather, with hurt— to Baba's news about his illness.

"I understand that they didn't want me to worry, but that should have been my choice. I should have been trusted to make that decision myself. For Allah's sake, they could send me to an entirely different city, by myself, to fend for myself, but they couldn't deem me capable of dealing with my father's condition?" Shadows form around my heart as Ma's anger heightens, her voice gravelly with pent-up emotion. "All I wanted was to make the choice myself, Zara. When your Baba said he'd been keeping his illness from me for two months? It was like I was nineteen and losing my father all over again."

My insides twist with sympathy. "I'm so sorry, Ma."

"I understand your father and he explained his reasons

for hiding it from me, that he didn't want to cause me undue stress, but all I want is the choice."

"Even when it's to protect you?" I ask, not sure if I have the right to question my own mother. But maybe that's just my own guilt talking.

"It's always nice to have somebody looking out for you, but there is a line when that becomes less about protection for them and more about protecting yourself."

Is that what I'm doing? Protecting myself?

Ma wipes away her tears with the ends of her oorna. "All I require from you is your honesty, beta. I don't think I could bear it if you were keeping anything from me."

I swallow. All this time I thought pretending to date Adnan would make her happy, but now it could be the thing that hurts her most. How can I make sure that my lies don't poison our relationship the way Nanu's lies did her relationship with Ma?

The logical thing would be to tell her. I could tell her about Adnan and Cami, swear her to secrecy with the exception of telling Baba. Then all the secrets and the lies would be over. At least at home.

But then I'd be breaking my promise to Adnan and, more importantly, all the progress that's been made to repair Ma and Baba's relationship will crumble. Their foundation isn't solid enough yet. Yesterday was proof of that.

No, I can't tell her. Maybe once they're in a more stable place, and the ruse is up, I'll tell them.

But for now, I'll have to keep acting.

"I would never lie to you, Ma."

21

A couple of hours later, Adnan and his parents are standing in our dining room.

"This looks delicious." Somaiya Auntie practically rubs her hands with excitement as she takes a seat at the dinner table while I retrieve plates and glasses from the cupboard. "What masala did you use?"

"I made a special blend using two large cinnamon sticks, twenty shelled cardamoms, two tablespoons of cloves . . ."

"It'll be quicker to ask her what she didn't use," I yell back.

"I heard that," Ma comments, her tone sharp. And then, remembering that she loves to boss me around, adds, "And oh, don't forget to bring the jug!"

After grabbing the plates out of the cupboard and placing them on the table, avoiding all eye contact with Adnan as I pass by, I return to the cupboard in the kitchen to fetch the jug. But for some reason, the stool I use to stand on when I need to reach stuff from the top shelf is nowhere in sight.

"Here, let me." Adnan comes up behind me and pulls out the jug, his bicep grazing my shoulder as he does. "I think Amma borrowed the stool from you guys a few days ago." He hands me the jug. "I'll get her to return it."

"Thanks," I mumble, unwilling to look him in the eye, the annoyance from yesterday still clawing at me.

I fill up the jug with water but just as I'm about to head back to the dining room, Adnan blocks my path. With a tilted head, I raise a questioning brow at him.

"Zara," he says, his voice pleading and assertive at the same time.

"Adnan," I reply with a swallow.

"Can we stop fighting?"

I lower my voice. "Can you admit that you and Cami were in the wrong last night by basically grinding and that I only did what I did for the sake of keeping up appearances?"

Adnan runs a hand through his hair in exasperation. "Maybe. Only if you admit that there were other avenues you could have taken to interrupt our so-called grinding."

"Maybe," I concede. I suppose I could have intercepted by telling Cami to back off, but after overhearing Ma and Baba's fight, spotting Yahya, and then seeing my fake boyfriend and his real girlfriend all over each other, my brain was pretty much scrambled. "But only if you also admit that you were a jerk for ignoring me last night."

Adnan grins. "Are you just going to keep one-upping me at every possible opportunity?"

200

"Yes. Because you deserve it." I playfully shove his chest. "You violated the number one rule of our friendship yesterday. Mates—"

"Before dates," he finishes with a long exhale. "I'm sorry, Z, for leaving you to deal with Sadie and for implying that Cami's feelings were more important than yours. They're not."

"They'd better not be," I reply with a little too much fire, and quickly add, "I'm sorry, too. For not seeing why kissing someone else's boyfriend might have been a big no-no."

Adnan smiles with a shake of the head. "Friends again?"

"We were never not friends, you dork," I say just as Ma yells, "What are you two doing in there?"

"What are they *not* doing in there?" Uncle fires back, the subtext unmistakably clear.

Adnan and I make our way to the dining room and take our seats at the table. I set down the jug in the center before taking my place next to Adnan.

When Uncle reaches forward to grab a blue bowl of creamy masoor dal, Ma redirects him to the bigger green bowl.

"Sorry, Sumon, but that one is for Arman," she says, swiftly moving the bowl next to Baba's plate.

"Sorry, my friend, but unfortunately this delicious low-sugar, low-salt, low-fat delicacy is all mine." Baba tries to sound upbeat, but his eyes betray him. Ma's got Baba on a new food plan, which she has named the Desi Diabetic Diet. Or, as I like to call it, the triple D.

"I thought masoor dal was already low in everything," Uncle comments.

"You can always make it healthier." Ma piles mounds of rice onto everyone's plates except for Baba's; his is overtaken by two plain-looking pieces of roti made with whole wheat flour. Ma glances at me briefly, probably remembering the conversation we had only a few hours ago. "I want Arman around for years to come, so if he has to suffer through food low in everything, including taste, he will."

Baba smiles at Ma despite the watery dal in front of him and the argument they had last night. I wonder why that's the case until he turns to Sumon Uncle and Somaiya Auntie and says, "It's all worth it if it means I get to live long enough to see our kids get married. Inshallah."

Ah, *that's* why.

"Inshallah," Ma echoes. "It can only get better from here."

I look down at my plate. How did this turn into a conversation about me and Adnan all of a sudden?

I guess, at least if they're talking about us, they can't focus on their own problems.

The parents chatter on about solidifying plans for the ridiculous dawat they're hosting to celebrate our "relationship"—Ma even gets the calendar off the fridge to look at dates—before moving on to discussing something they heard through one of the women at the mosque.

"Don't you think they're missing out by not taking the Auntie Grapevine online?" Adnan whispers.

"Oh, for sure. I even think they could give Thermae-Secrets a run for their money."

"To be fair, it doesn't take a lot to beat them. I wouldn't consider them factually accurate considering the number of times we've been on there."

I roll my eyes remembering how, now that we're actually "together," we barely make an appearance on there. Go figure. "True."

As I pick at the grains of rice on my plate, Adnan checks his phone underneath the table, the screen lighting up with both my face and a message from Cami.

A wave of guilt overcomes me at the sight of her name, reminding me of the messages from the day before. Of her hurt. "How is she?" I ask, making sure my voice is low enough that our parents won't overhear.

I don't even have to specify who I'm talking about for him to catch on. "She's fine. Still a bit upset but that's to be expected."

"You'll be OK, though, right?"

"Yeah, we will. It's just . . ." Adnan lets out a long sigh, his body shriveling up like a five-day-old balloon. "This is turning out to be harder than I thought."

"In what way?" I take a bite out of the chicken, my eyes rolling into the back of my head with enjoyment. Ma's really outdone herself.

"Like, it was her idea that you and I pretend to be together"—he pauses and turns to the glass in front of him, his eyes wandering but never landing—"but she doesn't want us to *pretend* to be together. If you get what I mean."

"I really don't," I say in between bites, keeping an eye on the parents and looking at their movements for any indication that they're eavesdropping on our conversation. Fortunately, they seem far too engrossed talking about natoks to pay any attention to us. "Elaborate, please."

"Basically, she hates seeing us together as a couple."

"But we're pretending."

"I know." Adnan sighs. "But it's hard for her to see. Especially after yesterday and the . . ." He clears his throat and looks away. "Kiss."

I squirm in my seat at the way he says the word "kiss." "Yeah, I get that. Like, I know it can't be easy to see your guy be with another girl, even when you're in on the whole arrangement, but it's not like I have feelings for you or anything. I mean, sure, the kiss yesterday was pretty good—"

My hand flies to my mouth before I can say anything else. Did I really just say that I *enjoyed* the kiss with Adnan? It was one thing thinking it but to say it out loud is a whole different thing.

"It was?" Adnan asks, his voice filled with surprise.

"Well, yes, *objectively*, I totally get why girls want to make out with you," I rush to add. "*Objectively*, you're a good kisser and, again *objectively*, I can see why she would be annoyed that I did, considering she can't. Not in public, at least." As I remember the kiss—viewing it *objectively*—my stomach simmers at the way his hand caressed my jaw only moments before we got lost in the kiss. "But it doesn't mean I'm in love with you or anything."

"That's not what Cami thinks. I mean, I don't agree, obviously. But the, uh, *kiss*,"—again, he says the word like it embarrasses him—"kind of just, like, solidified it for her."

I sit up taller. "What do you mean?"

"She thinks you're in love with me and that you only agreed to pretend to be my girlfriend so you can swoop in and be my actual girlfriend." The surprise must show on my face because he adds, "I keep telling her it's not true, I swear."

I know Cami can't be expected to be OK with the kiss, but it sounds like the kiss was the last shoe to drop, with her thinking I've had a crush on Adnan since before then. Which is just absurd! Especially when *I'm* the one doing *her* a favor! I leap to my feet with fury, knocking my knee against the table, sending a sharp pain through my leg, so ultimately I have to sit down again.

"Zara, are you OK?" Ma asks, her brows knit in concern.

"Yup." I squirm. "Fly buzzed near my ear."

"Oh no. There's a fly in here?" Sumon Uncle cracks his knuckles, hunting with his eyes for the imaginary fly. "Let me go get my swatter from the car. I will not let this fly ruin our delicious dinner with its diseases."

Uncle runs off before I can retract my fictional fly excuse, the adults getting up to grab plates to cover the food, not daring to have their dinner spoiled by a bacterium-carrying insect.

Even with the commotion around us, I can't stop thinking about Cami. In light of what Adnan's just told me, all of her recent behavior makes sense—the way she's been a bit colder toward me, how she inserted herself into the group without asking us first—but what doesn't make sense is that she'd make the accusation in the first place. How could she ever think that I'd be using my fake relationship as a ladder into a real relationship with Adnan? I thought Cami would be the last person to buy into the whole Adnan-and-Zara-are-meant-to-be spiel. Especially as we declared ourselves girlfriends-in-sync.

So, what changed?

"Z, you OK?" Adnan asks. "That looked like it hurt."

Amid fuming about Cami, I completely forgot about my knee. "Yeah, I'm fine."

"You sure?"

"Yeah. Let's just leave it." I pick at my food, moving grains of rice around on my plate but never scooping them into my mouth.

Our parents keep chattering, Uncle now back with his swatter tucked into his back pocket like he's a pest control representative. When the silence between Adnan and me becomes unbearable, I ask him to tell me a pick-up line. Anything to get us back to normal.

"I thought you hated them," he replies.

"Yeah, I do, but, like, in an affectionate way. I hate them in the way I hate how Ma fusses over me when I'm sick."

"So, you secretly love them?" he says with a wry smile.

I roll my eyes. "Just tell me a pick-up line."

"OK, here goes." Adnan clears his throat, his eyes shimmering with mischief as if he already knows I'm going to hate whatever he says next. " 'Hey, I just met you, and we're both Desi, but here's my data, so shaadi maybe?' "

My hand flies to my mouth. "That was *so* bad. You know that, right?"

"Are you serious? That was a good one!"

"It really wasn't. You're so lucky you're not single anymore."

Adnan clicks his tongue. "I'm a genius and you know it."

"Whatever helps you sleep."

Adnan shovels grains of rice into his mouth, a bit of sauce clinging to the corner of his lips. As he speaks about how he carefully crafts his pick-up lines, I'm unable to focus on anything but the speck of sauce. I try to ignore it, but my eyes keep drifting back to his lips.

"You've got some sauce, right here," I finally say when the image of his lips starts making me feel funny. I point to the corner of my mouth.

He uses the back of his hand to wipe away the sauce, but it still remains.

"Here, let me." I grab a napkin and wet it with some water. Adnan's hand rests on my knee for support as he leans forward, allowing me a better grip of his face as I gently wipe away the sauce. When I'm done, our eyes meet and my stomach goes all bubbly, just like when we kissed last night.

What is happening right now?

"Is it gone?" he asks, his voice husky as he narrows his eyes.

"Yep. All gone." I swallow, staring at the rice on my plate until this disaster of an evening is over and I can hide under the covers in my room.

Today 20:34

Zara

Hey

I just wanted to say I'm sorry about kissing Adnan at the disco

Cami

Thanks

Zara

I was just panicking

Sadie was going to do something if I didn't

Cami

I wish you'd done something else

Zara

I'm sorry

Cami

Yeah me too

SHAH RUKH KHAN 2.0

Today 22:46

Zara

I've had a thought since dinner

Adnan

?

Zara

Maybe, to be respectful to
Cami, we shouldn't hang out
by ourselves as much?

Adnan

oh

Zara

I don't want her to dislike me more
than she already does

Adnan

she doesn't dislike you

Zara

She doesn't trust me

And I don't want that

Adnan

i was thinking the same

i just . . . don't want to be a shitty friend to you, you know

Zara

I know

But this is just temporary, right?

Sooner or later, we're going to break up anyway

And all this tension will go away

Adnan

yeah

just sucks

you're my best friend

Zara

And you're mine

Adnan

can i still come to Sunday dinner?

Auntie's borhani is OP

Zara

That's a given

Maybe just like if we're gonna meet up to chat about things, we do it over text rather than in person

Adnan

maybe we should post more on social media too

ThermaeSecrets will know something is up otherwise

Zara

We can stage a photoshoot next Sunday

You know Ma will go senseless for the chance

Adnan

how could she not when I'm there?

Zara

I just threw up in my mouth

Adnan

hope it was tasty

Zara

Eww

And oh

Maybe at school we hold hands

But not all the time and especially
not when Cami is there

Adnan

i don't think she'll want to sit
with us at lunch anymore

Zara

Probably a good idea

Since Sadie now knows Cami likes you

It's just a bit shitty

I did want to be friends with Cami

Adnan

and she with you, Z

once this is all over, i'm sure you'll be fine

Zara

Oh btw, after you left, I spoke to Ma
and she set a date for the party

Adnan

the big Zara-and-Adnan-finally-
got-together party?

Zara

Yeah

Adnan

YEAH BOI

Zara

You're excited?

Adnan

any excuse for chotpoti and halim

when is it?

Zara

December 24

Adnan

christmas eve?

Zara

Not like we celebrate
Christmas anyways

And I thought since Cami would be preoccupied with her own fam it'd give you something to do other than mope about her absence

Adnan

you're clever

always looking out for me

Zara

What can I say?

I truly am the best fake girlfriend you've ever had

Also we'll have been together for like nearly three months by then

So it won't be weird when we break up in the new year

New year, new me, you know

Adnan

yeah

i guess

Zara

You guess?

Adnan

i'm not sure when Cami is going to tell her dad

and i don't want to push her

she's banking on us being her cover until she's ready

Zara

The longer this goes on, the harder it'll be for us to get out of this so-called relationship

Adnan

i know

i'll talk to her

dw i got you

Zara

You better

215

SolusZ26
Tell me something fun
Anything
Please

VelasY74
I see we're skipping introductions

SolusZ26
You're the one who said you never know
when I'm about to head off
I'm just being efficient, you know

VelasY74
True
Do forgive me for the accusation

SolusZ26
Will only forgive if you tell me something fun

VelasY74
The record for the longest conga line is 120000 people

SolusZ26
I think you added one too many zeroes

216

VelasY74

Nope

You read that right

120000

The year was 1988 and the people wanted to conga

SolusZ26

That is actually bonkers

VelasY74

Right?

It sounds ridiculous but if you google it you'll

see it's a real thing

Miami Super Conga

SolusZ26

I think you've broken my brain

Now all I can do is think about the conga

VelasY74

You better practice

You do owe me a dance

And I plan to cash in

SolusZ26

Keep dreaming

VelasY74

Oh, I will

Trust me

Sooner or later I will get you to dance with me Zara

22

After solidly chatting with Yahya every night for the past two weeks, I feel like every morning when I wake up I'll never get over this feeling of being on top of the world.

On Saturday, I start my day with a new holiday romance novel, and I feel like for the very first time I can personally relate to the emotions my characters are experiencing. Like the fear of not knowing what Yahya's going to say but being OK with that. Being excited to find out. The need to ask ridiculous questions and rehash stories of my past just so the three little dots on my screen will appear. The rush that races through my body as I imagine his reactions on the other side of the screen.

I feel all of it.

And even when Ma nags me about sorting out the recycling, I go downstairs without argument. I even teeter on the brink of dancing, thinking about how we stayed up until three in the morning just chatting, talking about our favorite movies (mine: *Angus, Thongs and Perfect Snogging;*

his: *The Social Network*), ideal stupid superpowers (mine: changing the channel on the TV with a click of my fingers; his: being able to see the topping of a pizza through the box), and funny childhood stories (mine: the time I ate powder detergent thinking it was salt; his: how he went through a phase where he was so into Egypt that he slept with his arms across his chest just so it would be easier to mummify him if he died in his sleep).

Even now, with my arms loaded with a mucky green recycling box clanging with glass jars and empty soup cans, I can't wipe the grin off my face just thinking about him. Talking to Yahya is . . . surprisingly easy. Even that first day I met him, I didn't find it difficult to chat with him. It's freeing, in a sense, that he's so far removed from anybody I know. I don't have to be a particular version of myself for him; I can just be me. I can let out my silly side with him, and I can be flirty with him, and his confidence makes me confident.

"Somebody's happy," Sadie says, sticking her head through the conservatory door and nearly scaring the life out of me.

"What are you doing here? We didn't make any plans, did we?" I sort the last of the recycling before guiding her into the house, heading toward the sink to wash my hands of the sticky residue that was stuck to one of the glass jars.

"You do remember that you promised me a tell-all on your relationship with Adnan, right? We talked about it at lunch the other day."

Oh shit, I did. But with everything going on I completely

forgot. "I thought you were interviewing other people before us?"

"I was meaning to but other than the people I interviewed at the silent disco for background footage and mini-scenes, which I've already started editing by the way, your and Adnan's story is the one I need before I can fully start framing the doc. I actually figured out that it'll come back to rom-coms and the media and how, like, people think the media has warped our sense of romance because we expect rom-com-esque love stories, but they don't realize that it's only that way *because* of how real life plays out. The Alphabet romance story wasn't a rom-com waiting to happen; the movie of the Alphabet romance story is the one waiting to happen. And the documentary will show just that!"

"Right. Framing of the doc. Media is wrong," I repeat like I'm a computer taking too long to process the information. "Let me call Adnan. He should be here as well."

Before I can call Adnan, Sadie covers my screen.

"I already interviewed him."

I roll my head in circles, easing out the knots that have suddenly appeared in my neck. "You did?"

Laughing, she asks, "Do you guys not talk or something?"

"Of course we do. I must have just missed his texts," I say, trying to keep my voice light. And sure enough, when I unlock my phone I see I have a flurry of missed messages from him.

sadie is on the prowl
you need to be ready
i told her—

221

"I wanted to do separate interviews," Sadie says, interrupting my reading. "Give the viewers different points of view, you know? We want to know how to achieve a romance like the Alphabet Couple by interviewing A and then Z. Stylistically, it'll look great as well. It'll be like those *Vanity Fair* interviews where they ask the person the same question two years in a row, with the then and now playing in split screen." Sadie's excitement rises as she babbles on about how she'll do the interview in that same manner, except it will be my story versus Adnan's, but she also hopes she can do a "Same Interview, A Year Later" with us, too.

Except there's not going to be one next year. Not that I can tell her that.

Nervousness trails me as I lead Sadie up to my bedroom. Adnan and I have that story we told our parents, but I can't really remember it off the top of my head. And while we gave Sadie and the gang a general overview, we never went into specifics. And then there's the fact that I can't lie to Sadie, not really. In all my years of friendship with her, she's always been able to spot a lie. It's a miracle really that she hasn't caught me out yet.

Sadie perches on the edge of my bed, adjusting the brightness, contrast, and all those other techy things on her phone, while I do my best not to sweat through my T-shirt.

Judging from the moist patches in my armpits, I don't think I'm doing very well.

Once she's finished messing around with her phone, she turns off the overhead light and instead switches on my desk lamp, illuminating me in an orange and pink glow. She steps back and views me from afar, a smile growing across her face. "I knew that would do the trick. Right, I'll count us in. Three, two, one . . ." Sadie presses down on her screen before she asks, "So, tell me, how did it happen? Because I've been on your case for years and you haven't budged. Why now?"

"Uhm." Without having even said anything, I feel like the words are scraping against my throat. "Well, it was after the movies."

Sadie's posture wilts as a line forms between her eyebrows. "Are you sure?"

"Yeah, why wouldn't I be?" I say with a nervous laugh.

"Well, you didn't end up going to the movies with Adnan. Your parents were fighting, right? I was texting you that night."

I swallow, the sound too loud as my heart beats in my ears. I suddenly feel like I'm in an interrogation that no lawyer could get me out of.

"Oh, yeah. This was a few days later. I went to the movie theater after I went to your house. I didn't really want to go home to my parents. Since they were arguing. Again. So, he thought it would cheer me up," I quickly amend.

Sadie scratches her cheek. "What happened next?"

"He . . . kissed me. After the movie, of course. We were walking home, and he just did it out of the blue. I was obviously surprised, don't get me wrong, but it just seemed right, you know? I think we were both inspired by the film

223

we'd seen." I use my hands for good measure, gesturing that there's nothing more to the story.

"It's interesting, you know," Sadie notes, tapping her pen against her bottom lip, "that you guys have the exact same story. There's practically no discrepancy, except for the fact that Adnan said you were the one who suggested going to the movies rather than him."

"Isn't that a good thing, though?" I twist the ring on my finger in agitation but stop when I notice Sadie's stare. "It'll make doing that split-screen thing more interesting, won't it? And the discrepancy could be one of those funny things that we as a couple can never agree on or something like that."

"I guess." Sadie tugs at her earlobe, the lines on her forehead indicating that her mind is whirring away. "It's just . . . ," she begins, but doesn't finish, tilting her head from one side to the other. "When you interview people and their stories are the same, it says something to the interviewer."

I swallow, waiting for her next words. And then, when she finally does speak, my stomach drops.

"It implies to the interviewer that the story's been rehearsed."

I laugh, but it comes out breathy and fake. "Sades. You're reading too much into it."

She opens and closes her mouth several times before forming any actual words. "It's just, you guys disagree on the movie invite."

I furrow my brows, not sure where she's going with this. "Yeah, I thought Adnan invited me because he thought it'd cheer me up and he obviously thought I invited him."

"Exactly, according to *me*. When I mentioned it to you, you didn't seem surprised or particularly fazed that he would say that. In fact, you brushed it off, like it didn't matter. So, while your story is incredibly similar to Adnan's, it's also not . . . How do I put this?" Sadie makes a steeple with her fingers as she ruminates on the right words. "It just seems like you would care more about the discrepancy. Like, you'd say your side was the right one like most couples do, rather than disregard it entirely." Sadie stops recording, locking her phone with a quiet click. "It just doesn't add up, Z."

Oh Allah, this is it. Sadie's figured it out. I knew she was going to figure it out sooner or later, but I didn't think it would be *now*.

"I don't understand what you're trying to get at."

Sadie's glance darts around the room with frustration, as if she's looking for answers I'm unwilling to give her, before settling back on me. "Z, is there something you're not telling me?"

I suck my cheeks in, my heart pounding in my ears. No matter how much I deny it, deep down she knows something's not right.

"Look, I can only think of one explanation for why your stories are identical down to a T." Sadie paces the room, her eyes not meeting mine as she whizzes through her theory. "Your actual origin story is so embarrassing that you're afraid I'll judge you or something and so you've come up with this ridiculous story about realizing you're each

225

other's soulmates after watching a movie. Because let's be real: after sixteen years, a movie would *not* be the reason you'd finally get together. Adnan knows you better than to give you vanilla when you are a toasted-coconut-chocolate-chip kind of girl through and through."

It takes a moment for me to compute what she's actually said, but when I do, I can't believe that this is the conclusion she's come to: she thinks we're embarrassed, that we actually have a different origin story that's juicier than the one we've told. That there's no way in hell I would finally get with Adnan after something so plain as a movie, and when I think about it I realize she's right—even though when Adnan described our origin story at dinner, I thought it was just what I wanted because it was effortless and easy. But now that Sadie's pointed it out, that's not what I want at all. At least, not anymore. I want somebody who will give me *passion*. Somebody who will kiss me in the pouring rain, because that's what happens in the movies.

Somebody who isn't effortless but who is worth the fight.

I refrain from holding a hand over my chest in relief and silently thanking Allah. I might not be out of the woods just yet but at least this way I won't have to lie, considering Sadie has reached the conclusion herself.

At the same time, some teeny-tiny part of me wishes she'd finally figured it out because at least then I could finally talk to someone about it all.

Sadie plonks herself back down on my bed. "I'm right, aren't I?"

"Yes, you are." I cover my face in my hands, overwhelmed by the disappointment that gnaws at me but hoping Sadie will just think I'm embarrassed.

"I knew it! I just knew something was off! I can always tell when you're lying to me."

"I'm sorry. I know I shouldn't have lied; it was just—"

"It's cool." She raises a hand, silencing me. "And even though it goes against my director's integrity, I'll allow you to tell your story again because, I'm not going to lie, the footage I've got does nothing but portray you as a terrible actress. And we can't compromise the documentary. If the committee even smells a fabricated documentary, they'll exclude me from the competition."

I hug myself as the cortisol in my body rises at the prospect of Sadie's work having been for nothing. I would hate to see her film excluded, especially after all the time and effort she's put in, just because of my lie.

"I do have one condition, though, since I'm doing you a massive favor by basically putting my documentary on the line."

"What?" I can't keep up with all these conditions that come with this fake relationship.

Sadie puts on her trademark grin as her eyes gleam. "You have to tell me the real story of how you got together."

SHAH RUKH KHAN 2.0

Today 18:49

Zara

If Sadie mentions anything about a
sippy cup, just play along

And act a bit embarrassed

Adnan

???

VelasY74

So I finally watched that rom-com

Your favorite

Angus, Thongs and Perfect Snogging

SolusZ26

What did you think?

VelasY74

I can see why it's your favorite

There are SO many terrible jokes in the film

It instantly reminded me of you

SolusZ26

Are you saying I'm not funny???

I mean, you're right, I do love the awful jokes BUT they're
not the only reason I love the film

VelasY74

It's the birthday party scene, isn't it?

When Georgia finds out that her best friend organized
the party?

SolusZ26

. . .

OK

How did you know that?

VelasY74

Nothing says "I love you" more than having your birthday party at a night club

SolusZ26
LOL

VelasY74

JK JK

It's because, as much as the film is a teen romantic comedy, it's about love in different forms, and for Georgia the heartbreak is when her and Jas are fighting

But then Jas organizes the party, making amends, and setting the record straight that no matter how much you argue with your best friend, they'll still always be your best friend

Even when they drive you up a wall, you don't love them any less

I think we forget sometimes that the love between friends, friends who are practically family, and the subsequent breakups that sometimes take place over friendships are just as difficult or even more difficult than a romantic breakup

At least that's my interpretation of it . . .

SolusZ26
Seriously
How did you know that's why the movie is my favorite?

Because not even my friend Sadie understands why I
love that scene so much

VelasY74

Guess she's not paying as much attention
to you as I am

SolusZ26

Or more likely I just talk about myself too much
Which I need to stop doing
Why don't you tell me something about YOU?
I feel like I hardly know you despite talking to you like
every night

VelasY74

What if I want to be mysterious?

SolusZ26

I'm really not a fan of mysteries
I much prefer rom-coms
I like getting to know my characters, minus the
brooding parts

VelasY74

Crap
I'm such a brooder
Or did sitting in a tree the first time you met me not tip
you off?

SolusZ26
Stop stalling

VelasY74
How about I show you?
VelasY74's TikTok

Today at 19:47

SolusZ26
Holy shit
Sorry for not replying sooner
But I haven't been able to tear my eyes away because
you can DANCE

VelasY74
I'm a beginner, to be honest

SolusZ26
How could you not tell me you have an actual talent?
YOU CAN DANCE
Like I know I saw you dance that one time
when we first met
But watching your videos and seeing that it's
like your THING . . .
I'm shook

232

VelasY74

Haha why?

Because I'm tall and lanky and look like I have no coordination?

SolusZ26

No, because you don't really see this type of dancing on TikTok

I mean, I know that's how Charli D'Amelio rose to fame

But usually you just see the trending songs with white creators ripping off creators of color

Or just general thirst traps

But you're like actually sick at dancing

It's impressive af

And you can tell you actually want to dance, and don't just do it for clout

Even I, who hate to dance, want to dance watching you

OK I'll stop now

VelasY74

Well, you do owe me a dance, remember?

SolusZ26

Oh, I am not dancing with you

Especially not now

Because you'll wipe the floor with me

Honestly you would cringe watching me

VelasY74

Like I said, you still owe me

SolusZ26

No way
I'd rather eat my own toenails

VelasY74

Best keep 'em clean then

SolusZ26

Back to your dancing skills
You're like really really good

VelasY74

Thanks
I wish my parents thought that

SolusZ26

They don't approve?

VelasY74

My parents don't see dance as something that will pay
the bills or help anybody
Not like their jobs

SolusZ26

What do they do?

VelasY74

Social work

But like all over the world

They basically say that dance won't help when the world
is going under and you're left fending for yourself

SolusZ26

But creative expression *is* important

I mean just look at what happened during the pandemic

Art was the only thing that kept everyone going

Like it wasn't just entertainment anymore

It comforted us

It connected us

VelasY74

Unfortunately my parents didn't see it that way

SolusZ26

That's so shitty

I'm really sorry

VelasY74

It is what it is

SolusZ26

But it shouldn't have to be

VelasY74

I know

But my parents are just different

What are yours like?

SolusZ26

They're really supportive, although it wasn't always that easy

Ever since I started reading, I knew I wanted to do something with books and I know that I want to do something good for the world, like increase representation in books on the market because even though society has come a long way, it's still difficult to find a rom-com with a South Asian lead.

So, when I did my research and found out what editors do, it just clicked into place for me

Now, my parents love that idea

But they didn't always

VelasY74

What changed?

SolusZ26

They did

When I first told them I wanted to work in publishing, they thought I was joking and then they said, "Publishing is a dying industry, everything is digital"

They were pragmatic, which I get since we're desi and
we can only be doctors, engineers, or accountants
So I wrote it off for a while, ignored my passion, but then
my dad came around

VelasY74
How?

SolusZ26
He'd seen me do my thing, make notes inside books
when I thought everyone else was asleep, or fall asleep
with a book on my chest
And he said it got him thinking

VelasY74
About what?

SolusZ26
About whether or not I was happy doing what I loved
Because he said at the end of the day, that's all that
matters
Embracing what I love

VelasY74
That's pretty sweet actually

SolusZ26

Yeah

He told me not to suffer through things just because it
was what people said was right

Or because I felt I had to

He told me to just dive in headfirst and embrace what *I*
loved

Ma came around in the end too

All this is to say, your parents might not encourage you
because they don't understand

VelasY74

You might be right

But, and I'm not trying to ruin your motivational speech,
they're probably never going to understand

They're just not like your parents

SolusZ26

☹

What are they like?

VelasY74

Difficult and distant

It's hard to explain

They travel a lot

Which means my uncle practically raised me

SolusZ26

How often do you see them?

VelasY74

At most?

A few months out of the year

It's also why they're never around to see me dance

SolusZ26

That's tough

VelasY74

Yeah

SolusZ26

Well, just know I think you're amazing

And I'd watch you dance anytime

You've got something special

SHAH RUKH KHAN 2.0

Today 22:09

Adnan

btw

Cami and i are planning to go out next Saturday if that's cool with you?

Zara

I'm presuming I'm your cover

Adnan

yes . . .

but also maybe a chance for you two to chat?

Zara

I don't think she wants to chat with me

Her avoiding me makes that abundantly clear

And she was pretty cold when I apologized

Adnan

just give her time

Zara

Right

At least tell me you're going somewhere fun this time

Adnan

we're going to Chippenham on a treasure hunt trail

Zara

Isn't that for kids?

Adnan

excuse you

treasure doesn't age

Zara

Sure it doesn't

But fine, I'll come with and just do my own thing

Adnan

thank you, Z

i knew i could count on you

SolusZ26
Hey

VelasY74
Hey
What's up?

SolusZ26
I was wondering if you'd want to do a raid sometime soon
Like next weekend?
I read on LeekDuck that they're rolling out a new five star
So, that could be cool

VelasY74
Yeah, I'm always up for a raid
We can do a remote one so I can join you from
wherever you are

SolusZ26
Remote raid
For sure
I'll invite you
Let's do that

Today at 23:19

SolusZ26

~~I actually meant to invite you to a physical raid~~
~~So we could, you know, hang out. Or whatever~~

Today at 23:47

SolusZ26

~~Can we do the raid in person?~~
~~I hear there are better rewards, like, more rare candy~~
~~And I deffo need them to evolve some of my Pokémon~~

Today at 00:14

SolusZ26

~~I want to ask you out but I'm scared~~

Today at 01:11

VelasY74

So, I've been mulling this over for the past couple of hours

SolusZ26

?

VelasY74

When you asked if I wanted to do a raid, you didn't mean a remote one, did you?

SolusZ26

No, I didn't

VelasY74

Ah, I see

SolusZ26

Yeah

VelasY74

I'll have to check my calendar

SolusZ26

Oh, OK

No worries

Maybe we can meet some other time

VelasY74

I'm kidding

I don't own one!

I just have dinner at my uncle's in the evening

So what time are you thinking?

Because, and do let me know if I have it wrong, I'm assuming we're not just doing a raid and then heading home?

SolusZ26

I've got bad news . . .

VelasY74

You only want me for my raid connections, don't you?

SolusZ26

Busted!

Only joking

We can do at least two

VelasY74

How generous

SolusZ26

That's me

I'll send you the details

GROUP

Today 01:26

Zara

When does that treasure thing start on Saturday?

And finish?

Cami

Starts at 3.

It's around two hours long.

Zara

Are you planning on doing anything after the trail?

Cami

Not that I'm aware of.

Adnan

i'd be down to spend more time with u, babe

Cami

I'll have to check with my parents tonight.

I think they might need me home in the evening.

Adnan

that's fine, just let us know

Cami

Of course, baby

Zara

~~Gross~~

23

"Did I ever tell you about the time I accidentally ended up in Melksham?" Adnan asks out of nowhere as we exit the train station.

I stretch out my neck after having leaned on his shoulder for so long. "We're not going to Melksham; we're going to Chippenham."

"I know, but again: did I ever tell you about the time I accidentally ended up in Melksham?"

I let out a guttural groan. I'm not sure what's worse about going on these dates as a cover: Adnan's ridiculous stories or having to figure out what to do. I'm leaning more toward the stories because at least this time I don't have to entertain myself for the whole afternoon.

Adnan elbows me. "Come on, you know you want to know."

He's not going to let up unless I let him tell me the story. And to be honest, we haven't got anything better to do. Cami's not due to arrive for at least another ten minutes. She's texted the group chat saying there is some delay on the highway coming from her house.

"How did you accidentally end up in Melksham?" I ask, taking the bait.

"I was on my way to Corsham an—"

"Why were you headed there?"

"Well, I was going on a ghost tou—"

"Since when are you interested in ghosts?"

"Are you going to let me finish the story?"

I hold my hands up in apology. "Go on."

"Like I *said* . . ." Adnan shoots me a side-eye before launching into his story, but I'm not really paying attention—too focused on what I'm going to say when I see Yahya in the flesh. The anticipation of being with him causes my butterflies to stir and I have to cover my stomach just to tell them to shut up. Despite knowing that I will feel at ease as soon as I meet Yahya, I'm still more nervous than I've ever been.

I just don't want to mess things up with him. It quite genuinely feels like he's walked straight out of a 90s rom-com without any of the problematic qualities attached. And something about him in general just feels like . . . home.

"Can you believe that?" Adnan says, jolting me out of my thoughts.

Not having listened, all I can say is, "What was the point of that story?"

"I don't really know, if I'm honest. I just thought it'd be entertaining and take your mind off being cold."

"It didn't work."

"Here." Adnan takes off his burgundy beanie and places it neatly over my head, careful not to mess up my loose waves, his fingers gently combing through my hair. "Amma always says heat escapes from your head."

"Is that why Ma always says that not wearing a hat will freeze your brain?" I readjust the beanie slightly, using the glass entrance of the train station as a mirror, but Adnan rearranges it again.

"Amma science is not to be disputed, you know that," he says, taking a step back.

"Hey!" Cami's voice is more high-pitched than usual as she approaches us and when I shift my gaze to her I see why: her dad's with her. "Dad, this is Adnan and Zara."

"Nice to meet you both," he says, but from the tone of his voice it doesn't feel like he means it. He's very tall and I see where Cami gets her sharp jawline from. They've got the same eyes, too, but where Cami's light up with excitement, his are filled with something else. Caution?

"Are you siblings?" he asks.

"No," I say at the same time as Adnan says, "We're a couple, sir."

He smiles thinly, like that eases any worries he might have had. He promptly turns his attention to Cami. "Remind me where you're headed to, again?"

"Just this treasure trail thing."

"Camilla, it's freezing. You should be somewhere warm, not outside."

"Dad, it's fine. I layered up. And I have an extra scarf in my bag."

Cami's dad looks at her with such worry it breaks my heart. "I expect you'll be done in two hours?"

"More like three?"

"Camilla, we have dinner to attend."

"I know. But Mom won't mind if we give her some extra time. Please, Dad?"

He sighs and looks pained for a second before reluctantly agreeing. "OK. But not a minute later."

What did Cami do that's got her dad so on edge?

"Of course, Dad. See you soon."

"Have fun," he says, looking at me and Adnan once again, assessing us almost, before disappearing down the street. At the car, he looks back one last time and waves goodbye to Cami, who reciprocates the motion.

"So, that's your dad," I say.

"Yeah. Are we ready to go?" She looks off into the distance, her eyes still on her father as he rounds the corner, before turning back to Adnan.

"Sure. Z, you going to be OK?" Adnan asks me, but I can tell he's eager to go.

"Yep, you two go."

They wave a quick 'bye and then practically sprint in the opposite direction of Cami's dad, leaving me standing all alone in the middle of Chippenham.

I stuff my hands in my pockets and stroll toward this little café I read about on TripAdvisor.

When I get there, I order a latte with extra foam and hide myself away at the back, letting my body dissolve into a giant leather chair.

I check my watch: 1:08. Two hours and fifty-two minutes left. That's a long time to spend with one person. Oh, Allah, maybe this was a mistake. And Yahya's probably realized that as well, which is why he hasn't shown up. I'll just leave. I'll text him and pretend I never showed up either, so it won't be awkw—

The bell above the door rings, the tolling more like a pair of clashing cymbals in the quietude.

"Hey, sorry I'm late. Traffic was awful." Yahya quickly unwinds the thick gray scarf from around his neck, shrugging off this gorgeous coat that hugs him in just the right places. Similar to the previous two times I've seen him, he's wearing a black oversize hoodie with some kind of anime print on it and mustard-colored Timberlands on his feet, and his hair is gorgeously wind-tousled. He looks good.

"Don't worry about it." Of course. Traffic. I really need to stop letting jumping to conclusions become my number one sport. "You're here now, that's all that matters."

"I need a drink to warm up. You want something?" he asks and then clocks the mug in front of me. "I've really got to get to you before you order a beverage." He goes to the counter and orders himself a drink. A minute or two later he returns with a steaming mug.

"What did you order?" I ask, cringing at my inability to make interesting small talk.

His cheeks redden. "A babycino."

"A babycino?" I can hardly contain the peal of laughter in my throat.

"Don't laugh! Milk is essential for growing."

"I don't think you need to grow any more. You're quite tall as it is."

"Fine. It's not the milk. I just really like cinnamon."

"How come?" I ask, genuinely curious.

"It reminds me of Christmas with my family," he says with a nostalgic smile. I want to ask him more about his family and his dancing, but it feels a bit too early to delve into the serious stuff.

"Well, cheers." I hold up my mug to his, a small clinking sound echoing as they meet. We sip in silence, neither of us quite sure of what to say. We exchange nervous glances and smiles, but even so, no words leave our mouths for longer than is deemed socially acceptable. I suppose when we've met before it's always been unplanned, accidental, but now that we're here with a purpose it feels more significant.

"I'm just going to come out and ask because it's been killing me ever since you sent me that message," he says. He rests his elbows on his knees, his gaze laser-focused on me. "This is a date, right?"

"It doesn't have to be, if you don't want—"

"So, it *is* a date?" He tilts his head in question and I have no other choice than to confirm his suspicion.

"Yes." I swallow.

He runs a hand through his hair as he furrows his brows. "I must say, I'm quite surprised."

"Why?"

"Well." He pauses, like he doesn't really want to bring

it up but knows that he won't get anywhere if he doesn't. "Because of the guy."

Now it's my turn to look at him with confusion. "The guy?"

His eyes drift to my phone, which has been lighting up with messages from Sadie. "On your lock screen."

Oh. *That* explains why he's been so weird since he walked in. I look down at my phone; Adnan's wide grin stares back at me. If Yahya were anybody else, I would have to say, yes, Adnan is very much my boyfriend. But Yahya doesn't know Adnan. I could actually tell him the truth. I could tell him how I've been roped into something that's snowballed out of control. How I can't talk to the people closest to me about how I really feel about it all. How I wish I wasn't such a fraud and could just be *Zara* rather than one-half of the supposed Alphabet Couple.

But if I do that, he might not see it the same way I do. He might not see it as me trying to fix things between my parents or helping a friend out while his girlfriend gathers the courage to face her own parents. He might see it the way Cami does: that I'm only doing this because I must be in love with Adnan.

"Look," Yahya says, leaning back in his seat, his body language signaling all kinds of defensiveness. "I don't want to be a home-wrecker, that's not my style. Maybe this isn't a good ide—"

"He's my friend," I blurt out.

So much for telling him the whole *story* . . .

254

"Your friend?" he repeats with a cocked eyebrow. "So, just to clarify, he's *not* your boyfriend?"

"Definitely not. Adnan's actually that guy I was telling you about at the silent disco. The one who was arguing with his girlfriend."

"Oh," Yahya says. He wipes his forehead with the back of his hand, his posture no longer rigid. "Well, that's a relief."

"It is?"

"Yeah," he says with an alluring laugh that disarms me. "Want to get out of here? Go for a walk or something? We don't even have to catch any Pokémon."

I grin. "Yeah, let's get out of here."

24

As our feet meet the cobblestones, my boot heels clacking along the roads of Chippenham, angry gray clouds gather overhead, threatening our excursion entirely. But we carry on walking aimlessly, my hands in my coat pockets as I kick a medium-size rock along, doing my best not to look at Yahya now that I know it's a proper date. I thought confirming it with him would put me at ease, but if anything, it's just made me more nervous, almost paralyzed by the sheer excitement of it all.

"Are you close with your friend then?" Yahya asks.

"Yeah, I am." Unintentionally, a smile stretches across my face. "He's funny without trying. He'll come up with the worst pick-up lines, and—" I shake my head. "I'm a walking red flag, aren't I? All I do is talk about my friend who just so happens to be a guy."

"Nothing wrong with having friends of the opposite gender," Yahya comments reassuringly. "Tell me about him."

"Well, we do practically everything together," I say.

"Have since we were kids. I don't think I could ever imagine life without him. He's practically the brother I never had."

"He sounds like a solid guy," he says with a slight nod.

Like me, he kicks a rock as he walks and, soon enough, he's kicked his a little too far and we have to battle over the one I've been kicking.

As we race to the rock in front of us, we playfully knock into each other, my competitive side coming out of its shell. But then Yahya's hand grazes my arm, his touch intoxicating as it awakens all my nerve endings, and I lose all concentration and he manages to kick the rock who knows where.

With the rock long gone, Yahya gives me a long look before deciding on his next words. "But there's something else going on, isn't there?"

I swallow. I play with the ring on my finger, trying to figure out how I can talk about this without giving away the truth. "Adnan's new girlfriend doesn't really like me very much, I think. So, we haven't been spending as much time together as we normally would."

"Ah."

"Yeah."

We walk in silence for a little while. "He's never been like this before. Nowadays, he'll only invite me somewhere if he needs me to—" The words die in my throat. I shake my head and rearrange them in my mind. "Nowadays, I'll be lucky if he actually speaks to me about anything other than Cami."

Yahya peers at me intently like he's giving his next response a lot of thought.

"Maybe she feels threatened by you." He lets his words hang in the air for a bit, the words dying in my throat as I wait for him to explain. "It's probably tough to be the new girlfriend—her name's Cami, right?"

I nod.

"Well, like I was saying, it's probably tough for Cami to be with someone who's so close to her friend. I mean, you feel edged out by your friend and what's to say she doesn't feel the same? Most likely, she's afraid that you're able to influence your friend in whether or not he stays with her."

His words make sense. "So, what you're saying is, I'm totally self-obsessed?" I say, a smirk playing on my lips.

"No, not at all." His mouth curves into a smile. "Sometimes you just need another perspective to understand how you really feel."

I smile to myself. It's thrilling that he listens—like, really *listens*—without interrupting me or making me feel like what I'm feeling is wrong.

My head buzzes in the ensuing silence and I have to fight against myself not to fill it. As our feet carry us forward, the intimacy of the moment is heightened, unaccompanied by external factors. That was always the thing with Adnan, why it felt like it could never work between us: everything would be loud. People were always watching, commenting, getting involved where they had no right to be.

"What are your thoughts on bowling?" Yahya asks as we come to a halt at a recreational center.

My toes curl in my boots at the sight of the building and all it holds. "I once dropped a bowling ball on my toes and am now scarred for life."

"You're kidding," he says, more a statement than a question.

"I wish I was. Luckily, nothing was broken. But I did lose one of my toenails."

"Ouch."

"Yeah." I make a small sound in my throat to shake off the image of a purple toenail.

"I'm guessing bowling is off the table then?"

"It's left the table and run out of the house."

"Good thing there's no bowling alley in there then."

"What?" I stop walking for a second. "One, what kind of recreational center doesn't have a bowling alley? And two, why'd you ask about bowling then?"

He shrugs, pretending to be casual. "Because I was trying to plan for our next date."

"Oh" is all I can get out before I force my brain to rewire itself and put together a proper sentence. "There's going to be a second date?"

"I hope so."

We keep walking, going past so many buildings I'm worried we've left Chippenham and ended up somewhere else entirely. It doesn't help that despite having these shoes for years, I've never actually broken them in, which means my calves are on fire with the arch of my foot feeling more stretched than usual. All that to say that I am in PAIN.

"There's a park just a little bit farther on that I thought might be nice," Yahya says, as if reading the concern on my face.

"How much farther exactly?" I ask. "Because I'm about two seconds away from swapping the excruciating pain of these heels for the agonizing pain of walking barefoot—"

Yahya stops in his tracks, and I do the same, grateful for the momentary reprieve. But then he does something totally unexpected.

He squats down and slaps his back. When I don't move, he swivels his head in my direction. "Come on, hop on."

"What are you doing?" I laugh.

"You said your feet hurt, so I'm giving you a lift. It's no Uber but at least I won't surcharge you."

I guffaw, not sure I'm hearing him right. "You can't be serious."

"Oh, I'm deadly serious."

Somehow, Yahya keeps surprising me. It's a little bit unsettling, not knowing what will come next with him. But it's also exciting as all hell, feeling like your story is yet to be written with an ending not even you know. No expectations and no disappointments.

"But I can only squat for so long, so you're going to have to get on quick. All that dancing's given me old man's knees, unfortunately."

"I'm too heavy—"

260

"This offer will expire in three, two . . ."

Before he can get to one and I can talk myself out of it any further, I put my arms around his neck and jump onto his back.

"I feel like a kid," I tell him, my chin leaning on his shoulder. "People must think we look strange."

"My lady must be comfortable on her journey," he says with a smirk that makes my insides spit with sparks.

As we near the park, I note that Yahya is a complete liar. When he said the park was "nice," he undersold it. Even with the overcast, cold weather, the autumn leaves are vibrant and bright as they fall in the wind, red and gold. Seasonal flower beds border the park in a circular shape. A flurry of people line up at a kiosk advertising hot beverages. There's a little bandstand, where a guy is playing an acoustic version of a pop song on his guitar.

We keep walking until we find a quiet spot by the fountain at the edge of the park, where he deposits me.

"How are your feet feeling? Still like they're about to fall off?"

"They're OK, I guess," I say with a shrug. "The ride definitely made them feel better."

"Good, because you still owe me a dance."

In the distance, the guy on the bandstand starts blaring out a trending song I recognize from my Spotify playlist. My foot taps along to the beat and I'm unable to stop myself from humming the lyrics.

"I'm not the dancer here. You are." I think back to the video of him dancing to "Beethoven" by Kenndog in the middle of a park somewhere, the way he elegantly twisted his arms and legs in perfect sync to the rhythm of the song. I tried replicating his moves in front of my mirror, but it looked more like I was having a spasm than dancing.

"Your own body is telling you it wants to," he counters, pointing at my feet. "Your feet wouldn't be tapping along to the beat if it didn't."

Yahya's grin grows devilish, since he knows he's got me in a corner. Fortunately for me, the music stops playing altogether. I turn to look for the reason and notice that the bandstand guy is packing up. Only a second later do I realize why: it's raining.

I throw my hands up in the air and a raindrop hits my palm. "What a shame. And I was just about to dance with you. Oh well . . ."

"You're not getting off that easy." Yahya pulls out his phone and opens Spotify. He scrolls through a few of his playlists before deciding on a song I've never heard before. After turning the volume up, he places the phone inside his coat pocket, the sound only slightly muffled, and stands up. He holds out his hand for me to grab and before I can talk myself out of it, I take it, following his lead. The song is slow so at least he's not expecting me to really dance, but rather sway. Even so, I can't stop my body from stiffening, the idea of people watching us making me slightly uncomfortable.

"People are looking at us," I whisper.

"Imagine they're not here. It's just you and me. They don't exist."

And soon enough, they don't. Just like the bandstand guy, they pack up, leaving me and Yahya alone in the park.

Yahya sways in time with the music, his movements considered and slow. He guides me in the little spot of the park that we've claimed, his eyes on me the entire time, the dimples in his cheeks charming me so I forget where I am. Soon I no longer mimic his steps, but rather take charge and lead us through the song.

"And I thought you hated dancing," he notes.

"Guess not anymore. How did you get into dancing?" I ask, to which he responds with a laugh. "What? Was that a stupid question?"

"No, not at all. It's just, ugh, it's genuinely not very exciting."

"Go on."

"Well, you know how my parents were away a lot?"

"Yeah."

"Well, when they were away in the summer, I used to go to sleepaway camp since my uncle tended to visit family abroad and my parents didn't want to offload me on them any more than they had to . . ." A flush creeps up his cheeks just as a raindrop slides down it. "Anyway, beyond all the educational stuff my parents signed me up for, like experiential learning and communication—whatever that meant—there was also dancing, which everybody had to sign up for as part of the sport requirement." His eyes flash at me with passion. His words are as fluid as his movements. "My parents don't realize it, but they're the ones who got me into dance. Purely by accident, of course, since they thought sport meant football or basketball, but even so. They're the reason I got into dance. And it was the perfect setting for it. At camp, it was like nobody cared. We were probably all not going to see each other again for another year so I could just fully get into it. I loved getting lost in the music while being able to push my body to the limit."

Yahya's retelling of how he got into dance makes me grin from ear to ear, despite its sad beginning. It was one thing to talk about his dancing when we were hiding behind our screens, but it feels more vulnerable to do it face to face, and being able to see how his features light up just at the mention of dancing makes me feel like I've got VIP access to an exclusive movie.

"What about you and reading?" he asks. "Did you always know you loved reading?"

"Definitely not. I wasn't a big reader when I was younger." I bark out a laugh.

"What?"

"I actually got into reading after spending too many afternoons at Fadiyah Auntie's. Ma and Baba would always drag me to her house, practically on a weekly basis, and it was so boring at her house. She had no TV—she was fundamentally opposed—and no kids I could socialize with, so all I'd do when I got there was try to entertain myself. Which, when you're eleven, is a hard task." I struggle to dance and speak at the same time but refuse to give up the lead. "But then, one fateful day, I stumbled upon the bookshelf in her office that was

just *stacked* with romance novels, and I picked one up."
I smile to myself, remembering how it felt as if I was
doing something illegal by picking up a book with a
man and a woman on its cover, their hair and faces wet
as they stared longingly into each other's eyes. "I sat
that afternoon in the dim lighting of Fadiyah Auntie's
office just reading, losing myself in the stories of these
fictional people.

"And I did the same thing the next week. And the
week after that. And the week after that, until eventually
I stopped doing it, as if it were a forbidden activity."

Yahya allows a small smile to spread across his face but
doesn't interrupt.

Despite the temperature and the increasing rainfall,
I feel all warm and fuzzy talking about it. Like I'm giving
him a part of me.

"I've always loved stories," I continue. "But there's
something about romance in particular. I love being
able to live a thousand different loves. I love that I get
to experience heartbreak from the safety of my bed, all
the while knowing that it's going to turn out OK. I love
sitting with the characters and being able to visualize them
without anybody else's input but mine and the author's."

"It's like dancing. It's a shared connection."

I nod. It's incredible to find somebody who just *gets* it.
"Exactly."

As Yahya continues to speak about dance, seamlessly
putting into words what I can't about my relationship
with reading, my heart increases in size. It's rare to

find someone who can not only perfectly describe their feelings, but also your own, making you feel like you're one and the same.

The clouds above thicken as the rain becomes increasingly heavier, but even so we don't let go to seek shelter. Instead, we keep moving, our feet gently swashing in shallow puddles as we make the park our stage.

"What song is this?" I ask as a new song begins, male and female voices coming together to harmonize, our steps slowing down as we inch closer to each other.

His eyes glint as he lets his head fall in my direction. We stay frozen in that moment, our gazes tethered together by an invisible string. "'This Is How You Fall in Love' by Jeremy Zucker and Chelsea Cutler."

That's the title of Sadie's documentary! Is this a sign?

"What are you thinking?" he asks quietly.

"I'm thinking that I want you to kiss me."

And you know what? He does, with no hesitation whatsoever. Like gravity itself demanded we drift together.

As the rain crashes down around us, he cups my cheeks with his hands, his thumbs resting just below my ears, the grooves of his palms scratching an itch I didn't know I had. His lips are tentative at first as they brush mine before they crush into me with a fire I didn't know he possessed. Cinnamon lingers on his tongue deliciously. Shivers run up and down my spine even though his hands remain where they are; the mere thought of them traveling across my body, underneath the thick coat, is enough to obliterate any brain cell I've got left.

We separate to come up for air, our eyes wild and our bodies soaked from head to toe.

"Again," I demand immediately, because Allah help me if this isn't what I've read about in the romance novels proudly displayed on my bookshelf.

"Again?" he teases.

I let out a slow and long, shuddering breath. "Again."

25

"What's, uhm, what's happening to your face right now?" Adnan gestures at my face as we walk along the train platform. "Does this have anything to do with the supposed friend you met? Also, why are you soaking wet? I thought you were going to a café?"

My expression changes from one of glee to a death stare. "I went for a walk." I'm careful not to reveal anything about Yahya because I know what Adnan will be like as soon as he finds out I've spent time alone with a boy other than him. In many ways, Adnan *is* like the brother I never had: protecting me from heartbreak by telling the guys I meet that he will crush them if they do anything to make me cry, which is sweet, I guess, but also infuriating.

Adnan ignores me, his fingers already typing away gross messages to Cami, and for a moment I can't help but feel a bit annoyed at him. Yes, I'm choosing not to talk about Yahya, but he could at least *try* to ask me about my day rather than immediately texting Cami. I mean, it's only been, like, ten minutes since they last saw each other! I guess I could open the channel, force him to engage with what's going on in my life, but what's the point? He's too occupied thinking and talking about Cami at every moment and it feels like since the kiss at the disco, that's just been exacerbated.

And I hate to admit it, because I was the one who set our boundaries in place, but I miss him. Our texts are few and far between, his replies slow or nonexistent. I can practically feel the strings that hold us together fraying, like at any moment they'll unravel altogether.

We've never had these kinds of issues before, and I guess we wouldn't have them in the first place if we didn't have to pretend to be a couple, because then this tension between Adnan having to choose between his girlfriend and his best friend wouldn't exist.

But I do know that for the first time since this whole ruse started, I finally feel like I have somebody in my corner. Not only because Yahya understands me in a way that extends beyond friendship, but also because his affection for me comes without any strings attached. Even with my parents and friends, I feel like I could never fully satisfy any of them unless I actually got together with Adnan like they've always wanted. But with Yahya, that Adnan-shaped cloud doesn't exist; my life is free to take whichever direction it wishes. And I didn't realize just how badly I needed that.

But beyond that, if we factor out Adnan completely, Yahya is just different from anybody I've ever met before.

It's not just that he understands me on an artistic level, or that he's understatedly funny; it's *everything* about him. It's how his mere presence calms me rather than putting me on edge. It's how he's attentive and listens to what I actually have to say, like when I mentioned in passing my favorite rom-com, only for him to watch it *and* be able to spot my favorite scene from a mile away. It's how he makes me forget about everybody else's needs for just one second and allows me to focus on what *I* need.

And I know Yahya and I might not work out, that we're not even in a relationship yet and I don't know if we ever will be, but even so, it feels nice to be more than a sidekick. I finally feel like the main character of my own story.

With Yahya, I don't have to pretend to be anybody else.

For the remainder of the journey back home, my lips tingle with the memory of the movie-perfect kiss in the park, and I think about how great it feels to live for myself for once.

"I'm home!" I kick off my shoes and deposit my jacket on the coat hanger. I run to the downstairs bathroom and grab a random towel on the radiator to dry my hair to the best of my ability before heading to the kitchen, where I throw my arms around Baba and smack his bald head with a loud kiss before taking a seat directly opposite him at the table.

Baba peers over his glasses. "What's wrong?"

"What do you mean, 'What's wrong'?"

"You never sit with us unless it's time for food. And, as I understand it, dinner isn't for another two hours." Baba glances at Ma, who confirms this.

"A daughter can't sit with her loving parents?"

OK, even I can admit I might have taken it too far with the "loving" bit.

"What did you do?" Ma comes up behind me. Her hands are on my shoulders, already anticipating that I will say something bad and then try to escape.

"Nothing! I promise." I shrug but Ma's grip is firm. "I just wanted to sit with you guys. I'm just . . . happy, I guess." I can't stop myself from smiling and doing a little wiggle in my seat.

"Our daughter's in love, Arman. You remember what it's like. Young love . . . ," Ma says with excitement, squeezing my shoulders a little too hard and causing me to yelp in pain. "It happens so quickly; you hardly notice it. One day, you're just in like with this person, getting to know who they are, and then the next you're in love with them."

That's it. That's exactly how it feels—except she's totally wrong about who the person is that I'm feeling like this about.

"When's that going to kick in with us then, huh?" Baba jokes. "Kidding, kidding!" he insists when Ma shoots him daggers with her eyes.

"You'd better be." Ma goes in for a wet kiss on his cheek, leaving her signature mauve lipstick on his stubble.

"Have you read your uncle's manuscript yet?" Baba

asks me as Ma goes back to the stove. "You know he needs some help."

"It's soooooo long." Rajib Chacchu's been working on translating a manuscript from Bangla to English for the past month or so, in order to sell the rights, but it's a first-hand account of the Liberation War and honestly it does little to enlighten me and more to depress me.

"Baba."

"And it's sooooooo sad."

"Baba," he repeats.

I pout and hope that if I widen my eyes enough he'll feel sorry for me like he did when I was a little girl and didn't want to sort the recycling.

"I can play that game, too, you know," he says. As if to prove his point, he mirrors my expression. "I think I might be better actually, considering you got my eyes and lips. You can never beat the original, you know. Now, go. Do at least a chapter or two. If you do, I'll fry some prawn crackers for you."

I groan but ultimately make my way to my room, my feet scraping against the carpet, making this horrible, slow *whoosh-whoosh* sound. I change into my pajamas before firing up my laptop and finding the manuscript just where I left it a week ago—still on page two.

I crack my neck left and then right and stretch my fingers out in front of me as if preparing for battle, a quiet LANY song playing in the background. I'm just about to start rewriting a sentence when the music subsides and is replaced by a quick pinging sound.

Messages: Cami

Huh. That's . . . random. Recently, anything she has to say to me goes through Adnan, and she barely said a word to me today. My gut instinct tells me to ignore the message, to wait until Adnan tells me in person whatever it is that she wants from me, but this other part of me, the part of me that is too curious for its own good, tells me to just click the message—get it over with.

That's the part that wins.

CAMI

Today 19:19

Cami

You need to stay away from my cousin.

Zara

?

Some context would be useful?

Especially since I'm pretty sure
I've never met your cousin?

Cami

Yahya. He's my cousin.

He was blabbering about you at dinner.

Saying you guys went out for coffee
and then some walk in the park?

He nearly blew my cover.

How dense are you?

Yahya and I have the same last name.

Our dads are brothers.

Wait. Hold up.
  Yahya is Cami's *cousin*?

As I reread Cami's messages over and over again, trying to make the pieces fit, my stomach finally drops.

His username, Velas, is short for Velasquez.

Cami

> He described you to a T.

> You're just lucky my dad was paying more attention to Adnan than to you.

> You need to stay away.

> You made a commitment to Adnan.

> Don't ruin it by getting involved with my family.

You'd think I'd revel in the fact that Yahya's been talking about me at family dinner. That he just had to let somebody know about our date and how good it was.

But no. Because all I can think about now is how Yahya is Cami's cousin. How this complicates things to a degree so exponential it's out of this world. How suddenly things with Yahya aren't easy anymore. How Yahya will probably find out, sooner or later, that I'm in a public—although fake—relationship with Adnan. Because . . .

Yahya

is

Cami's

cousin.

And oh, there's also the fact that I have spilled the beans on Cami's secret relationship to him without even realizing.

Cami

> And don't you dare tell him about me and Adnan.

> He's my dad's lapdog and will throw me under the bus with no regrets.

Zara

> ~~Well, it's a little too late for that . . .~~

> You don't know your cousin as well as you think.

> He wouldn't do that.

Cami

> Do you really think all those times you bumped into him were by chance?

What is she talking about? Are we even talking about the same Yahya?

No, Cami can't be implying what I think she is. That's just ridiculous.

The fact that Yahya and I kept meeting randomly was pure chance.

Wasn't it?

Zara

What are you implying?

Cami

You were just collateral damage.

A means to an end.

Zara

You're lying.

Look, I know you hate me and everything because Adnan and I are so close and you're convinced that I actually have feelings for him

(WHICH I DON'T)

But you don't have to go around making stuff up.

Cami

If you're so sure I'm lying, why don't you plan a date with him?

Adnan and I are planning to go to the movies in Swindon next weekend.

Why don't you ask Yahya to meet you somewhere else?

My body quivers with disbelief. Cami's lying. She has to be. She can't be implying that my meetings with Yahya have all been orchestrated. That Yahya's wanted to meet with me not because of me, but because he was actually keeping track of Cami. That I just happened to be, as Cami so delicately put it, collateral damage. She's still just mad about the stupid kiss with Adnan and is trying to get back at me.

But . . .

Whenever I've met him, it's been somewhere Cami's also been. Outside her house. At the disco. In Chippenham. And if what she says is true, that Yahya is her father's lapdog, what's to stop her parents from sending him to keep a close eye on her? Confirm that she is where she says she is?

I lock my phone and pace around my room, my hands fidgeting like there are ants crawling on them. It just doesn't make *any* sense. Yahya's not the kind of guy who would do this—he just wouldn't!

At the same time, how well do I really know him? Just because we've messaged and gone on one date doesn't mean I know him. Not as well as Cami does.

Why, though? *Why* would Yahya do that? What's in it for him? There must be an explanation for all of this. Maybe Cami's just got it twisted and Yahya's not actually been following her on his uncle's request. Maybe it was pure coincidence. You know, destiny and all that. Also, why hasn't Adnan told me about this supposed date in Swindon next week? He promised he would keep me in the loop whenever they made plans. But, again, he's left me in the dark.

I sit on the foot of my bed, cradling my head in my hands as I rock back and forth. This cannot be happening, it just can't!

There is one thing Cami's definitely right about, though. I can easily check if Yahya's been honest with me or not. I'll suggest another date like she said and if for some reason he proposes Swindon, then I'll know.

Yeah, I'll do that. It's the only way I'll get a definitive answer.

It'll be fine, I know it. Cami's letting her insecurities get to her. We all do outrageous things when we get jealous.

Right?

"Oh, Allah, if you're listening, please let this all be a giant coincidence."

SolusZ26

Hey!

VelasY74

Hey!

How are you?

SolusZ26

I'm fine, haha

Just been thinking lots, you know

VelasY74

Same . . .

I had a great time today

I couldn't stop talking about you at dinner

My cousin was side-eyeing me out

of jealousy

SolusZ26

Haha

Well I'm glad I've made it to dinner conversation

Listen, would you want to go out again?

VelasY74

Definitely

Saturday?

VelasY74
Sounds great
Want to go to Swindon?
We could go to the movies.

It's like my stomach goes into free fall.

No, not just my stomach: all my organs. It's like they shift around in my body, pushing against my rib cage, defying the laws of gravity.

Why did he have to say Swindon?

Why couldn't he say anywhere else?

It's probably just a coincidence.

I mean, Swindon isn't too far from here. Maybe it's a new hot spot for dates.

Whatever his reason, it's fine. I'll just suggest someplace else.

SolusZ26
Can we go somewhere else?
Not really feeling Swindon
I've had a pretty traumatic experience there

VelasY74

Bowling related?

SolusZ26

No, fortunately

Just had a terrible date there once

VelasY74

I see

What if I change that?

Overwrite that memory with a better one

I think I'm up to the challenge

SolusZ26

I'd just really rather not go there

Swindon is forever ruined for me

Why don't we go back to Chippenham?

I really liked that park

I might even give you another dance

OR

Let's go to the ice rink at Somerset House

You can show me your Hand Holder skills!

VelasY74

I'm just saying the movie theater in Swindon does
more flavors of the Tango Ice Blast than you
can imagine

Cami was right.

I was just a means to an end.

But the worst part? I can't even talk to anyone about it.

Not even my best friends.

26

All throughout Sunday, I feel like I'm drowning, with no amount of swimming getting me to the surface. No matter how many times I try to justify Yahya's actions or try to convince myself that it's all just a stupid coincidence, I'm hit with the reality of his messages. His insistence on going to Swindon despite my resistance is forever burned into my retinas.

I even miss Sunday dinner with my parents and Adnan's family, telling Ma I have horrible stomach cramps. I don't think I could get through dinner with everyone talking about how sweet Adnan and I are without breaking into tears.

I try to read, reaching for my books like the salvation they usually are, but everything reminds me of what a big fool I've been. Not only with Yahya but my entire life, to think that everything would work out.

Life is nothing like a rom-com and I'm the dork who thought it could be.

My phone keeps pinging with notifications, from whom

I don't know, but even with the ringer turned off, it's not enough. I turn it off entirely, refusing to look at the banners that have cropped up on my lock screen. I don't want to talk to anyone right now.

I toss and turn all night, and when I wake up on Monday morning, I feel no better. Cami's messages still ring in my head.

You were collateral damage.

A means to an end.

How could I have been so stupid to think I was anything else? I should have known that Yahya was too good to be true. I should have known that despite the picture-perfect kiss, my life would never be anything like a movie.

With my phone turned off, I'm not sure of the time. I power it on, feeling like I'm waiting for my doom as the screen goes from black to my lock screen featuring Adnan. It takes less than ten seconds for notifications to bombard my phone, but I don't pay any attention to them, especially the ones from Insta. I don't think I can take seeing everybody else's picture-perfect lives on my feed right now.

But as I clear the banners away, I see a text message from Sadie that makes the hairs on my arms stand up.

THE COOLEST PERSON YOU WILL EVER MEET (S♥)

Today 06:48

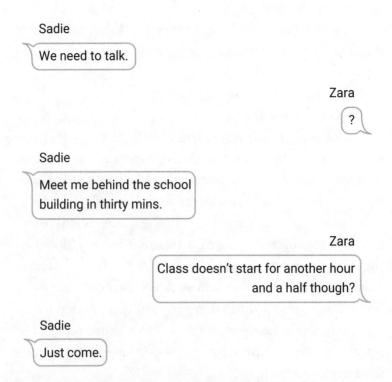

Sadie

We need to talk.

Zara

?

Sadie

Meet me behind the school
building in thirty mins.

Zara

Class doesn't start for another hour
and a half though?

Sadie

Just come.

To say I'm freaked out would be the understatement of the
year. I hurriedly get dressed, leaving a note on the counter
telling Ma and Baba not to make me breakfast, that I've
gone off to see Sadie for a coffee, before slipping into my
shoes and coat, and sprinting out of the door into the early-
morning darkness.

As I powerwalk to school, the wind howls lightly.
There's a light tapping of raindrops against my head, not

enough to soak it completely but just enough to cause some frizz as I arrive.

"Hey," Sadie says as I throw her a one-armed hug that she doesn't return. In fact, she practically dodges it.

"What's going on?"

"Have you been on Instagram since yesterday?" she asks, completely disregarding my question.

"No. I turned my phone off and this morning I had a bunch of notifications, but once I read your message about needing to talk, I was too anxious to do anything except get here and find out what was wrong." I go to unlock my phone, but Sadie puts a stop to that by covering my screen.

"Before you see it, I need you to be honest with me," she says with a gravity I can't ignore.

Everything feels like it shifts around me, reminding me of how I felt when I found out that Adnan had announced to the world that we were in a relationship. "OK?"

Sadie hesitates, swallowing a few times. "Have you been keeping things from me?"

I stiffen as a tingling sensation runs down my back. What does Sadie know?

"Because you can tell me if you have. I won't get mad. I'll be hurt, but—"

"Where is this coming from, Sadie?"

"I just need to know, Z. You've been acting a bit weird recently and if there's anything, *anything* at all, then you can tell me."

I bite down on my tongue. Surely, if she knew, she wouldn't have waited to see me at school? She would have just come straight to my house! Sadie is many things, but patient is not one of them. "I don't know what you're talking about."

"Right," she says, finally meeting my eye. "And you would never lie to me?"

I fiddle with my ring behind my back and silently beg for mercy. "Of course not."

Sadie shakes her head and reaches for her phone. "Then how do you explain this?"

On her screen is a ThermaeSecrets post. My stomach drops as I take it in: Yahya and me in the park, just as our lips locked, our hands tangled up in one another's hair, the passion of the moment captured so perfectly there's no way to talk myself out of the lie.

"When was this uploaded?" My voice breaks as I ask the question.

"Like, twelve hours ago," Sadie says.

Shit. Twelve hours is a long time. Long enough for pretty much everyone to have seen it! Oh God, what if Adnan's seen it?

And it's only then that I notice the post isn't just a single image, but a carousel. I swipe to the left and another photo appears. This one is of Adnan, who longingly looks at a girl with ash-blond hair. It's hard to see that it's Cami because she's not facing the camera, but there's no doubt in my mind that Sadie's figured out exactly who it is.

Fuck.

"Why?" Sadie finally asks.

I shake my head. "I can't explain it."

"Well, you're going to have to. Because people are going to want to know what the hell is going on. And to be frank, I'm in that category."

"God, can people just stop caring about my stupid relationship?" I burst out, unable to contain my anger with all the pounding in my head. Where is Adnan? I need to find him before class starts. "If everyone would just stop being so interfering, then none of this would have even happened. For God's sake, Sadie, you don't see me interfering in your life like you do mine!"

Sadie recoils. "What's that supposed to mean?"

"It means, while you're so busy butting into *my* business, you're too cowardly to delve into your own!" I'm conscious that other students are starting to arrive and are looking at us, but even so I can't stop. "I mean, how long are you just going to ignore the fact that Joe has actual feelings for you? Or that you have feelings for him? Because everyone else can see it, but you two are too scared to do anything about it!"

Sadie crosses her arms, her legs spread wide in immovable resolve. With a voice colder than the chill air, she says, "It's none of your business."

"Exactly, it's none of my business. And my relationship is none of *yours*." I let out a heavy breath and rush away before she can respond.

"Zara!" Sadie calls from behind me, but I ignore her, my heart beating too fast in my chest. I don't have time to argue with Sadie when Adnan could be intercepted by anyone at any moment who could tell him about the photo. If he hasn't seen it himself, that is. Which, admittedly, seems unlikely. We're not actually in a relationship, but this is not how I wanted him to find out about Yahya or how I wanted our so-called relationship to implode. I check my phone to track his location and find that he's already somewhere in the school. I scour the halls looking for him but find him nowhere. I call him in an attempt to pinpoint his exact location.

"I need to talk to you, now," I hiss down the phone, avoiding the stares around me. "Where are you?"

"Meet me outside the cafeteria," he says simply before hanging up.

I speed my way through the hallway, keeping my head down, my eyes firmly on the tiles beneath my feet. When I get to the cafeteria, Adnan is pacing.

"Where's Cami?" I ask, because if we're going to save this situation, we're going to need as much brainpower as possible.

"We broke up. The picture—"

Adnan shakes his head and it's only now that I really see him: for what must be the first time in his life, he looks a mess. His hair is disheveled, his tie is loosened, and his cuticles are inflamed from where he's been picking at them.

"It's over," he croaks out, his voice hoarse with devastation. Adnan shakes his head, all the while biting his lower lip. "She didn't want to risk it any further. The ruse is up anyways with the picture of you and that guy, so it would only be a matter of time before someone put the pieces together."

Is he trying to blame me right now? No, he couldn't be. He would never.

"I'm sorry that you guys broke up," I say, because I am. I would never have kissed Yahya if I knew it would lead to this. I feel too much loyalty toward Adnan for that. But when I signed up for this, I did not agree to having my intimate moment aired to the public. "But we need to strategize about how to move forward."

"What do you want me to do, Zara?" Adnan's body looks like it's wilting with pain.

"I want you to tell everyone the truth." I feel the pitch of my voice rise again even though I'm doing my best to keep myself calm.

"Why?"

"Why?" I repeat, startled by the fact that he's even asked the question. "Because I don't want people to think that I've done anything wrong!"

I refrain from adding the words *Especially now that everything's gone to shit and my life is crumbling right in front of my eyes. I was wrong about Yahya and his motives, but I was* not *wrong for kissing him in the first place.*

"What about Cami?"

"What about her? You said it yourself: the ruse is up; you guys are finished." I know I'm being unfair, but I'm so mad I can't think straight. Throughout this entire thing, I've been the sacrificial lamb, giving up everything just for him and Cami to have a shot at a happily ever after.

Adnan doesn't meet my gaze. Instead, he looks at the floor like it holds the answers to all his problems. But what is there to think about? His relationship with Cami is over and that's all that matters to him.

"Adnan?"

"Ki?" he answers in Bengali, something he only does when he feels at a loss for words. "Ki korbo?"

"Tell everybody the truth."

His face changes, his jaw transforming into a sharp, tight line so quickly that it makes my heart drum faster. He sucks in a deep breath as if trying to reason with himself and for a second I think he's going to place our friendship first.

But when he meets my eyes, I know it's a lost battle.

I stand tall, willing myself to be strong, and turn on my heel, marching my way out of school just as the first bell rings.

UNREAD

GROUP

Monday 16:49

CAMI has left "GROUP"

SHAH RUKH KHAN 2.0

Tuesday 09:35

Adnan

Can we talk, please?

I hate how we left it

UNREAD

SHAH RUKH KHAN 2.0

Tuesday 20:09

Adnan

Z, I need to explain

UNREAD

SHAH RUKH KHAN 2.0

Wednesday 19:36

Adnan

I told everyone the truth

Including Sadie

THE COOLEST PERSON YOU WILL EVER MEET (S♥)

Thursday 17:41

Sadie

Why didn't you just tell me from the start?

What, did you think I would judge you?

You know I wouldn't have.

But I'm not sure how we can recover from this.

I thought we never lied to one another.

I thought we were friends.

UNREAD

Friday at 16:17

VelasY74
Hey, is everything OK?
Haven't heard from you in a while
I miss talking to you

Friday at 17:03

VelasY74
Did I say something wrong?

SHAH RUKH KHAN 2.0

Friday 18:48

Adnan

I'm coming over.

27

The great thing about being the kind of kid who never lies about being sick at school is that when I do, my parents are supportive of it because they assume it's for an actual reason and not because I'm crying my eyes out over my best friend's betrayal/my own stupidity. It also helps that when I call Ma and Baba to tell them I'm going home, I sound like I have the worst cold in the world and have just thrown up. Which I do as soon as I get in, even though I've had nothing to eat all morning. And because school is the last place I want to be right now, I stay home all week, my phone out of charge and in the bottom of my bag, ruminating about the turn my life has taken.

On some level, when we began the ruse, I knew about the sacrifice I would have to make with all my relationships, but I never thought it would include the one I would develop with Yahya. In some twisted way, I thought this was the universe's way of giving me the rom-com moment I'd been waiting patiently for. That in return for the isolation and the inability to talk to my parents and friends about the toll all the lying was taking on me, I would be rewarded with a person who allowed me to be just myself. But no, apparently not. Instead, he was being anything but himself, only using me to get intel on his cousin.

Even worse, though, is how I can't talk to anybody about it. Especially Adnan, who is the reason we're in this situation in the first place. Even with the positive impact on my parents' relationship, if I'd known this was how things would turn out between me and him, I never would have gone through with it. Maybe then I wouldn't feel like I've lost my best friend. After all these years of friendship, I never thought we'd fall out over a relationship.

On Friday, after four days of wallowing in my own self-pity, I escape the confines of my bedroom and at least sit in the kitchen for a short period of time. But as I go to open the fridge, I see the family calendar where Ma has circled December 24 in a big, bright red circle for the dawat coming up.

Our dawat. Mine and Adnan's.

I rest my head against the cool refrigerator door, tears streaming down my face for so long that I hardly notice when Ma comes home from work at around five o'clock.

"Beta, what's wrong?"

There it is, my chance to let Ma in, my chance to expel all the secrets I've been holding onto. Everything inside me is pushing me to tell her, my stomach clenching as the words teeter on the tip of my tongue. But how can I? How can I explain to Ma the gravity of everything that's gone

301

down? Sadie hates me. Yahya used me to get in his uncle's good books. Adnan chose Cami over me. Again. And worst of all, I've been lying to my parents for weeks.

How could I tell her that after what she told me about Nanu? Could I really hurt Ma like that?

"Is it your stomach?" Ma asks, detangling my hair with her fingers.

I shake my head.

"Is it your head?"

Again, I shake my head.

Ma pauses before diving into what she's really been wanting to ask for the past few days. I could tell from each time she stopped by my room to check on me that she knew there was more to my staying at home than a stomach bug. "Is it your heart?"

I burst into another wave of sobs, unable to hide the reason for my pain any longer.

"Beta." Ma embraces me, steadying me as my entire body shakes. "Does it have anything to do with Adnan?"

I nod.

"His mother just called me. She said he's coming over."

"He is?" I ask, surprise making my knees go weak.

"If you want me to, I can tell him to go," she says, reading the panic I must be exhibiting.

"No," I rasp. "It's fine."

"You're sure?"

I'm not, but I'm going to have to see him sooner or later. "Yeah."

*

Half an hour later, Adnan appears on our doorstep and is swiftly ushered to my room.

"Did you get my texts?" he asks, not wasting a single second. He perches on the edge of my bed like nothing's changed and it makes my stomach turn with annoyance.

I open the window and let the breeze cool my face, my words subdued by the wind. "I haven't exactly been in the mood to talk to people."

"Well, I told everyone the truth."

"Yeah?" I turn around, my hands behind me as they rest on the windowsill.

Adnan's shoulders slump, his eyes cast down at the carpet. "I told them that we've been faking our relationship because I was in one I couldn't disclose."

"After everything, you still protected Cami."

"I had to."

"You had to?" I get off the windowsill, prompting Adnan to stand up. "We could have saved ourselves so much grief if she'd just been honest with her parents, or if she hadn't suggested we cover up your relationship with ours! Or how about if you hadn't gone and posted your relationship status on Instagram for the whole world to see without even consulting with me? God, how could you be so dense?"

Adnan pauses and swipes a hand down his face. "I wasn't thinking and that's my fault, but I swear it was with the best intentions."

"That's what murderers say."

"You're not really calling me a murderer, are you? Because, out of the two of us, I'm fairly certain *you're* the one who's the murderer 'cause you're killing me with those looks."

I let out an involuntary snort. "That was *awful*. And bad timing."

"Made you laugh." He grins but it doesn't reach his eyes the way it usually does.

"Momentary lapse of judgment," I respond as I pick at my fingernails; the skin around my thumb is stripped away to reveal tender tissue from anxiously picking at it all week.

Adnan clears his throat. "Like you not telling me you were seeing someone?"

"That was a conscious choice."

"Why didn't you tell me?" he asks, the hurt clear as day in his voice.

"I wanted to be with someone who wasn't subscribing to the Zara and Adnan hype. Someone who didn't know you."

"I get that. I guess that's why I was drawn to Cami so much," he admits with a swallow. "Her not knowing anything about the way people shipped us worked."

"Until it didn't," I remark.

"Yeah. We've really been through it, haven't we?" he asks, part serious and part joking.

The only way I can respond is by bursting into laughter that rocks my entire body. You couldn't write it; the whole thing is so ridiculous.

"Allah, I've missed your laugh, you know," Adnan says with a deep breath. I look up to see him looking down at me, the gap between us dangerously minuscule. When did that happen?

"I missed you, too."

Maybe it's the way he's looking at me. Maybe it's the way his breathing has slowed, no longer erratic but rather sedated and soothing. Or maybe it's something else entirely. Whatever it is, it doesn't matter. Nothing does, in this moment.

Except us.

His fingers cup my jaw, tilting my chin upward, and he looks into my eyes with his own coffee-colored ones. He looks at me for what feels like years, my heart beating in anticipation of what is yet to come. He bends down slowly, almost like he's asking for permission, before pressing his lips against mine as if they were the entrance to his home.

I comb my hands through his hair, not at all surprised at how soft it is, as he pulls me closer to him, reminding me of the moment we shared at the silent disco. After a week of being by myself, it feels incredible to be touched by somebody.

But as his hand comes to rest on my waist, something snaps within me. Suddenly, I step back and shake my head, on the border between rage and bewilderment.

"Why did you do that?" I ask, my words barely audible because of how breathless I am. "Why did you kiss me? We're not pretending anymore."

"Because I think I'm in love with you!" he cries.

"*What?*"

Adnan fidgets with his hands, his breathing quickening like he's stressed beyond belief. "After Cami and I broke up, I just wanted to speak to you, but you weren't replying and, I don't know, I missed you so much, and it got me thinking . . ." He lets out a deep sigh. "Maybe everyone was right all along. Maybe you and I are meant to be, Zara."

It's like everything stops as my brain processes his words, each letter entering my head as if typed incredibly slowly. Even sound stops: Ma clattering about in the kitchen, the soft rustling of the leaves outside—all gone.

"I mean, what are the odds that our lives would implode at the *exact* same time? It's like the universe did this to us. *For* us. Don't you think it's trying to tell us something?"

I face away from Adnan and instead look out of the window. How is this happening right now? How are we in this situation where we've just kissed and the idea of us being an *actual* thing is starting to make sense? I don't understand.

But I also do. When I add up all the little moments we've had together over the past few months, and how angry I've been at him this week, I can't help but finally understand. Involuntarily, my heart flutters in my chest.

Could it be that I love him, too? I've spent the majority of my life shutting everybody down when they've tried to insinuate that there's anything between us, but have I been wrong this entire time? Should I have listened to them from the get-go?

Is this my rom-com moment that I've just been too blind to see?

Adnan places his hand on my shoulder. "Say something, please."

Tears prickle at the back of my eyelids. I know that we make sense. On paper, we're perfect for one another. We love each other ferociously, but even so . . .

"What if it doesn't work between us?" I finally say as I begin tearing at my cuticle again, considering what a real breakup between us would look like. How it would also break up our families, create a divide between our friends. And with everything that's just gone down with Yahya, can I really open up my heart again? There's so much at stake.

"Shit." I flinch as I tear my cuticle, blood oozing out. But Adnan's quick to pull a bandage out of his back pocket.

"I always carry one in case I fall for you," he says, his trademark grin back in action. He lets his hands linger around mine even after he's tended to my injury, still waiting for me to say something more definitive. "We'll never know unless we try, Z."

He's right, I know he is. It can't be a coincidence that both of our relationships would disintegrate at the exact same time. And besides, how can you know if something is or isn't meant to be unless you give it a chance? It's what we should have done in the first place; maybe then this entire mess could have been avoided. I always thought being best friends would be enough for us. But what if it isn't? What if this is what we need to do? Not for everyone else, but for us?

"OK. Let's give this a go. For real this time."

28

On Saturday, I finally charge my phone and catch up on all that I've missed. The first notification that pops up is from Discord, a trail of unread messages from Yahya waiting for me. I hesitate to open them, not sure what there even is to say. Especially now that Adnan and I are giving it a real go. It's not exactly like I can say, "Hey, remember that guy on my lock screen? Yeah, not my friend. He's my boyfriend now. And oh, I know you weren't actually into me but were just making sure your cousin wasn't hooking up with somebody inappropriate."

Usually, I'd be asking Adnan for advice about everything boy related, but it feels like I can't ask him about this. And I don't feel like I can talk to Sadie either. Despite her messaging me that she knows the truth, I don't think she'll forgive me for what I did or what I said to her the day everything exploded. I even think she's taken me off her Close Friends on Instagram, because I haven't seen her post anything for days.

And Sadie *always* posts.

I clear all the other notifications, not wanting to bring myself down when I've only just gained some semblance of a normal life again. I watch TV, letting myself succumb to the darkness that is some new Netflix trash.

And then my phone vibrates. I'm afraid to look at it, scared another bomb is about to go off, but when I do, I see it's only Adnan texting.

Everybody misses you! his message reads, a photo of him and the gang hanging out on the steps of Cabot Circus. Even Sadie is in it, but she's not looking into the camera; instead, she's peering at her phone like it's a Magic 8 Ball. If she can't even pose for a picture, what are the chances she'll ever forgive me?

A second after I receive the photo, another message comes through. But not from Adnan.

From Yahya.

Can we talk?

I bite my lower lip, slapping the back of my phone against my palm in thought. It's not a question of *if* we can talk, but rather a question of *what* we would talk about. There's too much to say and not enough letters in the alphabet to express it all. I know I could ignore his message, delete him from Discord. Chances are I'll probably never run into him ever again. I could just forget about him entirely . . . But this pint-size part of me feels some loyalty to him even after the lies he told me. Some connection.

Like a tap that refuses to stop dripping, the nausea returns to me. I inhale deeply, but even that doesn't help. I know there's nothing to do but answer his messages. If I don't ask, I'll never know his motives, never know if what we had was all a lie or if there was ever an ounce of truth in it.

Today at 14:02

VelasY74
Can we talk?

SolusZ26
Hey.

VelasY74
Hey!
I was starting to get seriously worried!

SolusZ26
Been a little preoccupied.
Learned some things I'd rather unlearn.

VelasY74
Everything OK?

SolusZ26
Not really.

VelasY74
Anything I can do to help?

SolusZ26
~~Turn back time.~~

~~Tell me why you lied to me.~~
~~Tell my why you followed Cami around.~~
~~Tell me it's not what I think.~~
I know about Cami.

VelasY74
Sorry?

SolusZ26
I know you're Cami's cousin.
And I know you've been following her
because your uncle asked you to.

VelasY74
Following her?
That's not what I've been doing
Let me explain

SolusZ26
What's there to even explain?
Because it seems to me that you used me
to know more about Adnan.
You lied to me.

VelasY74
I never lied to you, Zara
Meeting you was pure chance

312

I could never have anticipated meeting you in
those fields

SolusZ26

But you could at the silent disco where Cami
had told her dad she was going.
And the park in Chippenham where Cami
was meant to be.
And let's not forget your insistence on meeting in
Swindon despite my reluctance to go there.
Because Cami conveniently had a date there.

VelasY74

You don't understand
That's not the entire picture
It doesn't mean my feelings for you aren't real

SolusZ26

I was a means to an end.

VelasY74

Don't say that
Can we meet up?
I want to explain in person

SolusZ26

I think we should stop talking altogether.

VelasY74
Zara
Please
None of my feelings have changed
I like you, Zara
I really like you

SolusZ26
~~I like you, too, Yahya.~~
~~I have a boyfriend.~~
Goodbye, Yahya.

VelasY74
Zara
Don't do this
Please

DISCORD DELETION

Disable Account   Delete Account

Are you sure you want to delete your account? This will immediately log you out of your account and you will not be able to log in again. Disabling your account means you can recover it at any time after taking this action.

YOUR ACCOUNT HAS BEEN DELETED

29

On Monday, Adnan picks me up before class and for some reason it feels like the first day of school all over again, especially with how clammy my hands feel just at the thought of walking through the main hall's double doors.

Leaves cling to my feet as we walk along the river to get into town; Adnan's hand rests at his side—he's not sure how to behave now that we're actually a couple. I thought it would be easy since we'd been pretending for so long, but if anything, it's made it more difficult. Before, when we needed to put on an act, it was easy just to hold each other's hands or slip an arm around the other's waist, but now that it's for real, it doesn't feel as intuitive.

"It'll be fine, promise." Adnan pauses before the entrance, hands now in his pockets, and I know he's waiting for me to do something. To solidify *us* somehow. I take a step toward him and plant a quick but delicate kiss on his lips—the surprise in his breath and the relief in his shoulders give him away. When I step back, he's quick to pull me back in—a hand lazing on my lower back like that's where it belongs—and kiss me again. His lips are warm against mine but still not entirely enough to make me forget what we're about to walk into.

I lace my fingers through his before letting him lead the way inside, dreading the day ahead of us.

Our morning passes without any trouble, just the odd whisper and glare here and there, but by the time lunch comes around, I'm not sure if I'm grateful or fearful to be speaking to my friends for the first time in a week.

"Do you want to grab our seats?" Adnan asks me as he eyes the snacks in the cafeteria like he doesn't already know what's on offer. "I'll grab you some chips, yeah?"

I tread to our usual table with heavy steps, reminding myself to physically put one foot in front of the other as the gang comes into view. The sight of Sadie makes my stomach roil with guilt.

"Glad to have you back, kiddo." Joe smiles at me and gestures to the seat opposite him, next to Sadie.

Ceri and Liam reiterate Joe's motion for me to sit. Sadie, to no surprise, does not. In fact, she doesn't say a word. It's only once Adnan comes to a halt at our table, balancing a tray while figuring out where to sit, that she even acknowledges our appearance by abruptly sliding to her right, leaving a gap for him to slip into.

"Thanks, Sades," he chirps, not noticing that it was more for her benefit than it was for his, as she's now further

319

away from me. Her obvious avoidance of me stings in a way I could never imagine.

"No problem," she replies, looking down at her miserable sandwich.

"So, are you sure you two are actually together now?" Liam fills the silence.

I stiffen, the comment stinging in an unexpected way. Adnan said he told the gang the truth—that he was dating Cami and used me as his cover—so I can see why the question is being asked. Even so, I feel like running out of here and straight into bed.

"Dude," Sadie says, her voice void of any emotion.

"What? I'm only joking," Liam guffaws.

"We're very much together, mate," Adnan responds, reassuring me by squeezing my hand under the table. After that, Ceri fills the silence with some long-winded story about her choir teacher, everyone momentarily glossing over the awkward tension at the table. I try to catch Sadie's eye, but she expertly dodges it.

After lunch, we split up, heading off to our different classes: English Lit for Sadie, me, and Adnan, while Joe, Liam, and Ceri jet off to Drama. Even though Adnan and I walk with Sadie to class, she doesn't acknowledge our existence by making any conversation. I knew she'd be mad, but I didn't realize she'd take it this far.

"I'm off to the bathroom—see you in class," she says, quickly shoving her way into the girls' restroom.

"Me too." I detach from Adnan's grasp and follow Sadie even though there's probably not any liquid left in my body, my sweat glands having secreted the water already during that awkward lunch. I tap my foot impatiently, waiting for Sadie to finish up, but she's taking forever.

"You don't actually have to pee, do you?" I ask after the last stall except Sadie's has emptied.

"Nope."

"So . . . are you coming out?"

"Are you leaving?"

"No."

"Then, no."

I register the time on my watch and figure out the magic words I know Sadie won't be able to ignore. "If you don't come out now, we're going to be late for class. And I know you're a punctual queen, Little Miss Being on Time Means Late."

She immediately steps out of the stall, bitterness curling her lips as she goes to wash her hands. "That was a low blow."

I shrug. "Desperate times."

"Seems you've had a few of those recently."

"I know." I let out a breath as I lean against the wall. "I'm sorry I didn't tell you."

"Pah! You think that's all I'm pissed about?" She rips sheet after sheet from the towel dispenser, aggressively wiping her hands but not drying anything because of how she's scrunched them up. "I showed you the picture and you didn't even explain! You just disappeared for a week. I'm your best friend, Z, and you just abandoned me like I was a day-old tuna sandwich."

"I know, I ju—"

"And when I texted you, you just ignored me. But worst of all? You made me feel like it was all my fault when all I've ever wanted is for *you* to be happy. I thought you would know that. I thought we were better friends than that, Z." She finally stops ripping paper from the towel dispenser and, rather than scrunching it up, she just lets it hang from her hands. "But it turns out I was wrong."

I want to keep apologizing, to explain, but I can see it won't go down well right now, so I decide to change the topic completely. "Thanks, for before. You know, with Liam."

"Whatever." She steps back in front of the mirror and brushes her hair away from her face. "You owe me a story," she says simply, with an unnervingly placid expression.

"OK." I stand up straight, seeing the olive branch she's extending. "Well, it started wi—"

She holds up her hand, pulling the plug on my sentence. "I should rephrase. You owe my *documentary* a story. I don't care what you have to say, but you owe the documentary the truth. Do you not realize how you lying to me completely ruined the integrity of the project?"

Sadie rolls her eyes, taking my silence as answer enough. Then she's on her way out, her hand pushing down on the door handle, and I realize I'm about to lose her again.

"When do you want to meet for the interview?" I ask. "I can do today, or if not today then to—"

"I'll decide when the interview is being held. And you'd better not lie to me this time," she says simply, as if my suggestions were merely white noise, and then she walks away, the door slamming with a loud thud behind her.

30

"Zara, will you grab the salad from the fridge?" Ma asks as she disappears to open the front door. "Top shelf in the big plastic bowl."

"Sure thing, Ma." I take out the salad bowl and when I hear Ma shout pleasantries to Somaiya Auntie, I grab a spoon and dig into the bowl of chopped cucumber, tomatoes, parsley, onions, and shredded carrots mixed with olive oil and black salt, no longer able to ignore my grumbling stomach. As I stuff my mouth, I play a soft tune in my mind, swaying from side to side.

"Are you . . . dancing?" Adnan grins as he catches me in the act, causing me to freeze with a wild look in my eyes. "I haven't seen you dance in years, Z."

"I wasn't dancing."

"Sure you were. I saw those moves," he teases, imitating me and making me feel embarrassed. "Since when did you start dancing again? When we were at the disco you were as stiff as a board and hardly moving."

Not wanting to delve into how Yahya was the one who got me to dance again, I simply say, "Just something I picked up on my week off."

"Well, I like it. It looks good on you. Dancing again, you know?" He puts his arms around me. "Also, you know Auntie is going to notice you've already started eating. The onion is practically radiating off your skin."

"You guys are half an hour late; can you really blame me?"

"Sorry about that. My fault, really." He reaches into his back pocket to produce a tiny velvet box. "I was rushing around trying to find a bow to tie around the box and Amma was busy doing her hair while Abbu was being unhelpful . . ." Adnan stops midsentence, catching sight of my curious expression. "Open it."

I set down the bowl on the table and run the spoon under the tap before tossing it in the dishwasher. As Adnan hands me the box, my heart speeds up. I delicately untie the golden bow and nearly drop to my knees at the sight of the dainty oval earrings.

"These . . ."

"Are my grandmother's, yes," he finishes for me.

I pick up the earrings, my fingers caressing the black onyx, fondly recollecting how his dadi used to wear them, right up until the day she passed. Disbelief at the gesture makes my stomach swirl like a tornado.

"They were the first gift my grandfather ever gave her, and before she . . ." Adnan chokes on the word "passed," his Adam's apple bobbing with remembrance. "She said

I should give them to somebody special. My parents and I agreed there was nobody better to carry her legacy than you. And, if we're going to be honest, Dadi always used to say they were for you anyways."

I'm rendered speechless, suffocated by the weight of what the earrings signify.

"I thought you could wear them to the party next weekend," he continues.

Right, the party. Our party. The one where we're formally announcing to friends and family that we're a couple.

"I know it's cheesy and everything but . . ." He's got his hands back in his pockets, his shoulders hunched as he waits for me to say something. For me to do anything except stand here like a statue.

"I didn't get you anything," I finally say.

"Oh, I didn't expect you to," he says casually.

But I should've gotten him something, shouldn't I? He's my *boyfriend* and it never even crossed my mind to get him anything. I should probably kiss him. But I'm not sure how, which sounds odd because I'm familiar with the physical mechanism of kissing, but even though it's been a while since that first kiss, we haven't kissed again. We've come close a few times, but it's always been interrupted by something. A blaring phone call. A sentence that just had to be said or it'd be lost forever.

And now, our parents cooing.

"I see Adnan couldn't wait to give you his dadi's earrings." Somaiya Auntie kisses me on the cheek as Ma takes the box of earrings out of my hands.

"Yes, thank you so much, Auntie. I know how much they mean to you and Uncle."

Auntie smiles softly. "Well, we would rather you wear them than have them wither away in my jewelry box."

"Allah knows she has too much anyways," Uncle comments, which elicits an elbow jab from Auntie. "What? You know it's true."

"Sumon, have you learned nothing after twenty years of marriage? Truths only come out *after* dinner, not before," Baba says with a hearty laugh, ignoring Ma's rolling eyes. "Come, let's sit. We don't want the food to go cold."

As usual, dinner flows on as if nothing has changed since that same dinner a few months ago when all of this was set in motion. The only evidence of a change being the pill Baba swallows with his water when nobody but me is watching.

And, of course, my and Adnan's relationship status, which, even now, never ceases to be the topic of the evening. You'd think that nothing else was going on in the world judging by how often our parents speak about it.

Honestly, I'm starting to see why so many celebrities keep their relationships on the down-low.

Our parents seem to have the exact opposite idea. As they debate whether or not we should get a photo booth like the Kardashians do at every gathering, a nervous lump settles in my throat, one that refuses to budge no matter how much water I drink. Underneath the table, I play with the box of earrings in my pocket just so my hands have something to do.

"Why can't we just have a small get-together?" I finally suggest when our parents reach a decibel far louder than necessary, worried our neighbors might call the police if the noise level doesn't reduce.

"A small get-together?" Ma tilts her head quizzically like she can't comprehend what I'm saying.

"I just don't see the point in making such a big fuss."

"Why not?"

I shrug, my throat drying up. Beside me, I notice Adnan's posture stiffening.

Ma's eyes flit between me and Adnan, trying to discern if there's trouble in paradise. "Zara, do you not want a party?"

What I want is for people to stop putting so much pressure on me.

What I want is to be in love.

And I'm not so sure I am. At least, not yet.

But I don't know how to tell them this without shattering all their hopes and dreams. Because it's about so much more than a party. Party or no party, Adnan and I would still be in a relationship—one I'm not feeling yet. And I know that we haven't really been together long enough, but surely I should be feeling something other than panic right now?

When Adnan pulled out that box of beautiful earrings, I didn't find myself tearing up with joy or love. I felt like I was being trapped. Trapped in a relationship—no, a *life*—I'm not so sure is for me. When I was with Yahya, I felt myself bursting with giddiness. I was excited to hear from him, constantly checking my phone for messages from him, looking for him wherever I went, and I itched to do mundane things with him like going for a walk because it felt new and invigorating in a way that everyday things usually don't. I found myself comfortable with being vulnerable, and not worrying about how that was going to make him feel and wanting him to feel the same way. And even now, when I no longer have the Discord app, when I know everything he's done, I find myself looking for messages from him.

I don't feel the way I should about Adnan, not like I did for Yahya, and I'm not sure why. My gut tells me that I *should* feel more for Adnan. I *should* feel like my wildest dreams have come true, that I am finally the main character in a romantic comedy. I *should* feel like the luckiest girl in the world.

So why is my heart telling me otherwise?

Across the table, I catch Ma's eye, wondering what she would say if she knew about the doubts assembling in my head. She'd probably say something like, "Relationships take work, beta. You can't expect it to be sunshine and rainbows all the time." And I know that. Not every relationship is plain sailing—just look at my parents. They've had their ups and downs, most recently a lot of downs, but now they seem to be in a better place.

Maybe if I believe it enough, if I give it more time and convince myself that Adnan and I truly are destined for one another, I'll fall for him the way he's fallen for me. I'll stop seeing him as just my best friend, but as my boyfriend.

We've gone through all this trouble for my parents so it's time we put in the work for us.

"Zara?" Ma prods.

"Sorry?" I shake my head, feeling the fog thickening rather than clearing.

"Do you not want a party?" she repeats, her eyes dimming by the second.

"No, I do. Of course I do." I swallow but still the lump persists. If anything, it's grown in size. "I just . . . can we make it smaller? Less flashy and more intimate?"

"So . . . eighty-nine guests instead of ninety?" Uncle teases, eliciting a slap on the shoulder from Auntie.

"Abbu," Adnan groans before turning to me, his eyes on mine with laser-like focus. "We don't have to have a party if you don't want to."

"Adnan!" the parents all burst out simultaneously, but it's as if he doesn't hear them because he continues talking to me as if we are the only two people in the room.

"If you don't want this, I'll understand, Z." He takes my hands in his, comforting me not only with his touch but with his words. "I'm here for you. Always will be."

My brain kicks like it wants to escape. Like it wants to travel downward all the way to my heart and challenge it to a duel, tell it that it needs to shut up and fight through the doubts, because how can I not see that I'm not the only one having to put in the work? Adnan is, too. He's making an effort to make us work and I need to, too. I can't sabotage our relationship just because I'm not where I want to be just yet with my feelings for him.

It's normal to have relationship anxiety, especially at the beginning, so what I need to do is push through.

For Adnan. For my parents.

But most of all, for myself. To prove that I haven't made a mistake. To prove that all the sacrifices haven't been for nothing.

I need to trust my brain. My heart's got me in enough trouble as it is.

"No, let's keep the party as it is." I squeeze his hand while our parents let out audible sighs of relief.

"You sure?" Adnan asks, worry still simmering in his eyes.

I nod. "I'm just overthinking it." I clear my throat and shake my head. "Actually, I think I might need some fresh air. It's probably all the spices from Ma's salad clogging up my thoughts."

"Hey!" Ma protests.

"Just kidding, Ma." I offer her a weak smile and take my half-eaten plate to the kitchen.

"You want me to come with you?" Adnan says, coming up behind me, his plate as clean as if it has just come out of the dishwasher.

I shake my head. "I'll be fine. I just want to listen to a chapter of my audiobook and do a loop around the neighborhood." I pause, not wanting to give away any hint of my inner turmoil. "It's just a lot with the parents. Especially when . . . it's all for real now, you know?"

He nods. "Totally. I didn't think it would feel any different, but it does."

"Yeah."

An uncomfortable silence washes over us and I wonder what he's thinking.

"Well, don't go too far, yeah?" He kisses me gently on the forehead, the comfort of his touch spreading across my skin.

How could I think for even a second that I don't love Adnan? Of course I love him. I do. I just need to work my way up into loving him as somebody more than a friend.

Movies and books tell us that real love can only be achieved at first sight. That you're able to fall deeply and wholeheartedly in love with somebody you don't even know. That you can have earth-shattering feelings for a total stranger. I thought I had that with Yahya, but it turned out not to be true. It's simply a fantasy the entertainment industry sells to us and we're the ones stupid enough to fall for it.

Real love, sustainable love, is something that builds.

I mean, isn't that why we sit on the edge of our seats rooting for the slow-burn romances? Isn't that why we wait with bated breath for the lead characters to finally seal their affection for one another with a simple kiss? Why we power through two hours of horrible dialogue, insensitive jokes, and a mediocre cast?

Slow-burn romances simmer over time.

But to create a fire, even the smallest one, requires heat.

"Actually, how about we go upstairs and watch something on Netflix?" I offer as he washes our dishes. "Let the parents be."

"Yeah?" He cocks his right eyebrow.

"Yeah. It'd be nice to have some"—I shut one eye with a cringe—"Zadnan time."

Adnan nearly drops the plate he's holding as he doubles over with laughter. "Oh, so we're going by that, are we?"

"I never agreed to Alphabet."

"Who said you could take the lead?"

I did. Because if I don't, I'm afraid of what will happen.

"That's besides the point," I tease.

"Oh, really?" He swivels around, putting his hands on my waist and sending a shiver up my spine. "What is the point?"

"The point is that I want to spend time. Alone. With you."

I plant my lips on his, slowly slipping my tongue inside his mouth, spelling out all my hopes. My hands roam around his back, his muscles tensing as my fingers trail down his spine. He pulls me into him as he leans against the counter, bearing the weight of my body on his. It's only when we hear the sound of chairs scraping against the hardwood floor in the other room that we finally pull apart.

"That . . . was something," Adnan says with a tantalizing chuckle.

That was fuel.

And if that doesn't ignite a fire, I don't know what will.

31

With the party tomorrow evening, my entire being crawls with dread. I don't typically mind the parties—you get used to them after a while—but usually I'd have Sadie talk me off the ledge or even attend with me and my family. But despite Sadie's vow to get an honest interview out of me, she still hasn't messaged me or even replied to my texts wanting to meet up and talk.

Because I do want to talk. I want to talk to her about everything that's happening with Adnan. I want to explain to her how I royally messed up by not telling her what was going on from the get-go. But most of all? I just want my best friend back.

I know I hurt her and that she made it clear she would be the one to reach out, but the longer she takes, the more worried I am that she won't.

I pull on my puffer jacket and slide into my Dr. Martens, the sharpness of the low December temperature hitting me as soon as I step outside, but to be honest I'll take it over the incessant party planning Ma and Baba have been doing all week.

As I wander in the direction of town, my fingers tingle with dread while my chest constricts with fear of the party. Of disappointing my parents. Of ruining my relationship with my best friend. Of losing myself.

I know that the party is just to celebrate our relationship, but I can't help feeling like it's something more than that. Like it's a ceremony that will tie Adnan and me together forever. And I don't want that.

Especially because, despite my best intentions, the fire I tried to light didn't start. I tried shifting my mindset to being ready to fall in love and I tried to open myself up to *his* love, but it didn't work. We even tried doing that intimacy exercise where you stare into your partner's eyes for four minutes before answering a series of questions that are meant to strengthen your bond.

But it didn't. No matter what I try, I can't make myself fall for Adnan.

But how could I ever turn around and tell my parents that? They've waited my entire life for this. Ever since I was little, this is all they've wanted for me. And then there's Adnan himself. He told me he loves me. My chest tightens at the thought of saying the words "We need to break up" to him. What if I do that and he walks away from our friendship, forever this time? I slide in my earbuds and click on a new rom-com. I try to focus on the story that's being told, allowing myself to be drawn into a different world, but the yearning I feel for a love like the one playing in my ears is overwhelming. I quickly tap out of the audiobook, unable to listen to somebody else's happily ever after right now.

I pass our neighbors' houses, their doors adorned with wreaths while their shrubs are lit up by Christmas lights. There's even one yard with an inflatable waving Santa Claus. I want to take a picture of it and send it to Sadie, and then I remember that she wouldn't answer even if I did. Somehow, even with this being the most joyous time of the year, the universe has filled me with everything *but* joy.

As I keep walking, I don't even realize where I'm heading until I get to the Royal Pavilion and the ice rink shimmers into view; the Bath on Ice event is in full swing. A giant Christmas tree, lit up with twinkling lights and festive decorations, stands right by the entrance. The usual Christmas pop songs play through the speakers as families skate together, shrieking as they try not to trip on the hard ice, while grandparents sit on the sidelines with their mulled wines and cinnamon doughnuts.

But what really steals my attention is a boy and girl holding hands while they skate. As the boy struggles with his balance, the girl guides him slowly across the ice with a strong grip and a beaming smile. She's his Hand Holder. The longer I watch them, the more my heart constricts with envy, especially when they pause to kiss in the middle of the rink. I'm about to leave the pavilion when I notice someone looking directly at me from the other side of the rink.

Yahya.

On the other side of the rink is Yahya.

We lock eyes for what feels like an eternity before he turns around, heading to the Ski Lodge where the refreshments are. It wouldn't surprise me if he were here with someone. Maybe even another girl. It's not like he cared about me anyway, clearly.

I hastily step away from the rink and find a seat on a bench near the entrance, so I can recover from the shock.

But a minute later, someone sits down beside me. When I turn, I'm surprised to see it's Yahya, holding a steaming paper cup of chai latte.

"Don't say I didn't keep my promise," he says, holding out the drink in my direction.

I don't know whether to accept the hot drink or not. I'm still mad at him and I don't want him to think otherwise, but at the same time I want to hold onto something to ground me, so I accept it. "Thanks."

The first sip of the chai latte burns my tongue, giving me something other than his eyes to focus on.

"Zara. I'm sorry. I really am. I didn't realize when—"

"What?" I interrupt, unable to hold myself back. "That when you were leading me on it just happened to be in close proximity to where your cousin was going to be—the same cousin you've been keeping an eye on like some narc?"

He lets out a heavy sigh and in that moment it looks like the last few weeks have been just as miserable for him. "I promise you, Zara, I didn't know who you were or that you knew Cami when we first met."

"Oh, right, as if I'm going to believe you," I say, fighting the urge to roll my eyes.

"It's true! I only put two and two together when we were at the silent disco when you mentioned your friends, but even then, I wasn't sure—"

"Then what? You just decided not to tell me and instead keep spying on her?"

"I wasn't spying on her, please believe me," he pleads. "When I realized your Cami was *my* Cami, I just . . . I wanted to make sure she was OK. She's like my baby sister. I had to make sure she wasn't off with a guy who was going to treat her badly again." Yahya shoves the hair back from his face in frustration. "Remember when we were talking about my parents? How they're never here?" He looks into his paper cup, unable to meet my gaze. "Well, Cami's family practically raised me. I owe them, Zara. They took me in when my own parents wouldn't. So, I would do just about anything for them. For her. And that includes making sure she's safe. Because I don't want her to go through what she did last year ever again."

Yahya falls silent. I don't know what Cami went through, and even though she isn't exactly my favorite person right now, I can't help but feel my heart break for her.

"What I'm trying to say," he continues with a shaky inhale, "is that I'm sorry I didn't tell you who I was, but I promise you, I wasn't spying on Cami, or using you to find out information."

Somewhere deep in my heart, the place that knows him best, I want to believe him. But I'm still so angry and confused, and I don't know if I can trust anyone, let alone myself.

More importantly, am I capable of opening my heart again to him? He may not have *intended* to hurt me, but he did nonetheless.

"You don't believe that I wasn't spying on Cami or the guy she was seeing, do you?" Yahya asks when I'm quiet for too long.

"Adnan," I say, feeling like I need to make his presence known in this conversation for some reason. "His name is Adnan."

"Right. Adnan." His face twists slightly as he says Adnan's name, as if it leaves a bitter taste in his mouth. He takes a sip of his drink before returning his gaze to me. "Cami told me what happened between them."

I swallow. "Then you know . . ."

He nods before I can finish my sentence. I wonder what Cami has told him about me.

"Then you also know that this conversation doesn't really change anything. I'm with him now."

Yahya doesn't even wait a beat before responding with "I don't think you love him, Zara."

His words are like a punch to the stomach. "And how would you know that?"

"Because when I kissed you, I could see that you'd been waiting for it to happen just as long as I had." The baritone of his voice sends shivers up my arms. "I could see it in the smile on your face after we broke apart. I could see it in the way you didn't want to let go of me at the train station. Zara, I could see it in *you*."

My breath gets caught in my throat just remembering the one and only kiss we shared. It was everything I wanted.

I try to brush it off. "How do you know that it's not the same with Adnan?"

"You don't need to lie to me, Zara. You never had to in the first place. Even when you were pretending to be his girlfriend, you didn't have to lie to me."

The paper cup shakes in my hands. "I'm not lying now. I'm with Adnan. For real this time."

He turns his body toward me, his eyes filled with torment. "Just answer me this and then I'll leave."

"What?"

"*Do* you love him?"

"Yahya . . ."

"Because I love you, Zara." The back of his hand grazes my cheek and I shudder. "I'm in love with you, SolusZ26. Have been ever since I first saw you, hunched under that tree waiting to raid that gym. I know that sounds clichéd and like a fuckboy thing to say, but it's true."

He sounds as if he means it, his words as comfortable as a freshly made bed. But after everything, can I trust him?

He inches closer to me, his forehead pressed against mine, the warmth of his breath beginning to thaw my heart. "I need to know, Zara, do you love him?"

The wind blows my hair across my face, and I use it as an opportunity to break away from him, to clear my head.

I want to believe that if I try hard enough, I can make myself fall in love with Adnan, just like everybody wants me to. That if I carve my heart out of my chest and stare into its four valves and command it to fall out of love with Yahya, everything will be OK in the end. That I can simply fix it all if I wish hard enough.

But I can't. That's not how it works. Not how love works. You can't force yourself to love somebody. And I know that now, because I've tried, again and again, to conjure up feelings for Adnan that simply do not exist, no matter how much I and everybody else wants them to.

And yet I still can't bring myself to admit it. Especially when I think of my parents making last-minute table decorations for the party to celebrate my relationship. I think of Adnan's family earrings in a box on my desk. I think of how our families' relationships would never be the same if I turned around now and broke up with him.

"Zara?" Yahya whispers my name.

"I can't do this." I shake my head and jump to my feet. "We can't talk to each other. We can't see each other. This is over."

And before he can persuade me otherwise, I run away, tossing the rest of the chai latte in the trash next to us, and leaving my heart at the feet of the only boy I've ever loved.

32

"Zara!" Ma shouts from downstairs. "Are you ready? Guests will be here soon!"

"I'll be down in a minute!" I yell back as I secure my hair in a messy bun with the help of a claw clip. With my hair parted down the middle, my bangs fall on either side of my face, framing my dark lips and highlighting my hazel irises. I hesitate to put on Adnan's earrings but ultimately decide it's the polite thing to do. I struggle to get them through the little lumps that have formed in my lobes from not wearing any for a while, but just like the past few weeks, I keep pushing, attempting to stick a key in a door it's not meant for.

"Zara!" Ma yells again just as the bell rings, as if she has a sixth sense for guests arriving.

Or, more likely, she's been peering out of the window, impatiently awaiting the arrival of all her friends. Ready to show me off to them as her golden daughter who has finally come to her senses and realized that the love of her life was standing in front of her all along.

"Coming!"

I take one last look in the mirror and attempt a smile, but it's not very convincing. I turn away and will myself out the door, hoping that everybody will be so swept up in their joy and "I told you so!"s that they'll forget all about me.

By the time I get myself down the stairs, holding onto the bottom of my lehenga as if I were a Disney princess, there is a queue at the front door. I don't know how many people I make awkward small talk with using my fake-friendly voice while they hang up their coats, but I must have been at it for the past twenty minutes because my feet are aching from the ginormous heels I'm wearing.

"Woman of the hour!" Auntie Zaria proclaims as she reaches the front of the queue. "You're all grown up. And look at that dress—stunning!"

Ma beams at Auntie's compliment. Earlier this morning, she was in a panic about which lehenga I should wear tonight. Ultimately, we settled on a simple yet elegant blue taffeta silk umbrella lehenga with embroidered mirror work all over, the matching oorna draped delicately across my shoulder.

"Nice to see you again, Auntie." We exchange European kisses on the cheek, careful not to smear each other's make-up. "I'm glad you could make it."

"Oh, I wouldn't miss it for the world!" Auntie's face lights up. "Your mother and I have been waiting for this moment since you were little, beta." She gently cups my chin. "It was written in the stars, I tell you."

I wonder what that says about the quality of the stars.

Once Ma has handed her a glass of sparkling water with blueberries, she disappears into the throng of people. Our living room is at max capacity and it's only twenty minutes past the time guests were originally due to arrive.

"He's here! He's here!" somebody shouts with fervor, breaking me out of my reverie.

I make my way through the hallway as the crowd parts like the Red Sea to come face to face with Adnan and his parents, my own standing behind me with a hand on each of my shoulder blades.

Adnan's navy-blue kurta matches my lehenga down to its embroidery. The mandarin collar elongates his neck and makes his shoulders look even broader than they already are. You'd think that the golden trousers he's paired with the kurta would look tacky, but if anything, they elevate the look into something classier. He looks amazing, but, like me, he seems tense. His posture is slightly hunched where it's usually tall with confidence. Perhaps he's just nervous about all the eyes on us and what this party means to our parents.

We step away from our parents, their hands dropping off our shoulders, and further toward each other. I swallow.

"Hi," he says.

"Hi." I look down at my feet, not sure if we should hug or kiss. I mean, Bengalis aren't exactly comfortable with public displays of affection.

Thankfully, he moves first and leans forward to give me a peck on my cheek. Then he whispers, "You look beautiful."

Despite the softness of his lips on my cheek and the warmth his words send through my body, I can't help but ache to see a boy in an oversize hoodie with an anime print on it in his place. I quickly excuse myself and run upstairs to my bedroom, and dramatically slither down my door as it slides shut. My entire body erupts with noiseless, convulsive sobs.

A minute later, two sets of feet pound up the stairs after me. Ma and Baba knock on the door, demanding to be let in. I push the handle down to let them in, before launching onto my bed and hiding my face in one of the giant throw pillows. On either side of me, I feel the bed depress with the weight of my parents.

They're quiet for what feels like forever, most likely silently exchanging parental glances while I do my best to calm down.

"Zara," Baba eventually coos, the deep bass of his voice quietly commanding. "Please, look at us."

I turn over but I don't look at them. I can't if I want to finally tell them the truth.

"What's wrong, Zara?"

I take a deep breath. "I can't do this anymore."

My parents' faces darken with alarm. "Can't do what? What's wrong?"

But the words are stuck in my throat like they always have been whenever I've tried to say them out loud.

"You're scaring us, baba."

I look at my parents, at the worry lining their faces . . . and the bubble in my throat finally bursts. "Adnan."

345

My parents exchange confused looks, and with their attention no longer on me, I plow on, afraid that if I don't get it all out now I never will.

"I don't want to be with Adnan anymore. No, I *can't* be with him anymore. I can't be in a relationship with him or I'm going to explode and all the pieces of me are going to—"

"Zara," Ma says, halting me midsentence. "Shash phelo." I do as Ma tells me and take another breath.

"Now," she continues, "what's going on with Adnan? Are you not getting along or are you having problems . . ."

"Is he not good in bed?" Baba unhelpfully finishes.

"Baba!" I groan, hiding behind my pillow again in embarrassment.

"Arman, chi!" Ma tuts before removing the pillow from my face, smudges of mascara coating the white silk. "But is your father right, beta? Are you and Adnan not having a good time in the be—"

"Please," I interrupt, "don't finish that sentence. I beg you." I sit up against the headboard of my bed, the congestion in my chest loosening. The world hasn't burst into a million pieces despite my confession about how I really feel. "I haven't been honest with you guys. About my and Adnan's relationship."

"What do you mean?"

"It hasn't exactly been . . . real. At least, not for as long as you think."

I fill Ma and Baba in on the details: how Adnan messed up by posting about his relationship on Instagram without asking Cami if that was OK; how he convinced me to go along with the ruse so he could date Cami and I could make my parents happy, all with the added bonus of getting people off our backs once and for all; how we realized that maybe there were some feelings there for each other and then finally decided to give it a real go.

"But now that we've tried, for real this time, I realize that it's not what I want at all. I love Adnan, I do—you know I do—I just . . . don't love him as more than a brother. As more than a best friend." The truth leaves a bitter taste on the roof of my mouth. "I want to love him as a partner, but I just . . . *can't*. I just can't. Which is ridiculous because we're meant to be a perfect match for each other. All the signs in the universe pushed us together and still I can't make it work. I can't make myself feel for him the way my head is telling me to."

When I finish, my parents are watching me in astonishment. I knew it: they're angry with me, disappointed. I should have just kept quiet and pretended like everything was OK. How could I be so selfish? Stupid, stupi—

"Beta." Ma places a gentle hand on my hand. "You don't *have* to love him as more than a friend."

Sorry, what? "I thought that's what you wanted."

Baba snorts. "If we got everything we wanted, I would be a millionaire right now."

"What we wanted"—Ma steers the conversation back, but not before glaring at Baba with her kajal-lined eyes— "was for you not to disregard Adnan as a romantic partner out of stubbornness. Falling in love would have just been

347

an added bonus considering he's like family already." Ma tucks a loose strand of hair behind my ear. "It wouldn't be fair to either of you if you didn't at least consider it."

I gape at them, unable to verbalize my surprise. All this time, I thought Ma and Baba were shipping me and Adnan just like everyone else, but it turns out they were just having my back, making sure I kissed every frog in case it turned out to be a prince.

"And now that you have, it's clear that sometimes friendship is better than fantasy," Baba adds.

I let their words sink in, wondering if maybe the fantasy of Adnan and Zara was just too good not to be drawn into.

"But, baba, why didn't you just tell us all of this? Why keep pretending?" Baba asks.

"Because I was scared. I was scared you would be disappointed. That I'd hurt Adnan. That the wound would open itself up again and I couldn't find another bandage to help you guys."

"Bandage? Wound?" Baba scratches his head. "What are you talking about?"

"Well. Uhm. I thought, since you guys were fighting, that I could distract you from your original argument with something that made you happy. I thought me getting into the relationship of the century would help you patch up your relationship."

"Oh, honey." Ma wipes tears from her eyes. But she doesn't seem sad . . . Are those tears of . . . laughter? I turn to Baba, who is unable to look at me, his hand obscuring his facial expression, but from the way his shoulders are shaking he seems to be having a similar reaction to Ma. "Maybe it's a good thing you're not going to be a doctor."

"OK, rude." I cross my arms over my chest.

"Bandages protect wounds from reinjury, but they do very little to speed up the healing process." Baba clears his throat and goes into full-on pharmacist mode. "Especially when it comes to small cuts or grazes. They would be useful if they were able to absorb more fluid from the wound or keep bacteria out, but unfortunately adhesive bandages aren't very good at those tasks. And actually, when it's time to tear them off, they might damage the fragile, newly formed skin."

"What your father means," Ma finishes, "is that our argument about your father's health wasn't your responsibility, Zara. It was ours and ours only."

"Yes, that is what I mean," Baba clarifies. "We certainly would never want to put the weight on your shoulders."

"We're sorry if we ever insinuated that the responsibility lay with you, Zara, but we certainly didn't need your lie"— I flinch at what Ma calls my solution to fixing their relationship—"to help us see that we were both in the wrong and hadn't been communicating properly." Ma cups my face in her hand. "Beta, people in good relationships, whether they be romantic or platonic, aren't just the ones who post fun selfies together or are at each other's sides twenty-four seven. They're the ones having uncomfortable conversations and helping each other overcome their problems. And your father and I?" Ma looks at Baba over my head with longing in her eyes, before meeting my gaze again. "We will never stop doing that. But that's because we chose each other. Because we truly do want to be with each other."

Baba gently takes hold of Ma's hand and kisses her palm, immediately making Ma's cheeks go rosy. My parents scoot in closer to me, despite the abundance of space on the bed, and I nestle in tighter between them.

"What if he hates me?" I ask after a while. The thought of telling Adnan that I'm not in love with him grates my stomach.

"He won't," Baba says simply and kisses the top of my head. "You two are best friends."

"But what if I tell him how I feel and all it does is drive a wedge between us?" I cry into his chest.

Baba says gently, "Just like your feelings for Adnan would have never become apparent unless you tried a relationship with him, you'll never know his response unless you tell him the truth."

33

"Hey, your parents called me up." Adnan gently shuts the door behind him, one hand resting on the knob as he debates whether he should stay by the door or sit next to me on the bed. "Are you OK? What's going on?"

I immediately burst into sobs again and he rushes over to the bed, wrapping one arm around my trembling body.

"Hey, hey, Z, it's going to be OK. I promise." He squeezes me more tightly, his hand stroking my arm as he speaks. "Whatever it is, we'll get through it. Together."

I'm unable to stop myself from violently shaking my head. I untangle myself from his grasp and stand by my desk, my hands clutching the back of the swivel chair for support. "I don't think we will."

Surprise crosses Adnan's face. "What do you mean?"

"I don't know how to say this but . . ." I stare at the ceiling as if Allah himself will be looking down at me with cue cards. "We need to break up," I blurt out, no longer able to keep the words in, for fear of never saying them at all. In an instant, the noise from the party downstairs—the incessant thumping of Bollywood music and the cackling of aunties who have had one too many appetizers—mutes itself. "I'm not feeling it the way I should. Not the way—" I stop myself from uttering Yahya's name out loud, not wanting to give Adnan more bad news. "I just mean, I'm not sure what we have is romantic, is all. I love you, Adnan, I always have, but we're just not meant to be. Not like this."

Adnan's gaze is focused on his feet, and I think for a moment that this is it. That I've lost him entirely. That I've stunned him into a silence we can never reel back from.

"I'm sorry," I tell him. "I didn't want to do this, trust me. I ju—"

He clears his throat and stares ahead at my untidy desk with its scattered notebooks and half-eaten bowl of chanachur.

It feels like an eternity before he says anything. Finally, looking up at me, his eyes slightly glassy, he whispers, "Thank you."

"Why are you thanking me?" I ask, feeling like I'm missing something.

"Because you just did what I've been too afraid to do. I can't do this either. Everything you just said, Zara, I've been feeling the same."

"Really?" I say, astonished and relieved at the same time, feeling the knots in my shoulders loosen after what feels like months.

"Yeah," he says, and I feel my eyes well up again—this time with gratitude. "Breakups are hard as it is, but losing your best friend at the same time? That's painful, man. I didn't want to risk it."

"But I thought . . . You just seemed to be actually into me. Why else would you give me the earrings?"

Adnan's shoulders slump forward. "I think, like you, I was trying to convince myself of feelings that weren't there. I was hoping that by giving you Dadi's earrings, I could, I don't know, fast-track my feelings for you or trick myself into realizing that I was in a serious relationship with you." Adnan shakes his head before looking down at his feet. "Actually, remember when you were asking about the party and whether or not we should have it?"

"Yeah."

"I was praying that you would call it quits then and there because I didn't have the courage to do it myself. I thought that maybe, I wasn't the only one not feeling it. But then you didn't and . . ."

"You kept pretending. Just like me."

Adnan looks at me with a sad smile and nods. I don't know what to say to him, so I simply throw my arms around him instead. He reciprocates the motion by hugging me tightly.

"Did you ever think we'd end up in a situation like this?" Adnan asks, his words muffled by my hair.

"Absolutely not." I pull away from him and wipe away the tears that have snaked their way down my face. "I've been trying to grapple with how we got here, but for the life of me I can't figure it out. I don't understand why we can't fit together the way everyone's always said we would."

"The reality is that we *don't* fit together. Not like that. Not as a couple, anyway." Adnan leans back on the bed with his hands holding him up. "If you think about it, we probably rushed to assume that with everything happening around us, we were meant to be. I mean, we were both going through breakups in one way or another. It's likely we projected our heartbreak onto each other."

I nod in agreement as the pieces I've been looking for fall into place like a jigsaw puzzle. "You're right. I think any romantic feelings I might have thought I had for you were warped by the loneliness I felt from everything with Yahya. And with how distant you'd been because of Cami, I guess I just wanted my best friend back in whatever form that was."

"You're telling me it wasn't because I'm such an amazing kisser?" he teases.

I shoot him a side-eye I hope will haunt him for the rest of his life. "*Objectively*, yes, I can agree that you are an *adequate* kisser and, *objectively*, I may have thought so at the disco since it'd been forever since anybody kissed me and, again *objectively*, when you kissed me at my house after everything went to shit, in a moment of weakness it may have swayed me to accept my best friend in the shape of a boyfriend."

"I'll take that victory," Adnan declares proudly, ignoring my glare. "Also, it was probably easy in that moment to think that the reason it didn't work between me and Cami and you and Yahya wasn't because of us, but because of them. Like, we couldn't possibly work with anybody else since we were destined for each other."

"I can see that. It's like we saw ourselves as each other's crutches. That the only way we'd ever find our true love was to finally realize what was in front of us all along. Not that it's true, but still."

"On top of that," he continues, "the pressure from just about everybody around us didn't help either. It was a formula for disaster, really."

"Hindsight truly is twenty-twenty." I rest my head on his shoulder.

"I've just got one question . . ."

I sit up, feeling like the other shoe is finally about to drop. I knew it was going too well.

"Did you really have to wait until the party?" he asks, and despite myself, I laugh, relief coursing through me, and punch him in the shoulder for scaring the shit out of me. "Ow, what's that for?"

"That's for making me do it instead and then complaining about the timing of it." I go to tuck a strand of my hair back, when I'm reminded of the weight hanging from my ears. "Oh, I should probably give these back to you."

I'm just about to hand the earrings back when Adnan stops me.

"Just because we're breaking up doesn't mean you can't keep the earrings."

I look down at the silver in my hand. "But your grandmother said to give them to somebody special."

"And you are special to me. Always will be," he says. "We're like the alphabet, yeah? It begins and ends with us."

"I read on BuzzFeed that actually the Swedish alphabet has three extra letters. So, technically, in Sweden we're not."

"Oh. In that case, hand them back."

I snort with laughter before putting the earrings back where they belong—in my ears. They already feel lighter.

"So, now that we're broken up, does that mean I can third-wheel your dates and tell any of your future boyfriends that I was your boyfriend first?" Adnan's face has split into a shit-eating grin. "I can weed out anyone who doesn't deserve you straight off the bat. Also, it would be hilarious."

"You can't do that!" I playfully swat his thigh as laughter rumbles through me.

"I'm only teasing, I wouldn't do that." He tries to adopt a serious face but fails miserably. "Until the third date, that is."

"You're horrible. You're not allowed to come along to *any* of my future dates."

"That's probably for the best," Adnan says with a laugh. "But can I at least meet your dates? I'd like to know what my best friend is up to."

"I think that can be allowed." I bite my lip before looking away from Adnan. "I think we need to think about our friendship, too, and what it's going to look like when we have partners. Like, even though I suggested we don't hang out as much, because of Cami and her feelings, I wasn't thrilled about it. But if we can talk through stuff like that, I'm sure we could work something out. I wouldn't want to lose you like that ever again."

"And I never want to lose you." I look back at Adnan to see the truth of his words reflected in his eyes. "But I guess we've just got to remember that we may not always be each other's number one all the time. Sometimes you can't always put mates before dates." He grins. "As we know all too well, sometimes your date is your mate, too."

I smile. "I think we just need to be upfront with each other. If we stew about things in silence . . ." I shake my head. "Nobody is going to be happy if we can't openly talk through what we're thinking."

"For sure, for sure." Adnan nods his head in thought. "We've got decisions to make about how we're going to move forward, but before that we need actual partners. Which, speaking of, what's the deal with lover boy?"

"I break up with you and you're already trying to pawn me off to somebody else?"

He rolls his eyes. "You're stuck with me forever, but I've got to make sure someone's taking care of you when I'm not around."

I sigh. "I'm not sure what the deal is, to be honest. I'm still confused about a lot when it comes to him."

"Why?"

My eyes feel like they're about to brim over again. "I'm not sure if his feelings for me were ever real or not. He says they were, but I don't know who to trust . . ." I take a shuddering breath. "Did Cami ever say anything about him to you?"

Adnan nods. "She mentioned him in passing. Just

that he's a great guy and she could always go to him for anything. She said he was protective of her."

That's the problem. In protecting her, he used me. Not that I say that. I don't think I can handle spilling my heart more than I've already done tonight. Maybe when this isn't feeling so raw, I'll tell Adnan about everything that went down with Yahya. For now, I switch the subject. "What about you? Are you going to try and win Cami back?"

Adnan shakes his head, the pain in his face evident as he clenches his jaw. "I miss her, far more than I ever thought I could," he finally says, blowing out a deep breath as his eyes become glassy. "But there's still the situation with her dad. And the fact that I did end up getting together with you after I told her there was absolutely nothing between us."

"Yeah, there's that." I feel awful thinking about how I made Cami's worst suspicions come true, but if there's anything I've learned throughout all of this, it's that talking is the only way to resolve anything. And that fake dating resolves absolutely none of your problems even if in theory it sounds like the best idea ever. "You've got some groveling to do, that's for sure."

"And I'm prepared to do it. Trust me."

And I do.

"Can you tell me a terrible pick-up line?" I ask to shift the mood.

"Anything for my bae of Bengal."

"I've said it before and I'll say it again," I tell Adnan after he makes me reconsider our friendship with his latest pick-up line. "I really can't stand you."

"I thought it was a pretty good one."

"No, definitely needs some workshopping."

"OK, well, what about this one . . ."

34

I warm my hands on the ceramic mug that rests on the table in front of me. I check my watch again, but the digits have yet to change since the last time I checked. Just as I'm about to give up, she appears.

"Sorry, sorry, we got stuck in traffic," Cami says as she barges in through the doors to Costa. She unwraps herself from her coat and scarf before taking her seat across from me.

When Cami messaged me on Christmas Eve, after Adnan and I had gone back down to the party, playing along for one final night despite our parents saying we didn't have to any longer, I nearly choked on the dal I was slurping. At the same time, I was happy she'd messaged me in the first place. Considering the deep, meaningful chats I'd had with both my parents and Adnan at the party, and before that with Yahya at the ice rink, it only felt right that I should have one with Cami as well.

"So," Cami says, breaking the silence. "I'm just going to come out and say it because there is no easy way to say this and I don't want there to be anything bad between us, so I'm really sorry."

I blink slowly, wondering if she spoke really fast or if my ears have somehow reduced their speed of processing by half. "I'm sorry, what?"

"I'm sorry, Zara. For . . . everything."

Huh. Out of all the things I expected Cami to say today, that was not one of them.

"I—or rather, we—shouldn't have dragged you into our mess. It wasn't fair of us to ask you to give up your life just to pretend to be Adnan's fake girlfriend. It also wasn't fair that I got jealous of you, after pushing you into the plan in the first place, or how I treated you after the silent disco. It wasn't cool of me to be annoyed."

I nod slowly. "Well, I'm sorry, too. For, you know, kissing Adnan and holding his hand and all, while you guys were together. I know we were doing it for show, but it wasn't cool of me to do it in front of you. I could just see it all imploding in front of my eyes and things were going down with my parents that made me desperate to keep up the act." The words are a jumbled mess as they exit my mouth. "And then, you know, actually getting together with Adnan. I'm sorry about that, too. I don't really know what we were thinking, doing that. Or, well, I do." I pause, trying to gather my thoughts. "We were lonely. And hurt. Adnan was missing you after your breakup and I was missing Yahya, but also I was missing Sadie, and with all that in the blender, we kind of just . . . fell into it. We're not together anymore, by the way."

"Oh, OK," she says, surprise in her voice, which surprises me. I would have thought he'd get in touch with her as soon as we left my room. Maybe he's just afraid to mess it up again. I'm tempted to put in a good word for him, when I remind myself that I really shouldn't. My days of meddling in other people's relationships are over. "Well, thank you for your apology. I appreciate it."

I take a sip of my coffee, the liquid scalding my tongue like a set of fireworks, which is appropriate considering New Year's is only a handful of days away.

"Well, this is awkward," Cami notes.

I chuckle. "Yeah, it is. Who knew fake dating would end with nobody staying in their couple, eh?"

"The films and books never show that part, do they?" Cami shakes her head. "It would have all been so much easier if my dad wasn't so protective, you know. If he just trusted me, none of this would have happened."

I bite my lip, not sure if I should ask what's on my mind, but I decide to do it anyway. "What's up with that? Why is he such a tiger dad?"

Cami inhales deeply. "I don't know how much you know . . ."

"Not much," I say.

"Yahya didn't tell you?"

"Nope."

"And Adnan?"

"He kept your secret."

"Huh."

"They both really love you and agreed it wasn't their story to tell."

Cami allows a gentle smile to rest on her lips as she settles into her seat, a faraway look in her eyes.

"I was seeing someone last year. Somebody older. *A lot* older." She swallows and I can see from how her back stiffens that this isn't something she likes to talk about. "I met him at a family wedding. He was the photographer, and he was really sweet. But I knew because of the age difference between us that my parents would never allow it, so I didn't tell them when we started seeing each other afterwards . . ." A tear snakes its way down her cheek as her breath catches in her throat.

"You don't have to tell me if you don't want to."

"No, I do." She wipes away the tear with the sleeve of her sweater. "I want you to understand why everything happened the way it did."

I nod but keep a watchful eye on her demeanor, hoping I can pull her back from the edge if need be.

"I saw him in secret for a few months. Back then, my parents weren't too protective about where I was going or who I was seeing because I'd always been such a good kid. It also helped that Yahya was around keeping them occupied." She laughs but there's something nestled underneath it. Regret. Guilt. "I thought this guy loved me, I really did. But then things started moving too fast."

My body fills with lead as I await her next couple of sentences.

"I was feeling all this pressure and so I asked Yahya for advice. And . . . let's just say that he wasn't the happiest."

"What happened?" I ask, although I could probably take a good guess.

She jiggles her foot, the thud of her boot against the floor a rhythmic soundtrack. "I made him promise not to tell my parents, but that's exactly what he did. My dad went mad. He found the guy and threatened him never to come near me again and then kept me under house arrest. My parents made us all move away and they enrolled me at your school for a new start. Until recently, I hated them for it—I thought they were ruining my life. But now I can see why they did it. Why Yahya did it."

"Wow, that's . . ." I'm at a loss for words. Not only because of what she's been through or what Yahya did, but because it finally explains why Adnan's been so protective of Cami. I thought he was being over the top keeping his relationship with Cami a secret, that he was prioritizing her feelings over mine, but now I understand that he was just looking out for her like the amazing person he is.

"Yeah. So, you can see why my dad is the way he is and why he's so overprotective."

"But would he have been that upset about Adnan? I mean, Adnan is your age."

"My dad didn't trust me. Still doesn't. So, it doesn't matter that Adnan is my age; all my dad sees is somebody who can hurt me."

God, that sucks. But I can also kind of see why her dad

would do it. It's his daughter; of course he'd do anything he could to protect her.

"Is that why you and Yahya aren't close anymore?"

She nods. "I was so angry with him when he told my dad." Cami throws a sheepish glance my way. "And speaking of Yahya, I need you to know that what I said about him, about him spying—it wasn't true."

"What do you mean?" I ask.

"When I told you about his spying, that's what I thought he was doing." Cami doesn't meet my eye as she speaks. "It was kind of a knee-jerk reaction, I guess, after he mentioned you at dinner. It just seemed like he was trying to provoke me, and it made me panic. It was easier to take it out on you, considering I was already mad at you, than actually talk to Yahya about it."

I slump down further into my seat as the realization hits me. So Yahya wasn't lying?

On some level, I knew that he was telling the truth at the ice rink. But my fear of being hurt all over again meant I completely shut him down while he was explaining himself, too focused on what I thought to be true to listen to him.

"But I spoke to him yesterday and it turns out I was totally wrong. It's why I'm here, actually. I thought maybe I could help clear some things up." Cami lets out a long breath. "He's really upset about how everything turned out, but he's not sure if you'll ever believe him that it genuinely was a coincidence that he bumped into you in the fields and then again at the disco."

I shake my head. "What about Swindon? He refused to budge."

"He knew I'd be going so he thought he could watch out for me, but he mainly just wanted to spend time with you."

"Two birds, one stone," I mumble.

"Something like that, I guess. But he did also say their Tango Ice Blasts really are the best and that there are some wicked parks for raids, or something?" She raises her hands in an I-don't-know motion.

I can't help a small smile. It's sweet in such a dorky way. Kind of like going along with a relationship you don't want to be in for the sake of your friendship.

"More than that, though, I need you to know, Zara, that he really does like you. I've never seen him like this before. I'm just sorry I got in the way."

As much as I appreciate Cami's apology and her coming all the way out to Bath to deliver it, I'm not sure what to do with it. It's done now. I've already walked away from Yahya.

"Well, I don't think he'll take me back now," I scoff, causing Cami to wince. "I wasn't exactly the nicest person to him the last time we spoke."

"I think he'd understand if you just talked to him."

"Yeah, maybe."

Cami cracks a smile that lets through the warmth I saw in her on that first day right here in this café when all of this kicked off. Since then, I'd thought Cami had grown cold toward me because of some irrational jealousy she harbored, but now I realize it's not that at all. She's

366

had a tough year with everything she went through with her parents and Yahya, and my and Adnan's behavior did nothing but make it more difficult for her.

And because I'm the reason Cami no longer sits with us at lunch, and because I know just how hard it is not to have anybody else to talk to, I abandon my rule of not meddling in people's relationships anymore for one final act. "You should talk to him, you know. Adnan."

"I don't know what to say to him. Especially since he moved on so quickly with you."

"But he didn't do it because he liked me. He did it because he missed you," I remind her. "I think it would be different for you guys this time, now that we've ironed out some of the kinks."

"Yeah. Maybe you're right. Maybe a twosome is easier than a threesome." Cami grins at me and I grin back. "I need to talk to my dad first, though. Nothing will ever work until we sort out our trust issues."

As we're leaving and I'm about to head one way and Cami the other, I ask, "Can we still be friends? It feels like a shame to do all this deep bonding only never to speak again."

Cami laughs loudly. "Yeah, I'd like that."

Sadie

My house.

In an hour.

And no more lies.

35

"You're late," Sadie says as I step into her room.

I practically sprinted as if I were in an Olympic race as I made my way from Costa all the way to Sadie's house, which is on the other side of town, for the final stop of my apology tour. When I got the text from her, I couldn't believe it. It'd been so long since we'd spoken that I thought she'd given up on me entirely.

"I know. I'm sorry but I was in town an—"

"I don't need any excuses. Sit."

I do as she says and take a seat in the chair next to her desk. As she sets up her phone on a tripod, I'm reminded that Sadie's not summoned me to talk; it's for the documentary. I thought when she texted me that she'd finally cooled down enough to hear my side of the story, but I guess not. But as saddened as I am that she only reached out for the documentary, I know this is what I need to do for her. Hopefully, it will be the first step toward repairing our friendship.

Sadie sets up the desk behind me, moving things about wordlessly. Even though we've aired all the lies, I can't help but feel even more on edge now than I did before. It's further exacerbated when she turns on the floor lamp that hovers just above me, illuminating me in the same manner as when a suspect is being questioned, and I don't know if it's even possible but it's like she's somehow made the clock on her wall tick more loudly than usual.

I try to shake off the tension by focusing on the items around her room, my eyes lingering on her shelf of romantic comedies she's bought and shared with me over the years. With each and every one of the films, I'm able to remind myself of what point in time we watched them and what was going on in our lives. But most of all, I remember how, no matter what, we always returned to them. We'd always find our way back to the stories and characters we loved.

Together.

"Are you just going to sit there or are you actually going to respond to my question?" Sadie glares at me from the chair she's sat down in.

"Sorry, what was the question?"

She rolls her eyes. "I asked you when it started. Your 'relationship' with Adnan."

"Oh." I sit up taller in my seat and cross my legs, elbows on the armrests of my chair as I look directly into the camera. "Well, it was pretty much straight after my parents had that big fight. You know, Baba suddenly announcing to Ma about his diabetes and her flipping out . . . Actually, can we scratch that? I'm not really sure we should include that in the doc."

"I don't think you're really at liberty to decide what I do or don't include at this point."

Her response stings. I know that she's still pissed at me about all that's happened, but I was hoping she'd have enough decency not to bring my family into it. "Sadie, please. Don't do this to me. You know what people will be like if they think I did this out of pressure from my family. It'll only feed the narrative that all brown families are controlling."

Sadie bounces her knees a couple of times in response. After a moment of tense silence, she asks, "Are you going to continue your story or not?"

I ignore her hostile tone and go on. "So, we decided to fake date because he was with somebody at the time who couldn't disclose their relationship."

"So you concocted this whole plan—"

"I wouldn't call it a plan . . ."

"—and then manipulated your way into making everybody think you were with Adnan when you weren't?"

"I didn't manipulate anybody."

"No?" Sadie hits a button on her phone, emitting a noise that indicates the recording has stopped, and leans forward, her star-sign necklace glinting in the light. "Then what would you call what you did by participating in a *fake* relationship? Did you just think that it would be funny tricking everyone you love into rooting for a couple that didn't exist? Did you not think that was a bit, I don't know,

371

calculating? Considering that at the end you actually *did* get together with Adnan and break up his *actual* relationship with Cami?"

I gawk at the accusation.

"Did you not think that was a bit mean?" she continues, taking my silence as an incentive to carry on. "You didn't hurt just one person, you know. You hurt—" For a second, Sadie falters, her own pain showing as she tries to keep her composure. "You lied to people for months. How is that OK?"

I've thought all this time that Sadie has been ignoring my messages because she was angry at me, but I realize now that isn't it at all; she's hurt. Anger is quick, a feeling that disappears as quickly as it appears, but hurt lingers.

"That's not how it happened, Sadie—"

"Isn't it?" she interrupts. "Because from where I'm standing, that's exactly how it played out."

I take a deep breath, trying not to feel too annoyed that Sadie isn't listening to me but instead is making assumptions, and remind myself that Sadie is doing to me what I did to Yahya. Just as I couldn't process what Yahya was saying at the ice rink because I was still reeling from the aftermath of it all, Sadie's hurt, and her feelings are getting the better of her. She's only human and, after all, I didn't only betray her, I also invalidated parts of her documentary, which I know she's worked so hard and so tirelessly on, learning a whole new craft just to be as authentic as possible.

"Sadie, I'm so sorry for hurting you, but please let me explain."

"Go on then." She clears her throat and presses on her phone, the recording live again. "Tell the documentary what happened, Zara."

"Well, like I said, Adnan had to cover up his relationship, so he posted on Instagram and, initially, I didn't want to do it, bu—"

Sadie rolls her eyes, dismissing my explanation entirely, and I decide that I've had enough. How am I going to tell my side of the story if she's so intent on believing a version of events that never happened in the first place? And wasn't that the point anyway, of breaking up with Adnan and coming clean to my parents, to not play along with the narrative everyone around me had constructed?

"How about you just answer *for* me? Since you're so hell-bent on telling a version of the truth that doesn't exist." I shoot up, my patience having ebbed away altogether. "If you want to tell me how you really feel, you don't have to ask questions using the documentary as a shield. Just ask already!"

"I'm just asking the questions the viewers will want the answers to, Zara," she says, stone-faced.

"No, you're asking the questions *you* want the answers to."

I make my way across the room and am just about to push down on the handle of her door when she shouts, "Zara, wait!"

I spin around with a heavy exhale. "What?"

Sadie is standing up, too, her arms crossed in front of her chest.

"Why didn't you just tell me?" she asks, her voice brittle with tenderness.

My grip on the handle loosens as I see the change in Sadie. How she switches from Sadie the Documentarian to Sadie the Best Friend.

"Friends tell each other everything and I'm one of your closest friends, Z." Sadie slumps back down into her chair. "At least, I thought I was."

"You *are* one of my closest friends." I shuffle across the room, the fibers of the carpet grazing through my socks. "Probably *the* closest friend I have. I just . . ." I shake my head. "There's no good way to explain it. Don't you think I wanted to tell you? It killed me not to talk to you about what was happening."

"Then why didn't you?" she asks, her voice cracking with pain.

I shrug. "I don't know. I really don't. I was scared?"

"I wouldn't have told anybody, you know that."

And I do. Sadie is and always has been fiercely loyal. If I ever murdered somebody, she's the person I'd call to help me bury the body, not Adnan. "I know. But I wasn't thinking. It all happened so quickly. Everyone was just so damn happy to finally see me and Adnan couple up that I didn't know what to do. My parents were speaking to one another again and you were acting like we were Machine Gun Kelly and Megan Fox. And although I thought it was stupid initially, I could see how it would benefit us."

I tell Sadie all about the plan Adnan and I had: how we were going to pretend to be together to get everyone off our backs while he dated Cami in secret; how we would break up at Christmastime after "realizing" we didn't actually belong together, finally showing everyone who has been pining for our relationship that sometimes what looks good on paper doesn't always work out so well in real life.

"And, I don't know, it just always felt like there was this massive weight on my shoulders and I *had* to go along with it. Not just for Adnan and my parents' sake, but also because people just would not stop shipping us."

"I'm sorry that I made you feel like you were pressured into pursuing a relationship with Adnan, I really am. That was never my intention; you know that, right? I just . . . I didn't want you to miss out on a chance to be with the love of your life by writing him off." Sadie pauses, and in that moment, I'm reminded of the fact that Ma and Baba said the exact same thing. I mentally kick myself for vastly underestimating my friends and family.

"Maybe you were right that day at school," Sadie continues, "about me butting into other people's business when what I should be doing is minding my own."

"I'm sorry about that, Sadie. What I said, I didn't me—"

"But you did. And you were right. I did force the documentary on you guys, and I shouldn't have." She laughs, but it's one of regret. "I don't know. Maybe I just thought . . . if you two could finally see it, what's to stop Joe from seeing it? But, you know, with us." Sadie's cheeks flush with heat like a little schoolgirl and it warms my insides.

"Sadie, you are the sweetest human on the earth, but you are also the dorkiest."

"Rude! But yes, you are right," she says with a little chuckle. "Actually, you were right all along."

"What do you mean?"

Sadie rubs the back of her neck. "I was scared of telling Joe about my feelings for fear of what might happen to our friendship and, well, I told him . . ."

"Oh my Allah!" I jump out of my seat. "What happened?"

Sadie's face breaks into a self-satisfied grin. "We're together now, actually."

I squeal and pull Sadie up by her hands and jump up and down on the spot. "You have a boyfriend!"

"I have a boyfriend!" she squeals right back, jumping up and down with me. "Who knew all it took for that to happen was you busting my ovaries?!"

Sadie and I let go and we both take our seats, slightly out of breath from all the excitement. "Well, next time I'll try to do it without yelling at you. But that's beside the point—how did it happen?"

Sadie's eyes light up as she recalls how she finally found the nerve to tell Joe how she felt. "I was so upset about what you'd said that I, unwittingly, went looking to him for comfort. And when I was talking to him, it was just impossible not to tell him about my feelings for him and, actually, I kind of did a Zara and busted *his* balls about not telling me about his feelings."

"You didn't?"

"Oh, I did." Sadie lets out a disbelieving laugh. "But

376

he was so focused on me admitting *my* feelings that he couldn't care less about being told off and just kissed me then and there with mascara running down my face."

"Aww!"

"And once it'd all calmed down, he did say that like me, he was just scared of what would happen to our friendship if I didn't reciprocate his feelings."

I grab Sadie's hand and give it a squeeze. "I'm glad you're with Joe and that you took the plunge. That's brave of you."

"Thanks, Z." Sadie's face is glowing with joy, and I feel my heart growing in size. "Hey, look at us! We've both got boyfriends! We're living our rom-com dreams!"

I lean back in my chair and groan. "Actually, I'm not living the dream. Adnan and I broke up."

"You did?" she asks, her eyes wide with confusion.

"Yeah." I let out a sigh. "But that's a story for another day. How about for now we just put on a rom-com and chill out for a bit?"

"I thought you'd never ask."

We watch an old rom-com on Netflix about a girl who falls for her charming neighbor. Halfway through, Sadie suddenly springs forward and asks, "Wait, what happened to the guy? The one from the ThermaeSecrets post?"

I blow out a breath as the memory of my last conversation with Yahya replays like a movie I wish I hadn't finished just so I can imagine it ends happily ever after and not like the dumpster fire it actually is.

"See, if you'd just told me from the beginning, I wouldn't

have to hassle you to fill me in on all the details at once," Sadie teases with a smile.

After I've told Sadie everything about Yahya, I feel like I could sleep for a thousand years.

"Dude," Sadie finally says, her eyes wild. "I'm not sure the documentary is going to be what we imagined it would be. I mean, especially since you and Adnan, and you and lover boy, are no more."

"Yeah, I know. I'm sorry. You put in all that hard work."

Sadie shrugs with a sad smile. "Maybe we can turn it into something else?"

"What do you mean?"

"Maybe we can still keep the documentary about love— that way, we can still use a lot of the footage I've shot—but . . . what if it was a documentary about different types of love?" Sadie shakes her head. "I don't know. I'm just spit-balling . . ."

"No, Sades, you're right. Who says love has to be *just* about romantic love? If we've learned anything, it's that love comes in different shapes. At the end of the day, whether it be romantic, platonic, familial, or whatever other types of love there are out there, it's still all *love*."

"Yes!" Sadie claps her hands in excitement. "That's perfect. We'll be able to explore more this way and it'll be more universal. Perhaps . . ."

"What?"

Sadie bites her lip in thought. "Maybe you could even give an exclusive? I mean, you've got such a good story with the fake relationship, the real relationship, lover boy, your parents . . . There's something there. Something I think people could benefit from."

I swallow. It was one thing to do the documentary for Sadie when it was under the pretense of being Adnan's girlfriend, but to do it now, when I'm just me—it feels different. It feels . . . vulnerable.

But I know it's what I have to do. Not just for Sadie or the documentary, but for myself.

I need to tell the honest and complicated truth of how I fell in love.

"Let's do it."

36

"Tell us the story of how you fell in love, Zara."

I look down the camera lens, take a deep breath, and finally tell my story.

"What you need to know about me is this: I love love. I grew up reading romance novels when it was way past my bedtime, huddled underneath my sheets with a reading lamp. I grew up watching my parents love each other day in, day out, listening to them bicker only to reconcile a few moments later through the power of cooking and long talks. I grew up watching rom-coms with my best friend, dreaming of the day I'd get my main-character moment in my own love story.

"But here's the thing: my love life has never really followed the tropes or the rules. Instead, it's done something different entirely.

"There are two sides to every story, and this is mine.

"This time, *I* tell my story. Not through somebody else or through an Instagram post, but through my own words.

"So, here it is—the abridged version: I entered into a fake relationship with my best friend.

"But then . . . I met *him*. Yahya. You might not know who I'm talking about so here's the lowdown: there was a guy I liked. A guy whose lips felt like clouds and who smelled like coffee infused with the tiniest hint of tobacco and chai with lemons. A guy who made me feel like myself at a time when I had to lie to just about everyone I knew. A guy who surprised me every day. I didn't anticipate falling for him, but I did.

"And then my world blew up. Suddenly, everyone found out about me and Adnan, and I went into hiding.

"Now, here's where the story turns: Adnan and I actually got together. Once the truth got out, it seemed like maybe, just maybe, the universe was telling us in its own twisted way that we were meant to be together. I couldn't be with Yahya, Adnan couldn't be with his real girlfriend, and all we had left was each other. So we thought: why don't we *actually* get together?

"I mean, everyone always said we'd be perfect for each other, so why not give it a go?

"So, we did.

"But here's the thing I've learned: you can't make yourself fall in love. Adnan and I didn't fit in that way, no matter how hard we tried. He's everything I could want in a partner. He's kind, funny, and ridiculously clever—but I don't love him. At least, not romantically. As a best friend, yes, and that's just as important. But as a boyfriend?

"No.

381

"I couldn't convince myself, and years of people telling us we were perfect together couldn't do it either. Which leads me to the next thing I've learned about love: people need to stay out of other people's business. Relationships are hard enough without everyone trying to butt in with their opinions. Maybe if they didn't, so many of us wouldn't break up or even get together in the first place. And I know people have good intentions, but if anything, it just applies a whole load of pressure that nobody needs.

"And for the love of Allah, stop photographing people when they're making out! We're not celebrities. We don't need you trailing us like paparazzi. It's unnecessary and, quite frankly, it's creepy. That's directed at you, ThermaeSecrets.

"But here's the most important thing I learned throughout it all: I did find love; it just wasn't in the form I was looking for.

"After all we've gone through, I fell back in love with my best friends. Their acceptance of who I am with no strings attached reminded me just how much I love them and how grateful I am to have them by my side.

"I also fell back in love with my parents, and along the way I got to know more about them. I gained an understanding of who they were at their core and why they acted in certain ways, allowing me to become closer to them. Things I probably would have never learned in other circumstances.

"Most of all, I fell in love with myself. I embraced that I am who I am, no excuses, and I realized I don't need to cater to what everyone else wants for me. I can still be loved by those around me while doing whatever the hell *I* want.

"So there you have it: the story of how I fell in love in all the ways except for the one I sought in the first place. I fell in love by finally listening to my friends and family, by speaking my truth, and realizing that as much as I wished my life would follow a rom-com storyline, the essence of love can't be manufactured or copied by using a blueprint. I'm not saying that I'm writing off rom-coms, just that there is no possible way that my story could ever match the books and films out there—because every love story is unique. *My* love story is unique.

"And oh, one last thing: I bet you're wondering what's next for me. Now that I'm no longer with Adnan, will I try to work things out with the guy who gave me butterflies when he kissed me?

"Here's the amazing thing: you'll never know.

"Because if you want a guide on how to fall in love *romantically*, you'll have to look elsewhere. This documentary isn't here to give you the cheat sheet on Romance 101; it's to remind you that falling in love is acknowledging that it comes in all shapes and forms and opening yourself up to those around you.

"And besides, I don't owe you the story of how I fell in love romantically, because that's *my* story.

"And the story of how you fall in love is *yours*."

DISCORD RESTORATION

ACCOUNT SCHEDULED FOR DELETION

Your account was scheduled for
self-destruction . . .
Are you sure you want to restore it?

I AM SURE!

Today at 00:02

SolusZ26

Hey, happy new year!

I was wondering if you'd want to ring in the new year
with a raid?

And to clarify this time: not remote . . .

VelasY74 *is typing . . .*

Acknowledgments

The truth is, writing a book is never a solitary endeavor, and I couldn't have written this book without the wonderful team of people who have stood by and helped me in various ways.

Absolutely none of this would have been possible without my incredible agent, Alice Sutherland-Hawes. Thank you for your support and guidance over the years, for reassuring me that I'm not a terrible writer, and for believing in my stories. I cannot thank you enough for all that you do for me.

An immense thank-you to my editors, Emma Matthewson and Ella Whiddett, for somehow transforming my jumbled words and plotlines into an actual story. A massive thank-you as well to the rest of the team at Hot Key for all their work. Sophie McDonnell, your initial design with the stickmen had me cackling with joy. Talya Baker and Holly Kyte, thank you for copyedits and for spotting things I never would have thought of, and for making my English sensible and grammatical. And finally, a massive thank-you to the SMP team for working harder than I ever could at making sure my book reaches my readers.

An enormous thank-you to Bhavna Madan, who created the cover of all covers. I can't express how heartwarming it is to see Zara and Adnan come to life.

Thank you to Berättarministeriet and Bath Spa University for helping me find my voice and realize that I could write stories for and about brown girls.

To my Cinnamon Squad—Eve, Fox, Kate, Lis, Steph, and Zulekhá: I cannot thank you enough for encouraging me to keep writing my stories and for listening to me rambling on about my characters. You've kept me sane in ways you don't even know.

To my agency sister, Ravena, for being there to answer all my stupid questions and for making me feel a little less alone as I try to navigate my way around what it means to be an author.

To my amazing former roomie, Sami: thank you for everything you have provided to me, from food and awkward hugs to the best trolley ever—my life would not be the same without you. Foxy Ladies forever!

To my work wife on the other side of the city, Kim: thank you for always believing in me and pushing me to do what's in my best interest even when I'm too scared to do so. Thank you for helping me grow.

To my *straight girls, Freddie and Ida: thank you for being the best former locker buddies a girl could ask

388

for and for being on hand for ridiculous chats that leave me with stomach pains for days.

To my Yugifriends—Taha, Tasnim, Tausif, and Ohi: thank you for letting me steal your dreams in one way or another and for loving me anyway.

To my in-laws: thank you for accepting me into the family without a second thought. I'm so lucky to have in-laws as amazing as you.

To Mum and Dad: I don't know how to thank you enough for pushing me to follow my dreams even when it wasn't traditional and it meant I would have to leave behind all that I knew. Thank you for all the trips to the library and for encouraging me to keep jumping into the unknown.

To my brother, Nahian: we've been through a lot but we're both smashing it. Thank you for dreaming big with me. The world isn't all rainbows and sunshine, but even so, we'll keep moving forward.

To my husband, Martin: no words will ever be able to express how grateful I am for you and all that you've given my life. Thank you for being my own personal PR manager and for never once telling me to stop following my dreams. Thank you for being sensible and telling me to write when I procrastinate and for taking care of me when I'm deep in my writing. But mostly, thank you for teaching me how to open up my heart, to be vulnerable with my emotions, and for showing me that I too deserve my own love story.

And finally to my readers, my Desis: this one is for you.